The Red Cathedral

A Hunter, Hawk & Hound Novel

K. Clopton

Clockwork Heart Publishing

For my wife Rebecca, who made it possible.

And for my sister Sheila. I wish you could have been here to see it.

Contents

Prologue

923CE, Northumbria

Kenric's feet bled as he ran. He and Drustan had been running since sunset, long miles ago. The drizzle that had started at twilight was now a steady downpour. His torch guttered and hissed, but he could still see Drustan's cornsilk hair through the branches ahead. Gods only knew how his brother could tell which way home was.

They shouldn't have stayed out until dark. A lot had happened lately that shouldn't have. Crops had blighted. Game bore strange wounds and evil eyes. People disappeared. Father had disappeared. Who could fault his eldest sons for daring everything to look for him? They had left the shelter of the family home that morning, determined and strong.

The evils of the world care not for daring or fault. Fell beasts care only for fear and food. So they ran, brave young men of the morning, hunted in the night. If they made it home alive, ealdmodor would lash them for their over-reaching, their foolishness. Kenric considered it fair trade to be safe behind her wards again.

A twig snapped somewhere in the dark, the soft sound hitting Kenric like an arrow, and he stumbled. "Right!" Drustan shouted. Kenric charged through the bushes to his right, hoping that had been his brother's intent. He slammed into Drustan's back ten paces later. Drustan whirled and clamped a hand over Kenric's mouth hard enough to bust his lip. "Shh," he murmured, barely audible in the rain. "There's more than one."

Low growling reverberated around them just under the sound of the wind in the leaves. One of the creatures made a series of small yips and another answered with a howl. Moments later, half a dozen similar calls answered. The brothers were surrounded. Somewhere in the night, one of the beasts laughed, almost human. Not nearly human enough.

Drustan held his torch high, staring into the dark. "Kenric, listen to me," he said. "You're going to have to make it back alone. You have to. You have to warn them, so ealdmodor can try to ward them off."

"Tell them what? What's out there?" Kenric was afraid he already knew. "What are you going to do?"

"It's Father. He's with them now." Drustan gave Kenric a hard shove and yelled, "Go!" as he darted into the wood, trying to lead the pack away. Kenric ran. He saw the beast that took Drustan from the corner of his eye. Gray furred, tall, muscular. Missing an eye and an ear. Father. Tears could come later. The whole family was in danger now. Father would want them for his new pack.

By the time Kenric saw the torches of home, he could no longer run. One foot didn't work quite right, and he drug it across the ground, limping for the door. He knelt before the great wooden planks and pounded his fist on them. "Ealdmodor," he called, "It's me. It's Kenric. Let me in. Please."

For long moments there was no sound. Was he too late? He hadn't noticed any signs of destruction around the cabin, but he was hardly capable of walking, let alone much observation in the dark. His heart pounded and he fought not to even breathe, listening hard enough to make his ears ring.

"Tell me, by Lugh, god of oaths, that thou art thyself, mine grandson, Kenric."

The voice was ancient, almost indistinguishable from the sound of the bare branches of the forest creaking in the late autumn wind. Still, it held power, and to Kenric, it was beautiful.

"Ealdmodor, by Lugh, I am your grandson Kenric, and I must come inside. Death follows close at my heels!"

The door flew open and a pair of dry, heavy knuckled hands shot out and pulled him through. For a split second they grasped for a brother who wasn't there, then quickly retreated inside.

Kenric heard the door slam and the heavy crossbeam fall. He felt the searing heat of the cookfire. Many hands pushed, led, cradled him as he staggered toward a pallet. He was so tired, soul and body. He tried to resist, he knew there was something he had to say, but it wouldn't come forward in his mind. Then the room spun. His vision darkened. Perhaps he fell, but he didn't feel it. After that, only nightmares.

He woke screaming an hour later. Sisters and cousins were close by to comfort him, and soon he was quiet again. His ealdmodor was chanting, sitting cross-legged before the door. For long moments he couldn't remember where he was and for worse moments after, couldn't remember what he was supposed to do. Something important, something vital was trusted to him, and he could not remember what. His eyes would not still, casting about the one room home.

Drustan wasn't there.

"Ealdmodor!" he called. "It's father!"

She turned sharply to look at him. "What meanest thou, child?"

"He's with them, ealdmodor. They're coming here. Werewulfs."

Fear paled the old woman's gnarled features. She'd been chanting protection from spirits, and even from werewolves. But Wymond, her dead daughter's husband, would still hold some authority and power over the house. She'd thought him slain. To have him taken was a weight her soul baulked against.

Revna, the old witch of the woods, spun back to the door and began chanting a new warding as fast as she could. She wove Wymond's name into it, and tied his name to the wolves. Years of magic her mother and grandmother had taught her, decades of communing with magic and the forest on her own, she poured it all into the grating song coming from her dry lips.

Not fast enough.

The sound of claws came though the door, sliding slowly from the top of the frame down to the threshold. A low, rumbling growl became words, formed in a half human throat. "Revna," the beast said. "Open the door for thy sunu. Fetch me meat to eat by the fire."

The old woman got shakily to her feet, but when she spoke, her voice was firm and steady. "And art thou thyself, mine sunu? By Lugh, art thou the husband of mine daughter, Wymond, son of Orvyn?"

For a score of rapid heartbeats there was no answer. Then Kenric heard the low, rasping laugh he had heard in the forest. "Thou wouldst seek to compel me by Lámfada, by Long Hand, and Lonnbéimnech the Fierce Striker?

I answer thee by Conmac Hound-Son, I am myself. I am thine sunu Wymond, and I am more. I am brother in the pack. I am fear in the night. And I am lord still of this clan, mine sons and daughters. I will not be denied, witch."

Kenric heard howling all around the cabin. They were trapped, and it was still many hours to dawn. Could ealdmodor hold them? Surely if father could just walk in, he would have. How much strength still rested in the twisted and shriveled body of the once powerful witch?

Barely a finger's breadth of candle remained. The old woman had chanted through nearly the entire night, and it showed on her. Her voice barely crept out through a wheezing rattle in her throat. She rocked back and forth as she sat and her granddaughters sat beside her, supporting her withered frame. The werewolves had made many attempts on the home through the dark hours, clawing at the door, climbing to the thatch roof, howling down the chimney. Each time the old woman's power had swelled to meet the challenge.

Kenric prayed for a swift dawn. But then what? His ealdmodor's strength would not last another night. He had to take the family away from here, as soon after first light as possible. They would have to leave much behind. Likely Revna would need to be carried. He and the two oldest of his sisters would have to take turns with that. Could they even reach the nearest village before nightfall?

Suddenly the oppressive darkness of the room lifted. Pale light glowed in the cracks in the door and the roof, pulling him from his thoughts. It felt like he breathed for the first time in many hours. The dawn was beautiful.

The beams of light shone on his sister's face. Then they swung across the floor, and climbed the wall. The light moved quickly over the roof, shining through holes and cracks, swirling around the house. The howling of the wolves retreated into the woods, small and scared. The cabin shook, and a terrible song filled the air, like women wailing in chorus.

Revna ceased her chanting. She looked around at her family, all their eyes on her for an explanation.

"It is an Angel," she said. "It has driven the werewulfs away."

Tears rolled down her time worn face.

"We are doomed."

Part One

Clockwork Heart Publishing

Chapter 1

Dylan glanced over from where he was leaning against the brick wall of a roof access stairwell. The woman to his left, thin and dressed like some cyberpunk comic hero, was fitting an antique looking metal disk into a clamp on an electronic gadget. Wires ran from the device into a black box, which sprouted wires out to an antenna and a laptop. Dylan Carter didn't know how the gadget worked, couldn't run most of the programs on the laptop. But, he knew what the disk was. Maybe better than the young woman, Ariel Ikeda, did.

He turned his head and looked at a random building, trying to hide a smile. "Now, I KNOW that one's illegal," he said.

"Your stupid hat should be illegal," she replied, not looking up.

"I ought to turn you in for having that, it's black market, and it should be locked up," he said. He was leaning back again, eyes closed.

"Are you gonna hide all the illegal stuff you're carrying when you take me down to the Confessional?"

It was true, he was a walking felony, according to Order Pure laws and regulations. The knife he carried was magical, possibly haunted or possessed. A smith couldn't get silver and copper veins into steel like that without alchemy. He carried ancient charms, was covered in warding tattoos, and even had an old fashioned dime with a hole in it tied around his ankle. No one knew just how many weapons he had hidden in the pockets of his long, brown leather coat, but everyone knew he bought them at Underground markets. No, he wasn't going to turn her in, just like he hadn't the dozen times they'd bantered like this during other missions. He was just interested to see if she'd try to explain the how, the what, and the why of the contraband. Or simply change the subject.

Besides, they weren't going to find the guy they were looking for without bending rules. That was the way it always worked. The good ideas in R&D either got tied up in red tape, got labeled heretical, or were worth more in the private sector: both civilian and black market. Since Ariel didn't want to talk about where she got the medallion, Dylan guessed it was black market contraband.

The medallion was linked to the Demon, had been for several hundred years. Losing it had either been sloppy or a tragedy, possibly theft. It would "want" to get back to him. Ariel knew that much and knew how to utilize connection. If she knew the full extent of what could be done with the piece in experienced hands, she'd be afraid of it. Dylan chose not to burden her with this knowledge, not yet. She was safe enough handling it and he was there to make sure no one came looking for it.

"Getting something," she said. "Very strong Nether presence. Same wavelengths as the medallion." She glanced at the metal disk. It was vibrating subtly in the clamp, making a rattling sound. "The bauble looks excited too."

"Clocking in," Dylan said, rising. He sounded at ease, looked relaxed, but breaching an enemy compound always scared him. This mission was doubly frightening. The Demon's home area would be in an alternate dimension, a literal hellscape, sitting alongside the real world. Dylan couldn't afford to even wonder about what might happen if he died inside it while taking down the target. So he put on a careless smile, checked his gear, and walked to the roof access door. "We're up, King."

A large Black man who had been leaning on the railing around the roof turned to look at him. Matthew King was in his mid twenties, a Hercules cut in onyx. "On it, chief," he said, giving one last look at the night view of the city from his vantage point. He crossed the roof in heavy but quick strides, meeting Dylan at the door.

"You ready?" Dylan asked.

"Got your back," Matthew answered. Together they entered the flickering stairwell, Matthew ducking as he went through the door. No wires to lower them from the ceiling, no night vision, none of the complicated stuff to breach a Demon's lair. If you want to visit Hell, you just take the stairs.

"Why do you always wear that coat?" Matthew asked as they wound their way down. "HQ hands out free gear like it's candy. Could get some proper tactical clothing."

"Not enough pockets in Order uniforms," Dylan replied.

"Not supposed to need so many," Matthew said. "On that note, you carrying anything that's gonna explode on us today?"

"Not today, but I'd watch Ikeda and her doo-hicky up there."

They were casual but quick in their descent. They'd gone down twelve flights when Dylan stopped and tapped his headset. "Floor ninety-six, we still good, Ariel?"

"Nothing changed, you should be good to go, ninety-three still green."

The two men moved more slowly now, but weren't sneaking. Until they focused on it, they wouldn't be in the Demon's artificial hellscape. This was supposed to make the space more secure for the Demon. No one could accidentally find their hiding places. That essentially put a wall between them and the outside world, and Dylan and Matthew could do whatever they wanted on their side without notice. In the normal world, the building was a legitimate business tower, full of busy, oblivious humans.

Ninety-fourth floor. This was where the job would start.

"Hope that hat at least gets lost," Matthew mumbled.

"Focus," Dylan said. "Head in in three...two...go."

Both men focused their intent on entering the hellscape. They set their will on it, like walking into a room in the dark, but knowing where everything was. This, and knowing which floor held the hellscape, were the only things required to enter. If one didn't know it was there, they'd never accidentally walk into it.

As reality in the staircase twisted around him, Dylan reached into an inner pocket and pulled out a silver spike, about the size of a letter opener, with a milk white quartz gripped in silver talons on one end. Matthew followed with a silenced pistol drawn, but pointed at the ground. They would stay quiet as long as the situation allowed.

Their first engagement materialized a foot in front of Dylan, rounding the banister headed up as they came down. It was a tall, thin goblin with a face that could pass for an ugly human, if it was dark. Its face registered shock as it collided with Dylan. Dylan's wore a smile. After a half second, they looked down together to where Dylan's fist was wedged between their chests, holding the silver spike. It was buried halfway to the crystal in the Nether creature's ribcage. The pale crystal turned black as it leached away the Nether's life, and the goblin's yellow eyes rolled up. Dylan caught it as it fell and eased it to the floor. As he stepped away, he tapped the blackened marble, now full of the Nether creature's life essence, against the concrete wall. It shattered and he offered the eager talons another white quartz from the same inner pocket.

The ninety-third floor was thickly carpeted in burgundy, dark wood paneling, and hung every few meters with expensive art. This ninety-third floor, at any rate. The one outside the hell dimension was some sort of firm dealing in financial legalities. Still, the physical layout was expected to follow the same map, and after ten meters a hallway branched off to the right.

Before making the turn, he and Matthew stopped and hugged the wall. Dylan handed forward a small flexible tube with a lens on the end, then turned on the screen he held in his hand. As Matthew fed the camera around the corner, Dylan said, "Ariel, I count two, 45 Celsius, confirm?"

"Roger, King, reading forty-five point three Celsius, probably ghoul. Confirmed Nether and recorded."

Dylan nodded at Matthew, then dropped into a runner's crouch. Matthew checked the safety on his pistol once more, then held up three fingers. Two. One.

Matthew moved around the corner in a half crouch, four quick, short steps that took him a third of the way down the hall. As the two ghouls, dressed in navy suits, jerked toward him and reached for their shoulder holsters, Matthew put blessed silver rounds into their hearts. The pistol was silenced but not perfectly soundless, and there was nothing to be done about the bodies falling to the floor. Dylan had to hurry. As he heard the first shot, he raced forward, using his left hand to push off the corridor's wall rather than try to turn against momentum. By the second shot he had sprinted past Matthew. He reached the door as the first body hit the ground, Matthew two meters behind him, moving into a sentry position with his pistol raised.

Dylan slammed a short tube into the door directly over the lock, setting off a shotgun breaching round that bucked against the lead weighted end he held. The door swung in and he rushed through.

What should have happened next was the sound of Dylan's Order-blessed .454 revolver going off a split second after sighting on the Demon in the room, who ought to be behind the big mahogany desk. The whole mission depended on speed, precision, and efficiency. The team had run simulations over and over for days, based on extensive intelligence and predictive strategy reports.

The reports were flawed.

The woman was very pale white, with curling black hair, blue eyes, thin lips, and a straight nose. She sat in a chair to the side of the mahogany desk, no emotion registering on her features as she stared straight ahead. Dylan froze, his eyes going wide with recognition. It didn't matter that his mind knew she couldn't be who she looked like. Who she looked exactly like. No one else should have been here at all, but this person absolutely could not be.

There was indeed a large man behind the desk wearing an expensive charcoal suit, a smile on his handsome face. As he stood, he reached for a large ring with a blood red gem, prominently displayed in the center of the desk. He slipped the ring onto the middle finger of his right hand and reality shifted. The Demon's Temple descended. His human appearance faded away.

Dylan, distracted, confused, had hesitated too long.

"Boss!" he heard from the door.

The room darkened, fast.

"Boss!" Farther away, quieter.

Despair became an entity as the Demon invoked its greatest weapon.

"Ikeda, it's Carter, he's in..." The rest was too far away.

"Shit," Dylan said.

Chapter 2

The temple had no windows. The ceiling, if there was one, was lost to darkness. Concrete walls rose to Dylan's left and right, smoked, filthy, and smooth, with square pillars ten meters apart. All light emanated from a tall, thin being standing where the businessman had stood moments before. It was a sick, gray light. Back-alley light. Sewer light.

The thin being was tall, too tall to be human. It wore robes that reached down and pooled on the floor. They may once have been white, but now were covered in soot and swamp water stains. Yet there was still power, dignity. The creature's posture was straight, arms held forward and open, palms up. Not offering. Receiving.

Dylan's eyes were locked on the Demon. A fog of despair clouded his mind. A name dominated all his thoughts. Klarisvan. In putting on his ring, Klarisvan had freed his power from the shackles that made him look like an ordinary human, and brought his temple fully into reality. Once Dylan was trapped, the Demon had unleashed one of the most feared supernatural attacks known. Worship. It forced a worship of fear, of despair, and of a ruined angel. This was why the plan had called for such speed. Dylan knew a Demon had to be killed before it had time to even reach for that ring. But Dylan had committed a terrible sin. He had become distracted.

He realized he was on his knees. He had gone down hard. It should have hurt, but he didn't remember the motion at all. Through the fog in his mind, he realized he'd holstered his weapon. His heart weighed an eternity. He was just a man; what on earth was he doing here, thinking he could fight creatures like this?

A powerful force struck his consciousness. He had been reprimanded.

"Creature?" a silky voice said.

It was beautiful, yet it filled Dylan with nausea.

"You call me creature? You fear to oppose one like unto me. You are so close, so almost right. But you are too high in your own thoughts. Am I not strong? Am I not beautiful, so much more than you ever dreamed? Your world does not even know of beauty, yet I have allowed you a glimpse. Respect your betters, human. Accept your weakness and filth; give yourself to me. You may yet have the mercy of swift death. Even in your annihilation, I will keep and hold you. Worship me. You cannot win. You cannot fight, or run, or resist. Worship."

Dylan knew he would. He could give himself over now. He had opposed such strength for too long, been a fool for too many years. Impudent. Wretched. Bathed in hubris. All he had to do was stop. Let it happen. Fall. What could be easier than falling?

His muscles slackened. This was the final moment. All done. Until he saw the black, wavy hair across the room, only just in his peripheral, but so stark and beautiful. Real beauty. Clean and pure and so familiar. His mind no longer recognized that it could not be his sister, lost to him so long ago. In the little bit of his mind that was left to him, in his heart that was dragging him down like an anchor, there was a foundation, a place to stand. He had stood there for years. His sister, who had been killed, murdered, years ago, had become the symbol of his calling and the driving force in his life. She was a pure element. Love for her and grief over her had fueled his conviction, his sense of justice, his rage. It gave him rage now. He slammed against the stone of that foundation as he fell to Klarisvan, and held.

The Demon's face, so serene and confident, betrayed the smallest mote of confusion. It was not that no one had ever resisted before. Everyone resists. But no one had ever taken their inner eye off of him before. Klarisvan curled his fingers, just tugging on the webs of control, the bond, that had been forming between himself and the human. Dylan moved a few centimeters closer to the ground, but it was like pulling a tree branch down toward the ground. The more Klarisvan pulled, the more resistance he encountered. Too late, he realized he was only making things worse. The human creature was getting angry.

Dylan shakily looked up at the Demon, trembling with effort and emotion. His eyes continually shot back and forth from the woman to the fallen angel, but were lingering longer each time on the gray, shrouded face of his assailant. He was still himself. Still alive. He grabbed hold of the rage and fear he felt inside, and slowly climbed it, like a mountain, as he worked to own himself again. He wasn't here to bow for his enemies. He hadn't brought mercy with him.

Klarisvan tilted his head, the silk robes around it snagging and shifting. "You're strange," he said. "I commend you. You've shown me something new. And you may have honor for it, if you come to me. Even now, you know your strength to be finite. You do not look well, human."

He wasn't. It would be so good to rise up and put a blessed round through the masked eyes of the beast before him. The best he could do was hold an awkward, painful half kneel. His knees were grinding into the concrete, and as much as he wanted to strike out, he couldn't muster the concentration to form a plan. All he could do was see how long he could hold out.

In one small corner of his senses he was aware that the room had started to flash different colors. Firelight reds and electric greens blinked across the floor. A deep, pulsing blue lit the upper walls. It took strength he couldn't spare to lift his head. He saw that Klarisvan had also noticed the lights and was looking in confusion at the walls. Dylan strained to twist his head to the side. Now he shared the Demon's confusion. Huge runes blinked inside the walls like neon lights, almost pushing their way through the concrete and granite into the room.

His coms suddenly crackled to life in his ear.

"…-mething's happening, I think the wall's thinning!"

"What col-…is it?!"

"Red and gre-…no! It's open! I'm going!"

A racing heartbeat later something huge and loud slammed into the Demon. He folded in half over the charging bulk, and let out a grating cry, like breaking stone. The pressure on Dylan suddenly released and he accidentally flung himself backward, landing with a crunch on his left shoulder. Gasping for air became his whole world for the next two seconds. It was almost too long. As the ringing in his ears died, he heard the angry but frightened voice of Matthew King shouting to him.

"Carter! Get up and help!"

Crunching blows were landing as Matthew pounded his fists into Klarisvan's face, kneeling on the Demon in an attempt to pin it to the floor. "I don't really know what to do here Carter, get up!"

Fresh adrenaline flooded Dylan, and he jerked to his left, coming up on his left arm, wincing. Matthew sat like a mountain on the Demon, but it wasn't going to last. As Dylan watched, Klarisvan gave a lightning fast open handed slap to Matthew's face, throwing him off balance and off guard. With no visible sign of effort, the Demon grabbed the front of Matthew's combat vest and lifted him straight up, then threw him to the side. "Cart—" Matthew shouted, before crashing into the steps that led up to the still silent, motionless woman.

It was a race to see who would gain their feet first now, Dylan or Klarisvan. Dylan came up running at the same time that the Demon had almost levitated back to its feet. Dylan was no expert at combat magic, but he gave it his best shot. He raised his hand straight over his head, palm down, then slammed it back toward the ground, shouting, "Karteus mekia dai!"

Klarisvan was turning to him, snarling and fangs bared, when suddenly his head snapped back and slammed into the stone floor, sending out a spider-web of cracks. He lay there writhing as though chains held him by the neck to the ground.

Dylan made a desperate leap the last two meters to the struggling Demon, reaching into his coat for a gray bladed knife strapped to his side. Almost on top of the creature, he heard a strangled, "KRATHNAEM!", and Klarisvan shot off the floor toward him, the magical bindings shattered. They crashed together mid-air, spinning and slamming into the ground, Klarisvan pinning the Hunter to the floor. The Demon's hands, so smooth and ready to receive his offering minutes earlier, were now gnarled and clawed. It stabbed its dagger-like claws into Dylan's shoulders and raked his chest and face before he could orient himself. He forced his left hand between himself and the Demon, trying to push it up from his chest, desperate for air.

"They can have your body. You're not worth bringing in alive now!" Klarisvan said, screaming in a voice like snapping rocks. "I should never have agreed! It is an insult! Nothing is wor—"

Klarisvan's voice gurgled to a stop as Dylan slashed his blade across the Demon's throat. The knife was very old, and terribly angry. It cut deep into the hard flesh of the Demon, and as it cut it pulled, drinking magic from the creature. Drinking quickly. It couldn't kill Klarisvan, but he couldn't withstand the blade's strength. His attacks ceased.

Blood splashed down from the opened throat onto Dylan. It was hot and vile, and smelled of sulfur and burning flesh. It filled his mouth and coated his body. He was barely aware of it, fully transfixed by what he saw on Klarisvan's face. A smile. A horrible, fanged, wide smile.

"Well then," Klarisvan rasped. "Let them deal with you."

Dylan shoved the Demon off of himself and stood quickly, spitting blood and filth from his mouth. Klarisvan lay laughing quietly, staring up at nothing. "Matthew, you ok?" Dylan shouted.

"Yeah, I think so," Matthew said, standing slowly.

"Can you get the woman? See if she's hurt?"

"Woman?" Matthew said, looking around. "What the...why is she here? There's not supposed to be anyone here!"

"No idea," Dylan said, "but it can't be good, and we gotta take her with us. See if you can get her to move. Wait, what the hell are YOU doing here? Wasn't I locked in with this thing?"

"Yeah, but Ikeda got me in somehow. I didn't ask questions."

"She got you in, and now she needs to get you out!" a voice shouted in their coms. "Keeping a tunnel open to you guys hasn't been easy, I haven't been sitting here watching anime you know!"

"Ikeda, what-"

"Kill the bad guy and run out the door, now!"

Dylan yanked the revolver from his shoulder rig and pointed it at Klarisvan's head. "I don't wish you peace, Fallen Angel," he said.

Klarisvan laughed and spat blood. "Nor I you, Hunter, and none shall you have. Run, little human. Give your masters my regards. They don't know what they keep on the leash."

Dylan looked at him a moment longer, and pulled the trigger. The blessed .454 round went through the Demon's head and sent more spiderwebs crazing out in the cracked stone.

Then Matthew was sprinting past him, the unresponsive woman over his shoulders, shouting, "Come on, boss, here!"

Dylan was suddenly aware that the runes on the wall were blinking and changing colors. In his ear Ariel shouted, "Guys, now or never, I'm out of tricks!" Spinning fast, Dylan ran for the glowing portal, gaining quickly on Matthew. They made it with time to spare. A whole second and a half.

With a crackling sound, everything behind them disappeared.

They were in a normal office building again. The place they had been no longer existed, having died with its master. That much tracked with the original mission plan. What didn't, was the near catatonic woman over Matthew's shoulder. Shaky as he still was, Dylan ran past Matthew to the corner, hand signaling for him to wait while he checked the route back to the stairs. A sick bile sloshed in Dylan's stomach. He could still taste the Demon's blood in his mouth. It took a lot of concentration shove that aside and concentrate on checking the halls up ahead. After precious seconds peering left and right, he signaled Matthew forward, and they both jogged back to the stairwell. Dylan kept a floor ahead of Matthew on the way up, looking and listening for movement. Supernatural security was no longer a problem; humans ready to call the police for what must look like a kidnapping were.

Even burdened with an extra sixty kilos, Matthew wasn't particularly strained. Dylan, however, was gasping harder with each new floor. He hadn't ever experienced an attack quite like the Demon's before. Not many Hunters had in recent centuries. The assassination of a high-level Demon was a once in a century event. The team had trained extensively for it. Dylan was supposed to have gotten the shot off before the Demon even realized he was there. Instead, the woman in the room had provided enough shock and distraction to turn the tables on Dylan. If intel had said she was going to be there, that some kind of ritual was going on, or whatever it was, Dylan would have prepared for that. Intel had said nothing about it. Intel said a normal business merger was supposed to be happening today. Dylan was going to have a long, serious conversation with someone in the intelligence department.

Finally at the roof door, Dylan tapped his ear bud for Ariel. "We're here, coming out. One extra friendly, no alarm."

"Extra friendly? What do you mean—"

Ariel's jaw dropped as she saw Matthew jog out with the limp woman over his shoulder. "What did you guys do?" she said.

"What did you do?" Dylan countered. "I've never seen those runes. How did you even get King in? There's supposed to be no way you can affect a Demon's temple, it's on a whole other plane."

"'Thank you, Ikeda, you're amazing, I'd be dead, can I buy you something?' You're welcome!"

"Seriously, how?"

"I—"

"Guys, maybe in the car?" Matthew said. He was now carrying the woman like a child in his massive arms, far more gently than one might expect from a big man covered in armor and weapons. That was Matthew. He knew easily how to hurt, so he had practiced gentleness.

"Right," Dylan said, shaking off his lingering shock. "Let's get out of here. King, you're between me and Ikeda for this one. Ikeda, draw your sidearm, you get to guard King."

Ariel quickly stowed her gear in her bag with a practiced efficiency, then pulled her 9mm with somewhat less confidence. Matthew and Dylan always had her surrounded and protected: she guarded them with computers and gadgets. Still, she had put in the required hours with her pistol. She was ready to fight in whatever way she had to. Even if it meant walking across the shaky-ass bridge Dylan and Matthew had strung across an alley earlier that evening.

The setup was an Order approved high altitude urban infiltration bridge. Carbon fiber, steel cables, and plastic, pulled from Dylan's backpack, and arranged into the approximation of a rope bridge between the office building next door and the one they currently stood on. Unfortunately the building next door was two floors shorter, turning the tried and tested bridge into a poorly designed ladder. With only a small, strangled sigh, Ariel racked the slide and followed her teammates.

Dylan led the way to the bridge, giving it a once over before stepping onto it. The bridge was a dusty black color, meant to match the night sky and dirty buildings around it, so no one should have noticed it to tamper with it. Still, enough had gone wrong tonight, and Dylan was feeling extra cautious.

Crossing the bridge at a downward slant was awkward, especially with his .357 in his right hand. The .454 was much too big to be Dylan's everyday piece, but the job had called for hunting-caliber rounds, so he had pulled one of the big revolvers out of the Order's arsenal and spent some time on the range with it. It was now safely snapped back in his shoulder holster. The .357 also carried blessed rounds and was more than enough to take down anything or anyone else he was likely to encounter on the way to the garage.

They reached the adjoining roof with only a couple of slips between them, and headed for a freight elevator that accessed the roof. This building was older than Klarisvan's and constructed with more of an idea of utility in mind. The freight elevator ran all the way down to the three levels of parking garage in the basement of the building.

Dylan strolled out at parking level two, looking casual and a little tired, like anybody else who belonged in the building at that time of night. Then he lit a cigarette, using the hand covering the flame as a blind to take a quick look around. Nothing and no one. He could feel the knot of nausea in his gut tighten a little more. His system had kept pumping micro doses of adrenaline into him all the way back from Klarisvan's temple, then dropping him like a rock when nothing happened. He was exhausted from it, and done.

He gave a small whistle and Ariel came out with her pistol held low, then Matthew. The big man had been stooped in the elevator all the way down, afraid his head would touch the top. He had refused to put the woman down. Now he stretched tall, still carrying the woman like a sleeping child, and made his own inspection of the garage. Level two was roughly half full, middle managers staying late hoping for promotions and their assistants hoping for bonuses. The team's gunmetal gray sedan was parked by the far wall. A smaller car might have been less conspicuous, but neither Matthew nor Dylan were small men.

Matthew placed the woman in the back seat, then slid into the driver's seat. Ariel was on her phone in the front passenger seat, trying to find something on what had just happened in the Order's database. Dylan got in behind Ariel and glanced over at the woman. She wasn't unconscious. She just didn't react to anything. Apparently if you sat her up straight and buckled her in, that's how she would stay. It was giving Dylan a bad case of the creeps. Demons and monsters, they acted like, well, Demons and monsters. A human acting like a big robot or doll was not ok in his books.

He snapped his own buckle in, listening as the wheels made unnecessarily dramatic screaming sounds as Matthew backed out and took them home.

Chapter 3

The Red Cathedral was founded in 1596 CE as a pillar of defense against the supernatural evils found in the New World. After the ambush and loss of the colony at Roanoke a decade earlier, a veritable army had been sent across the Atlantic. Engineers, soldiers and, most importantly, senior Clergy and Hunters landed on the east coast of the mostly unexplored continent. Then began the arduous trek inland to find a suitable convergence of ley lines and a defensible position to establish a city of protection.

A capital grew on the shore of one of three giant lakes in the center of the continent. Present day Chicago was the hub around which the wheel of North America rotated. The spokes of that wheel, which formed many of the modern travel and shipping routes, were once important roads for dispatching soldiers and Hunters. Conquerors. The Order allowed only one colonial loss before slamming its fist down onto the land. The taming was swift and ruthless.

The Red Cathedral itself was an amalgamation of many religious, administrative, and military buildings and systems that had slowly merged into one giant institution over the centuries. Most of the buildings weren't red. The name began with the original Cathedral building, which had a constant blood mist glow, inside and out.

The complex was a small city within the city. Most of it didn't matter at all to Dylan. The only parts important to him were the armory, the training area the Cathedral security forces shared with Hunter teams, and the Cathedral itself. This original structure was now a workplace for the Clergy that comprised the backbone of the Order Pure and, for some of them, home. Many of the senior Clergy stepped outside of it only every few years, and rumor had it that some never left at all. Dylan's business here was always conducted in the east wing, where Clergy met with Hunters to give them missions and consecrations. Technically Dylan and other Hunters were expected to spend time in the Cathedral basilica, studying ancient texts and meditating. How much time was not stipulated, however, and Dylan typically considered his thirty second walk down the aisles to be enough.

As he made his way to High Cleric Postan's office to make his report, Dylan noted that Matthew was already seated in a pew near the front. Matthew couldn't stand the residual feel of the supernatural on his skin, as he put it, and almost always hurried to this central chamber as fast as he could, seeking peace. Matthew even made use of the Hunters' barracks available on-site for team members, living within the sheltering walls of the Order. Dylan respected Matthew's right to his beliefs, but didn't understand them. He was here for wholly different reasons than religious fervor.

Dylan entered the east wing ground floor corridor, a well lit, well adorned hallway that led to various meeting rooms, alcoves, libraries, and a reliquary. Most of this floor was for the sake of impressing visitors. His destination was down the stairs at the end of the hall.

High Cleric Postan's chambers consisted of a suite of rooms five stories down, deep in the most solitary parts of the Cathedral. Descending that far was like a trip back in time. Electric lights had only been run to the third level down a few decades ago. Past that, one relied on gas lamps from the early 19th century. The Clergy that lived in the deepest halls preferred the dimmer light and the quiet hiss of the flames to the buzz of electricity. Dylan could well believe that Postan hadn't left his chambers since he or his team members were born. Most Hunters didn't have to report to senior Clergy, and could stay comfortably in the modern world above. Dylan Carter was just one of a wretched lucky few.

In contrast to the passageways, the High Cleric's chamber door was undeniably a thing of beauty. Intricate scrollwork and relief carvings told a story across the broad expanse of dark oak. The beginnings of the Order Pure were shown there in images of Demons, Vampires, werewolves, ghouls, and creatures Dylan couldn't even identify. Presumably long ago wiped out by the work of the Order. Opposite the monsters stood the Clerics. Rays of light shone from their foreheads and outstretched palms as they blessed groups of Hunters, the holy soldiers. Dylan always assumed it was meant to inspire those who walked through the doorway, and even for him, it worked. He didn't adhere to the rules and guidelines of the Order as given to the populace at large, meant to show them the ways of purity and safety from the forces of the Nether. But, he still felt a sense of pride looking at those early Hunters, his occupational ancestors. Without judging others' beliefs or creeds, they had protected those who couldn't stand against the supernatural alone. He hoped each day he could live up to that standard.

There was a large iron knocker wrought in the shape of an impaled imp. Dylan only hesitated slightly these days before touching it. He gave a single rap against the ancient wood and waited. He never heard the door being unlocked. It always took exactly to the count of four to swing open. It swung silently inward now, and as always, there was no one on the other side pulling it, neither the High Cleric nor some servant. There was only the slightest creak of hinges. The old man was sitting in a wingback chair in front of his small fireplace, reading a book.

The chamber was slightly brighter than the hall outside, and much more richly adorned and furnished. Museums would have been tempted to commit atrocities to get at the artifacts contained therein. The tapestries along the wall told the whole of Europe's history. Shelf after shelf of books filled any other available wall space, and tables held what the shelves no longer had room for.

Most interesting to Dylan were the ancient tools of the trade displayed in cases and on mannequins. Ancient Vampire hunting armor was something to see, with its reinforced neck and bright silver spikes. Armor for tracking and killing a werewolf, by contrast, was less ornate but much sturdier, as much to protect one from the brambles and branches of the forest as from the claws of the beast. Heavy swords hung from the walls next to delicate daggers. Dozens of types of arcane, magical, and blessed warding tools filled shelves and small alcoves. What would the Order Pure's modern armory look like, he wondered, to the Hunters who would come along hundreds of years after his death.

A voice like crushed flint pulled him from his contemplation. "Though I did not want to damage your confidence in the days leading up to this previous nights' work, I will admit to you now, my son, that we had worried much for your safety in this most difficult of struggles." Looking up, he smiled and said, "I see now that we need not have."

"I dunno," Dylan said, taking his usual place standing by the fire. As usual, there was no chair for him. "I worried. To say that things didn't go according to plan...yeah. I'd rather missions didn't get that off balance again."

"Ah, yes," Postan said. "You refer to the woman." His tone was not entirely approving.

"Yeah," Dylan said. "I got some funny looks when I handed her over to Doctor Arthane in the hospital ward. Between you and him, I'm getting the feeling the Order doesn't approve of me having brought her back here. What was I supposed to do, drop her on some back street and wish her luck?"

"Absolutely not!" Postan snapped. He took a breath and composed himself, but his tone was still tight. "I cannot at this moment tell you what I think you should have done for the woman, as this is not a situation I can recall having occurred before. But for that same reason I am disturbed by the thought of having her in this holy citadel, in what ought to be a place of safety and purity. I can appreciate that you have a tendency toward human compassion, Hunter," he said, leaning on the old title, "but let us use this as an opportunity to consider other options for future difficulties, and focus more strongly on the priorities of your station."

"Fair enough," Dylan said, staring into the fire.

The old man regarded him for a few moments in silence. "What of the Hound and the Hawk?" he said. "Were their individual performances acceptable?"

Dylan winced at the use of the old titles. In ages past, all Order Pure teams had consisted of three members, a Hunter, Hawk, and Hound. The Hunter's job was mission planning and coordination. Hawks were spies and intelligence and Hounds were the muscle. The lines between those roles blurred considerably with modern strategies and tactics, so the terms were only historical now.

"Matthew King," Dylan said, "Performed admirably as always. Fast, smart, and hard hitting. Ariel Ikeda..." He paused. "She got us in and out smoothly and ran proper interference. Top marks for both of them."

"I see," Postan said. "The woman, then, was the only matter of note. I understand correctly?"

Dylan could feel the Cleric's sharp eyes on him. "Yes, High Cleric."

The fire snapped and sparks rose up the chimney. "Very well, then," Postan said. "File a detailed report with my aide, for the records. You may go, Hunter. Good work."

As Dylan made his way back to the upper Cathedral, he thought about what he would, and wouldn't, be putting in that report. He thought about the fight with the Demon and tried to figure out why the woman had been there

The west wing of the Red Cathedral was home to the medical ward. It was, in fact, a small, but state of the art hospital. In centuries past as Hunter teams had been injured in the line of duty, it had become necessary to employ physicians to sew them back together, or sedate them when night terrors kept them from rest. Over the years the villages and towns that grew around the Cathedral came to rely on the charity of the Order and the skill of their doctors. That charity was somewhat more costly now, but the best treatment could be found in an Order Pure hospital and being cared for at one was a privilege and a blessing.

Four stories below the hospital wing was a suite of rooms. An apartment with bedroom, kitchen, bathroom, and office, all well furnished. And a laboratory. The Inquisitor of the Order Pure stood in the middle of the large room, surrounded by equipment both new and very old. A cursory inspection of the lab would show that the work done here was also medical in nature, but not concerned with healing.

The man was unremarkable. His height was average, and his weight perfectly suited his frame. He gave no impression of physical prowess underneath his white coat. His steel gray hair and round glasses gave him a fatherly, pleasant look. When he moved, it was with grace. His smile, while small, was always genial.

There was a chair in the middle of the room, very similar to what a dentist might use. The addition of the leather ankle, wrist, and head restraints spoke of a more custom purpose. The woman Dylan and his team had rescued was strapped into the chair; the man, standing over her and injecting something into a vein in her arm, was made all the more sinister for his pleasant appearance.

The man set the empty syringe down on a nearby cart, then folded his arms behind his back. He waited and watched as the woman's open eyes went from dull and unfocused, to confused, and finally to awake and frightened. "Hello, my dear," the man said, and her eyes snapped to him. She couldn't quite open her mouth with the leather brace wrapped around her head, but she made a whimpering, questioning sound.

"I understand that this is unpleasant for you," the man said, his German accent only somewhat noticeable. "Though I assure you I do not endeavor to make it any more so than necessary." He pulled a metal stool close and sat down on it. "Do you remember at all how you got here?" She shook her head slightly. "Well. You were, unfortunately, made captive by a Demon lord, and only rescued earlier this day. Yes, I know that is confusing and startling news, and unfortunately I don't truly have much time to explain. What it boils down to is this: this Demon lord was the object of an assassination mission given to one Cleric Dylan Carter. You were not a part of the reported intel package. After Cleric Carter subdued and killed the Demon, he retrieved you and, somewhat rashly, brought you back to the Red Cathedral - ah, yes, I see you must know the place, resident of Chicago then, I presume? So then, Cleric Carter thought it best to bring you to the medical ward to have you checked over. You were rather unresponsive, you see.

"However, my dear, and this is the truly unfortunate part, it was not in the jurisdiction of the ward to treat you. You have been inside the personal temple of a denizen of the Demon realm, and worse, you were present when he was slain." The man then swiveled the stool toward the nearby cart and began taking various tools and other objects out of cases and small leather bags. "Therefore you were handed into my power. I am not a doctor. My name, or rather at least what I have been designated in my employ by the Order Pure these last one hundred and fifty years, is Inquisitor. It is my job tonight to see if, upon his death at the hands of the Cleric, the Demon Klarisvan hid any part of himself in any part of you, in order to facilitate survival and escape. It has been known to happen, if only rarely, and it causes a great deal of trouble." He looked at the woman then, over his glasses. "I don't suppose you'd like to admit if you're in there, Klarisvan? Just to save time?" There was no answer, and the Inquisitor gave a small chuckle as he turned back to his tools. "Where would be the fun in that, anyway?" he muttered.

"I want you to know that I'm not here to torture you, my dear. I'm not trying to wring any confession or truth out of you through pain or fear. My job is to take you apart, piece by part, mind, body, and soul. I will look inside those pieces, and see what I find there. You will think me cruel before the end, and I do not judge you for that. I do not intend cruelty. Only thoroughness. If you must direct your feelings to someone, I recommend Cleric Carter. He should not have pulled you out of that hole alive."

Perhaps it was morning by the time Inquisitor was close to finished. Dawn meant nothing down in those rooms. The woman was still alive, but the Inquisitor had made good on his promise. She was alive because he had the skill to not kill her. He had torn apart nearly everything not essential for the function of the mind, body, and soul. He was not done yet. Everything had to be examined, in detail.

He rolled his stool close to the woman's head. She could still hear. That was the last non-essential part of her left. He always left his victims the ability to hear up until the last. He had a message to send.

"We part ways here, my dear," he said gently. "You are about to enter the undiscovered country. You will meet a gray man there. He is the only certainty. When you do, I must request of you that you speak to him on my behalf. Please ask him...if he is willing to reconsider yet."

Chapter 4

B y the time Dylan got back to the upper halls of the Cathedral, Matthew King had finished his meditations and gone. He wouldn't be hard to find. Ariel Ikeda would be miles away by now, but Matthew would still be in the complex. He rarely left when not on a mission.

Matthew had a routine. Coming here to meditate and get his mind right after an assignment was always first, but after that came his weapons. Matthew was not a fool. He believed the Order could bless him, bless his friends, and bless his guns, but that all that would fall apart if he couldn't pull the trigger when it was time. So he always took extraordinarily good care of that trigger.

It was one area that the two men agreed on firmly. Dylan and Matthew differed in armament philosophy in that Dylan rarely used Order standard weapons, instead relying on an esoteric collection of what he called the "tried and true tools". Some were ancient, with questionable legality and provenance; while others were nearly brand new. His favorite was a very long barreled .357 revolver, what Ariel called his "ego gun". There was a knife made by David Bowie and a Native American shaman, and a strange silver spike with a crystal in the end he sometimes called a "soul sucker". A dozen other pockets and hidden sheaths held increasingly strange artifacts. No one knew exactly how many or what kinds of weapons Dylan carried and he liked to keep it that way.

Dylan knew exactly what Matthew carried. It was in the Order Pure Field Agent Handbook for that year. One silenced 9mm semiautomatic handgun, one smoke grenade, one flash-bang, and two salt grenades. Long gun options were an Order Light Assault in 5.56 or Nether Ward shotgun with over-under twelve-gauge buckshot and silver spike launcher. Knife options were a silver dagger or iron long knife. One med kit including mission specific antivirals and supernatural reagents. Then a page long list of various items, depending on the Cleric's specialty and training. Matthew was always by the book.

Dylan didn't hold that against him at all. Matthew got top marks in all combat proficiency tests, and Dylan didn't care at all what tools he chose to use.

Matthew wasn't as certain about Dylan's choices.

"Not carrying anything that'll make this place blow up, are you?" Matthew asked as Dylan walked into the armory. "Or get anyone haunted? Again?"

Matthew was seated ramrod straight at a metal table covered in every conceivable weapon maintenance tool available. Everything got cleaned, every mission, whether he used it or not. Everything got re-blessed by a Battle Priest. Everything was inventoried and locked up in Matthew's personal locker afterwards. Dylan suspected Harold Tomlinson, the Order Armorer, wanted to adopt Matthew by now.

"That wasn't a haunting, exactly," Dylan said, "and no, everything's pretty standard today. I'm even putting up Tomlinson's gun, see?" He held the massive cannon up in the air by two fingers and waggled it back and forth. "I'm a good boy."

Matthew smirked and went back to his routine. It was an old running framework of a joke that helped them both reconnect after the stress of a mission. Dylan filled out the paperwork at Tomlinson's cage and handed the old man the gun, unloaded but uncleaned, and went to sit by Matthew. Tomlinson gave him a customary sneer and went to take care of the weapon.

"Did the High Cleric have any explanations for what happened in there?" Matthew asked.

"No one has any ideas so far," Carter said. "I left the woman with Doctor Arthane, hopefully he'll get her up and around soon and we can question her. In the meantime, I assume Ikeda's gonna be wringing info out of the archives."

Matthew nodded and began reassembling a handgun. "She's really good at that kinda stuff."

"You're both really good at what you do. None better." For a few moments there was only the clink of metal parts sliding back together. Then Dylan said, "You wanna ask me about it? I don't have an answer, but…"

Matthew put everything down and stared at the lockers across the room. "I'm not gonna put that part in my report, about how she got me in there, or how we all got out. I don't wanna get her in trouble. But...I was pretty freaking sure stuff like that was impossible. You either kill a Demon before it raises its temple, or your friends check your will for what they get. And I am not complaining, Carter, I was trying to break down the office door, I was trying to get to you. I'm glad she did whatever she did. But I've never even heard of anything like that. Is that...I mean, are we ok?"

Matthew would never outright accuse Ariel of going gray, of borrowing black magic or making Nether deals. But Dylan knew what he meant.

"I think she's just that much ahead of us, man. I dunno, whatever she did, it was all her. I think we're ok. Though I do plan to find her and talk about it. If she can do more stuff like that, I dunno, maybe she's better than this. Maybe she needs sent up to R&D or something. In the meantime, she's keeping the two of us alive, and I'm making sure she gets a bonus. You too. Thanks. Really. I owe you both."

He rose and patted Matthew on the shoulder as he headed for the door. He saw the big man was smiling as he worked now. "I don't have a will, though," he said as he reached for the door handle, "So you can all just fight over my record collection."

He heard Matthew mumble, "Record collection?" as the door clicked shut.

Back on the street, Dylan made a stop by the Cathedral security building, situated at the main entrance gates. Certain items were strictly prohibited from entering the Cathedral premises. His cigarettes were one such item. He had checked them in the previous day and had no time to pick them back up after the mission. Now his hands visibly shook as he lit one up and pulled slowly on it.

Dylan knew it was a bad habit, but in his line of work, not an uncommon one. He always said that at least he wasn't into any of the stronger vices that a lot of Hunters fell to. Ariel and Matthew were neither of them mollified. Matthew had finally convinced him to at least try getting them consecrated. For a ten percent surcharge anything could be "blessed" and, theoretically, made safer or better or whatever. Dylan wasn't sure he really believed that. It was almost certainly just a money-making system for the Order. Then again, a blessed bullet would kill a Nether and a street bullet generally didn't. So, he got his cancer sticks blessed.

While the nicotine did its work, he set about finding Ariel. She wasn't quite so easy as Matthew. She usually didn't want to be found. If he was hunting her on the web, she'd dance around him and he'd never even know it. In the concrete world, a little familiarity and observation would go a long way. He was also going to cheat.

He pulled a small bronze box from a cargo pocket on his left leg. He cupped his hand around the box and whispered something to it, then held it out and spun slowly in a circle.

Nothing.

The guards at the gate were looking at him.

Dylan shook the box and held it up again. Still nothing. "Hey!" he said, and slapped the box in his palm. A moment later it began faintly buzzing, more so as he held it out to the west. Dylan smiled at the guards and started walking toward 57th.

When he found her, she was sitting in a back corner of a coffee shop, well hidden behind a large laptop screen. He ordered a black coffee, then sat down on the other side of her screen and waited. All Hunters came back from every mission shaken to some degree. What took Matthew and him a dozen hours to get over might take Ariel days, and usually he'd leave her alone. This time, he needed to talk sooner.

"That didn't take long," she said. Her eyes peeked over the top of the screen. "Did you follow me? Have me followed?" She looked around, suspicious.

"No, and no way," he said. "I sank much lower than that. Straight up cheated." He set the bronze box on the table and shook it gently. It vibrated and skittered gently an inch toward Ariel's backpack.

"Ok, freakin' creepy," she said. "What is it?"

"Scarab in a pillbox," Dylan said. "Or at least that's what the guy I got it from told me it was. I've never opened it to check. Anyway, had it get the scent of Klarisvan's medallion before the op. Didn't wanna lose track of something like that."

"You didn't think I'd turn it in?"

"You didn't turn it in," he said.

"I'm gonna," she said, not embarrassed to be caught red handed. She went back to her screen. "I just wanna check some more stuff on it." She reached down and shook some cables that ran into her backpack.

"Just be careful with it, underground stuff like this can be dangerous. Is almost always dangerous."

"You're one to talk." She smirked.

"I am, as a matter of fact. Blown up my fair share of ancient artifacts, sometimes with as little as careless salt spilled on the table." He paused. "If you find anything good though, maybe hang onto it. I can fudge my report a little."

She glanced up. "For real?"

"Yeah," he said. "Especially if it has anything to do with, you know, how you got King in. And me out."

She bit her lip. "Am I gonna be in any trouble for that? I didn't mean to do anything unauthorized or whatever, I just wanted to help."

"You're not in trouble with me, and me and King are the only ones who know about it. But just what did you do? Was it the medallion, or something else you've got hidden up a sleeve?"

She looked down at her bag. "I think it had something to do with the medallion," she said. "That's what I wanna find out. I know officially there's no way into a temple once it's up. But here I had this thing wired into my computer, getting a signal from Klari-whosits, and then you went quiet and Matthew started yelling that you were trapped. But I was still getting a reading on the Demon, so I figured the link was still active, and that seemed a lot like remote access to a system, and...I dunno. I made up some code. Like, totally made up on the spot, don't think I've seen it before. And I got it to access the walls of the temple. I guess. It's like the medallion is full of spells written in the Demon's personal magic, and I was making up spells in that language. Because the temple should have been written in the same magic, right? I don't know, that doesn't sound like it makes a lot of sense now, but it seemed right then. And then you guys were back, and I shut it down."

Dylan sat back. "Huh."

Ariel blinked. "'Huh'? That's it, oh wise and glorious leader? Shouldn't you explain to me what I did and tell me not to dabble in the dark arts or somethin'?"

"Doesn't sound all that dark to me," he said. "Saved my ass, too, and I don't wanna be ungrateful." He looked at the bag. "Huh."

He took a slow sip of coffee and studied her. Ariel was a short Japanese-American woman of twenty-five, with shoulder length hair on the top and right side of her head and a close buzz on the left. She always dressed like she was going to an cyberpunk convention and smiled easily when things weren't too work related. If he'd just met her, he'd assume she was a web designer or social media guru. Instead, he knew he was sitting across from one of the best intelligence and infiltration agents in the Order. Hacking magic, which he had never heard of, added a whole new page to her resume. One, he decided, that needed to be carefully guarded.

He set his cup down. "All I wanna tell you is thank you, Ikeda. Missions that sideways don't usually end with coffee the next day." She stared at him with big, serious eyes. "You're both receiving commendations on your records and pay bonuses. And I take it back, telling you to be careful. Sounds like you're the best person to have hold of that thing right now. Good job."

He stood up and smiled at her. "Just keep your report vague and leave all that other stuff out. And you are filing a report this time."

Ariel let out a groan and thumped her forehead onto the table. Dylan grabbed his scarab and left.

Interlude – Dylan Carter

Dylan was sound asleep in his sister's house in Florida. He had just turned eighteen and his birthday present was a summer spent on the beach. He was exhausted every day from fighting waves in the Atlantic. His Illinois skin was badly burned. He had tried to get the attention of a dozen girls and failed miserably. It was a nearly perfect summer.

His sister was twenty-nine and working as an assistant in an advertising firm. While not quite in Miami, it was Miami adjacent, and they'd been making weekly trips into the city for dinners and shopping. Dylan hadn't gotten to see Linda nearly enough since she graduated college and moved south. She was his "older twin," as they liked to say. Same eyes, same slightly crooked teeth, same dark hair. Hanging out with her was making life feel whole again.

Dylan's room was on the other side of the house from Linda's, on the second story. His usual nighttime routine, even on the long days at school or on summer break, was to stay up reading for a couple of hours. When sleep finally got the better of him, he was still propped up at a neck breaking angle on his pillow. As the night wore on his sleeping frame explored a dozen variations on the shape of pretzels and various sailors' knots. Nobody could out sleep Dylan Carter.

It was about 3AM when the noises woke him. They didn't seem like much. Some quiet scuffling. Maybe racoons in the attic. For a moment he didn't remember where he was. Then Linda screamed.

Dylan was bursting through the doorway to his room before he even realized he was out of bed. The house was darker than it should have been and way too hot. Later, his mind would register that this meant the power was off. Not yet though. All he knew now was terror.

Linda's door was closed. Dylan tried to turn the knob and push through without stopping. The handle didn't turn, and he slammed into the door painfully, cracking the thin wood, bouncing his head off of it sharply. There was a grunt inside the room, a man's voice, and Linda screamed again. Dylan slammed his shoulder over and over into the door. Finally, it flexed in its frame around the crack he'd made, and the latch slipped loose.

The streetlights through the window illuminated a scene his brain didn't want to comprehend. Four men surrounded Linda. They dressed in all black, with lots of belts, lots of pouches. Guns.

A split second after Dylan entered, he saw Linda's balled fist come down on one man's shoulder, close to the neck. There were snapping sounds and the man crumpled to the ground. Linda swung a wild right hook at another man who was stepping in. He must have been looking for it, because he stepped outside the punch, looping his right arm up through hers, and slamming her back and down over his leg. Linda's head made a sickening crack against the footboard of her bed. She went still.

Dylan screamed. He rushed in at the intruders and straight into a sweeping backhand. The blow stopped him in his tracks. Suddenly, the air exploded from his lungs as the man followed through with a hard front kick, and Dylan went flying back through the splinters of the door.

He was only vaguely aware that the man who struck him was pushing through the wooden wreckage. He pulled something silver from his belt. A knife? Gun? There was no way to tell in the dim light filtering into the hallway.

"No."

Someone in the room had spoken to the man looming over him. The man stopped and looked back over his shoulder. Dylan was fading out.

"Not…-thorized. H-…owing any signs. Just th-…ster."

The darkness he fell into was haunted with the echoes of his sister's screams.

When he woke, he was still lying in the hall. Crusted blood covered the left side of his nose and mouth. His chest hurt too badly to take a deep breath. Everything was completely quiet and still. He crawled into Linda's room, but there was nothing there. No man crumpled and broken on the floor. No sister. Hardly even a mess, except what he'd done to the doorway.

Dylan went downstairs and phoned the police. He waited for them outside, sitting on the curb. He wasn't sure if staying in the house was the safe thing to do.

He answered endless questions after they arrived. Then he answered them again. The officers took him to a station, where he answered the questions for a third time for someone who must have been of higher rank. He could begin to see why they kept asking. He was basically a teenager describing what sounded like an action movie. They wanted him to remember what had really happened. By the end of the morning, he did too.

That Linda had been assaulted and probably kidnapped was obvious. The power had been cut at the outside junction box and the front door lock picked, albeit skillfully. There were some boot scuff marks, signs of a struggle in the bedroom, and a little blood. Not enough to justify Dylan's story, however.

Dylan went back home to Chicago and waited anxiously with his parents. Anxiety became fear, then heartache. Finally, as the year ended and no progress was made on the search, despair.

Dylan never quite gave up. As unlikely as finding Linda seemed, he always hoped for that newspaper miracle, his sister's name in bold print, followed by "KIDNAPPED WOMAN FOUND". He would go through periods of manic research, trying to figure out who took her, trying to find something that matched the unlikely events that were all he had to go on.

Three years later, in an obscure online chatroom, he did. People with stories. Of family members acting not quite normal. Of armed abductors in the night. Of being left alive, left behind, for reasons they couldn't understand. People who knew someone who knew someone who heard something. And a name. The Sons of James.

The SOJ, as chat members called them, were an obscure group of religious zealots who followed the teachings of King James, a notorious Demon Hunter of the 16th century. They claimed to hunt those afflicted by the Nether. Rumor said what they really did was kidnap and murder humans.

It was another three months before Dylan had tracked that name, that group, as far as he could on his own. Another dead end. But not for long. Days later, a man in a blue suit knocked on the door to his trash apartment, offering a job. An opportunity. All the resources he could ever need to find those who took his sister, in exchange for hunting other monsters. For the Order Pure.

Chapter 5

Dylan was already awake when his cellphone rang at 5AM. Not because he was habitually an early riser, but because he had been having dreams so boring he couldn't sleep through them. His sleep patterns and dreams had been erratic and disturbed ever since the event with Klarisvan a month before. Some nights it wasn't worth it to keep trying to rest.

He slid the green bell symbol across the screen and said, "Carter."

"Cleric Carter, this is Order Assignment Sector, 11-0-35K. Please confirm agent code."

"Katie, it's early, and I know you know it's me, can't we just—"

"Dylan, you know this is being recorded. If you get me in trouble again, you'll be hunting cursed rats in the sewers. So, please, *Cleric,* confirm your agent code."

Dylan sat up and rubbed a hand over his face. "Dylan, 27-5-91T. What's up."

"Intelligence has sent compelling evidence of an impending Vampire gathering. Field agents confirm activity consistent with such. Order leadership would like your team to determine the night of the gathering and intervene."

"You're throwing us an easy one? Aw, you guys really do have a heart, huh?"

"Well..." she said.

Dylan slumped. "You don't have hearts, do you?"

"It's because it isn't easy that it went to your team."

"Ok," he said. "Tell me in what awful way a gang of bloodsuck punks isn't going to be easy to kill."

"It's not a street gang," she said. "It's a Coven. With an Elder Vampire."

By 8AM Dylan, Matthew, and Ariel were in a private strategy room at the Red Cathedral. Matthew was apparently the only professional member of the team. He had on his usual khaki cargo pants, black t-shirt, and clean, polished combat boots. Dylan was wearing a coat that he had explained several times was a custom outback leather duster, which he'd had made for all its extra pocket space. The wide brimmed leather hat on the conference table was because he burned easily, he said. Ariel was wearing pajamas and fuzzy slippers.

"How did you get in here like that?" Matthew asked. He had his big brother smile on to soften his serious tone.

"Frank, the security guard. He likes me. He's almost always on duty at this wretched hour. I wanna know how you," she waggled her coffee at Dylan, "keep getting in here like that."

"Frank's scared of me," Dylan said without looking up. He was digging through a library cart of old books he'd wheeled in.

"Are we doing book reports today, boss?" Matthew said.

"No," Dylan said. He looked up, scowling. "Fuck no, man. Don't talk like that." He carefully set two large volumes on the table. "See, the thing is, we have become the Order's favorites for digging ditches, taking out the trash, and killing the scariest, slimiest monsters. Because we are just that good." He waved a finger back and forth between Matthew and Ariel. "I blame you two."

Ariel raised a hand. "I'd like to confess to cheating on my exams, please. All of them."

"I heard you re-wrote one of your exams from memory to 'make it right,' and turned your version in to your prof the next day," Matthew said. "No one's gonna believe you cheated."

"That guy was an idiot," Ariel said, scowling at her coffee.

"Anyway, it's too late. You're stuck with us. If I have to carry you around in a backpack, I will." Matthew smiled wide, and Ariel stifled a giggle.

"You guys up on Vampires?" Dylan asked, bending over an open volume.

Matthew blinked. "You mean the skinny little punks that fight ghouls for dead rats in back allies? The things they send out Junior Hunters to kill for practice? That's your big scary. Bloodsucks. Do we, what, have to fight them naked?"

Ariel winced. "Uck, my eyes," she said, pinching the bridge of her nose. "Think of my innocent eyes."

Dylan flipped a few pages. "That's why we have the old books. It's not as simple as your basic Nether ragdoll on the street. Apparently Chicago is about to be visited by an Elder Vampire."

"Oh," Matthew said. "I'm gonna need a refresher on that, I guess."

"I thought Elders were kinda just mostly legends?" Ariel said. "Movie stuff?"

"Generally speaking, yes," said a voice from the door. "Would that it could stay that way." A tall, thin man was leaning against the frame, sleeves rolled up and arms crossed. He had curly brown hair down to his jawline and very pale skin. He was dressed in early 20th century trousers and a brown waistcoat over a white button up shirt. What could be seen of his arms and chest were crossed with tattoos, symbols and lines of text in some arcane language. Matthew stiffened as the man strolled into the room. Ariel stared, wide eyed.

"Guys, this is, uh...Blood. The Order calls him Blood. Which, you probably already knew, but..." Dylan said.

"The Order scores no points for originality," said the man. "They intend the term be felt as a slur. I prefer James Wilson Clarke. You may call me James."

"Dylan, we're good on our own. We don't need him here," Matthew said.

"And what is it you think you know of Vampires, Matthew King?" James said. As he smiled, two white, long, sharp teeth showed at the corners of his thin lips. "Far less than I, certainly."

Matthew stood very still. Only Dylan noticed the slight tremble of anger in his hands.

"You're a Vampire," Ariel breathed. "Like, the Order's Vampire."

"James is the resident specialist, yes," Dylan said quickly. "He works with the Order and has since before any of us were born. And he's a friend of mine," Dylan said. Matthew's gaze snapped over to him. "So let's all be friends."

"And you stop that," he said, pointing at James. The Vampire was smiling at Ariel, who was shrinking in her chair behind her coffee. She was smiling back. "Her eyes are very innocent, and she reads too many romance books. Sweet mother of hormones, I'm too old to deal with all of this. Elder Vampire," he said loudly. "Professor Clarke, would you please give us a basic rundown here."

Ariel winked at James, and he grinned once more, then walked over to stand by the books Dylan had brought.

"Cleric King is correct," he said. "Normally your average Vampire on the street is nothing to worry about. Many don't even know they're monsters, having only a mild manifestation of abilities and weaknesses, lying to themselves and claiming some mystery illness. Even the Vampires that your groups usually hunt are weak and uneducated shadows of the Vampire legend, and therefore generally easy to put down. Then there are cases of the afflicted limiting themselves to animal blood and eventually starving because of a lack of necessary nutrients, et cetera."

He thumbed through the yellowed pages of a book. "Nevertheless, caution is exercised even in the hunting of lesser Vampires because of post feeding aggression and manifestation of invulnerability. Immediately after feeding, most Vampires will display a marked increase in strength, resistance to attacks, and aggressive behavior, usually lasting—"

"Can we skip to the part we need to know?" Matthew said impatiently.

James eyed him. "Never skip the basics, Matthew King," he said. "You never know when they might save your life."

Matthew and James glared at each other, neither man breaking eye contact. Finally Dylan said, "These guys are considered above average on lore and technique, James. Why don't you tell us about the Elder, and we can do a Q and A later, ok?"

After a moment James said, "Elder Vampires. Elders are, as you would guess, very old. More than ten centuries at the youngest. Elder Vampires are almost exclusively sanguine, not psychic. Whereas a common Vampire may display strength and fortitude following a kill, the manifestation is usually short lived and there are reliable methods of overcoming these defenses. An Elder, however, is much more dangerous after feeding. The strength of an Elder after ingestion of blood is many, many times higher than the average human, often more than nine hundred percent so. Further, while I am loath to say that they are invincible, there has not yet been discovered a method of killing one after it has fed. Whatever magic drives such a creature, it renders their bodies impervious to blade or bullet. If one does manage to inflict a wound on an Elder, it will heal as quickly as it appeared. As to aggression," he added, "it will not manifest in the rage and recklessness shown in young specimens. Think of it more as a terrible madness bound to a focused will to do harm."

Everyone sat quietly for a moment.

"Boss, about my PTO I've got built up," Ariel said.

Dylan was sitting with his arms folded, leaning back and looking at James. "This doesn't sound like an assignment, James. Sounds more like an execution. Our executions."

"Only if you don't get to him before he feeds," James said.

"About that," Matthew said. "Why wouldn't they just feed every day, stay like that all the time? They could rule the world."

"I think you could say that's exactly the problem," James said. "Elder Vampires could. They almost did. In the 14th and 15th centuries there were, relatively speaking, many Elder Vampires. The world was essentially divided between their rule and the rule of the Order Pure. However, Vampiric territories began to clash. At that point Vampires began to be hunted, not just by the Order and villager, but by their own kind. Vampiric assassins for hire.

"Soon it was obvious to the Vampiric lower ruling class that either a peace must be found, or extinction accepted. Treaties were made, councils convened, and a decision reached. Open rule was untenable. Even without the interference of humans, the strength and volatility of the Elders was a danger to the species itself. This was the beginning of the Coven system. An Elder is ostensibly the head of a Coven, but he or she is also subject to the guidance and control of these lesser, but still immensely strong, Vampires.

"A resolution was passed to…reduce…the number of Elders to a controllable level. These Elders would then provide a focal point of governance for the Vampire community, and provide a certain amount of protection when needed. Their lesser numbers would attract less attention from human governments."

"You make it sound like Elders actually work for the coven," Dylan said.

"In a way, yes," James said. "A fully fed Elder is a danger to even other Vampires. Covens therefore restrict Elders' feeding frequency, using their combined strength and magic to control the Elder until the effects of fresh blood have worn off. Most Elders are only allowed to feed once every decade or so. At those times, a blood ritual is employed to magically extend the life-giving powers of the blood consumed, without extending the strength it gives."

"How long will the Elder be invulnerable when it does feed?" Dylan asked.

"At least a couple of days," James said, "Though it depends on the Elder. Do you happen to know which one you're going after?"

"Info packet calls her Jelena," Dylan said.

James' lips formed a thin frown, and he looked down for a moment. "Almost regrettable," he said. "One of the few Elders who could be called reasonable, at a stretch of the term. Still, we have our orders, don't we?" He ran his long, thin fingers over the volumes in the library cart. "I will help you as I can. But of all of them, that you should be sent to hunt an ancient Serbian Vampire is problematic. Their magic, their proclivities, strengths, weaknesses, all of these will be very hard to define.

"It's possible, likely even, that my kind, originated in Serbia. The magic that governs our being therefore also began in that area. Full Serbian Vampires believe magic is what you will it to be. If Jelena wants something badly enough, there will probably be no way to predict how she obtains it."

"What are our surest weapons against her? And the Coven?" Matthew said.

"As for the Coven, garlic and its derivatives are the best defensive measure. I believe the armory stocks a garlic extract suspended in a gel, yes? Stakes made of hawthorn will perform well for close fighting, if it comes to that, though you should hope not to be caught close to any of them. Coven members must be strong enough to collectively control an Elder, and that is no mean feat. As for Jelena," he thought for a moment, "I cannot imagine anything but fire will ultimately do the trick. That's how the early Serbians attempted to prevent their loved ones from becoming Vampires. Likely in her mind it will be the only thing she believes will kill her, and her magic will be shaped by her belief."

"So, like...you want us to burn her at the stake, or something? I thought that was witches," Ariel said.

"Firstly," James said, "please don't do that to any malignant witches you may encounter, they started that rumor, it's just an escape ploy. Secondly, flaming arrows would be a better option, if you could manage to hit her. Any of you good with a bow?"

Matthew and Dylan looked across the table at each other and smiled. "Cherry bombs," Matthew said.

"Cherry bombs," Dylan agreed.

James and Ariel looked at them, puzzled. "Fireworks?" Ariel said.

Dylan took the key from Tomlinson and walked over to a heavy door in a back corner of the armory. The key was nearly the size of Dylan's hand and etched with several lines of runes. He slid the key into the door and turned it.

For several seconds mechanisms in the door and wall clacked and whirred, then the door swung open. Fluorescent lights stuttered and buzzed to life. Matthew and Dylan strolled in with big grins on their faces. Ariel followed behind more cautiously, hands in her pockets. "Is this you guys' secret clubhouse?" she said.

"You know how you and I have our own toys, and King has his 'daddy says it's ok' stuff?" Dylan said. Matthew punched him in the arm as he walked past. "Well, this stuff sort of falls in between. Failed experiments, weapons deemed generally obsolete but kept for special purposes, and ordinance considered too destructive for widespread use. We're here for the latter."

"Found 'em," Matthew said. He came out from behind a row of shelves with a satchel over his shoulder and two hardcase gun carriers. Dylan took a case and set it on a nearby table, popped the latches, and lifted the lid.

"Interesting," Ariel said. "Kinda looks antique, kinda looks new."

"They're new," Matthew said, "It's just the Order exerting its traditional style. They're based on old blunderbusses."

He set the other case and the satchel on the table and unzipped the bag. "They fire a couple of different ammo variants, either scattershot or what Carter and I called cherry bombs. Both use a special impact trigger system and thermite core to thoroughly cleanse whatever you shoot them at with fire." He stared lovingly at a red, golf ball sized pellet in his hand. "Always hoped we'd find a reason to use these."

"Ok, so what's the catch with these then?" Ariel said

"They were developed to quickly control ghoul and zombie hordes," Dylan replied, "But after the first few deployments the damage to surrounding property was considered to be just too much. However, because I am a senior Cleric and we have special circumstances, we get to take them out to play." He took a deep breath and let out a satisfied sigh. "It's good to be king."

"I'm not cleaning you two children off the walls," Ariel said. "I don't do cleaning."

"We'd be dusty ashes anyway, just turn on a strong fan," Dylan said. He looked around at the shelves full of weapons. "I don't know that there's anything down here like what you use though, I think it's mostly guns and swords and stuff."

"Oh, that's fine," Ariel said. "I make my own toys." Her grin was just as big as Matthew's was.

Interlude – Matthew

Matthew sat on a bench in his high school locker room. It smelled damp, with notes of rusted metal and gym socks. Usually this was his favorite place in the world. Right now being here did nothing to calm his shakes, to ease the weight of his football pads on his shoulders. He didn't know why he'd been pulled from practice and told to meet his coach here. He didn't smoke, drink, or party. He hadn't missed a practice in two years. He had turned in a paper late a couple of weeks ago and coach had high standards for academics. No, he decided. He really couldn't figure out why he was waiting here. And that was awful.

When Coach Roberts walked into the room, Matthew jumped to his feet. "Hey coach, what's up?" he said, trying to sound casual.

"Matthew. You need to come with me, son. I'm gonna give you a ride," Roberts said. "It's, uh …son, your mom's been hurt. She was attacked at the laundry. She's at Newmann Memorial. She's stable, as far as I know, but you're done with practice for today. Let's go."

He led Matthew out to the car with a hand on his shoulder. Matthew's mouth hung open, slack. There was a sick knot in his stomach. His brain didn't seem to want to process what he needed it to explain. His mother had been fine yesterday, planting flowers and singing lame oldies from her teen years. This morning she'd kissed him goodbye and driven off to work while he'd eaten his breakfast. Now she was in the hospital? Coach couldn't tell him more than that. He didn't know more. He was just the ride.

Matthew had been sleeping on the floor of the hospital room for two nights in a row. There was no way to pull the small visitors' chairs around to accommodate his two-hundred-ten--centimeter frame. Rhonda King had not woken up yet. It was hard to even tell that it was her under the thin blankets. Under the blue hair net, oxygen mask, IV's, drainage tubes, casts, bandages, and so much tape, tape everywhere, all Matthew could see were her closed eyes. Since he'd gotten to the hospital he'd stared at her eyelids between bouts of crying, holding her hand and willing her to wake up. It hadn't worked yet, so he kept trying.

Sometimes he would look down at the bandages and the plaster around her leg and forearm. Only two broken bones, but so many cuts. Lacerations, the doc had called them, and he thought that word fit better, sounded more like what covered his mother. Deep, wide lacerations, rows of them, across her shoulders and abdomen, raking the muscles and tendons of her limbs. Mom had held their lives together since dad died. Now she was held together with stitches, like a dilapidated marionette.

The cops had told him it was some kind of knife attack. They hadn't found the weapon at the scene but they had forensics on it. A customer coming into the laundromat had heard screaming and rushed to the back room where Matthew's mother folded the laundry she was paid to wash. The customer said Rhonda was lying on the floor with someone crouching over her, swiping at her. They described the man as shaggy, long haired, wearing some kind of dirty old fur coat. Matthew couldn't remember how they'd scared the guy off. Beaten them with a jug of detergent maybe. The cops thought it was a homeless guy, maybe mentally ill, maybe looking for money. Maybe, possibly, could be.

Matthew held his mother's hand and cried.

On the morning of the third day, Matthew woke to see a man standing at the foot of his mother's bed, going over her chart. At first, he thought it was a doctor. But the docs so far hadn't come in wearing navy suits and red ties.

"Mr. King," the man said, as Matthew got clumsily to his feet. The man in the suit looked up from the chart to Rhonda, then over at Matthew. "I am Shepherd Hendricks, of the Order Pure, stationed at Red Cathedral. I have a proposition for you."

Chapter 6

Matthew King had only been down these corridors once before, at his assignment to Dylan's team. His size made them feel especially cramped and, more than once, he had to duck or turn sideways to avoid rockwork or lighting fixtures.

His cell phone had buzzed with a private message an hour after he and the team had inspected the weapons they planned to use to hunt the Elder Vampire. Matthew rarely got personal messages. To get a message that wasn't from Dylan or Ariel was unusual. Getting a summons from the High Cleric's aide had never happened before and was unnerving.

The heavy wooden door was exactly as he remembered it. Even though he was going to have to duck to get through it, somehow it was still imposing, as though the wood held some power of its own. Old as it was, it must have heard its share of secrets, seen enough strange times. He reached out for the knocker, pausing only a moment before grasping the iron and rapping it against the door. The door opened, but whoever had opened it was already gone.

"Come in, Cleric King, come in," a gentle voice said from inside the chamber. Matthew crossed the floor carefully, weaving between furniture. He knelt before the old man in the high-backed chair and carefully took his withered hand, touching it to his forehead. Then he stood and crossed his hands behind his back. "How may I serve, High Cleric?" he said.

Postan smiled at him. The old man was wrapped in a wool blanket and held his pale hands out toward the fire. After a moment he nodded to himself. "How long have you been with us now, Cleric? Ten years?" he said.

"Eleven, sir."

"Eleven years," Postan mused. "Do you know, I do not recall a more decorated Cleric as young as you are? Some nearly so, of course, but you are exceptional. I wanted to take a moment to personally congratulate you on your achievements. And also to apologize."

Matthew's face had begun to burn with embarrassment at the praise, but all thought of that was suddenly wiped away. "Apologize, sir? There's nothing…sir, you would never need to…"

Postan gently waved a hand to silence him. "Perhaps for nothing direct, but I have had some conversations with your superior, Cleric Carter, lately, and he has had cause to chastise me for some of my more archaic ways. Particularly my use of the old titles associated with your profession. You are aware of the historical designations of team members, I suppose?"

"Hunter, Hawk, and Hound, sir. My role would have been designated as the 'Hound' of the team."

"Yes," the High Cleric said. "Well, as I say, I sometimes lapse into that old terminology, and I did so during Cleric Carter's last discussion with me. He reminded me that those terms took on negative aspects some years ago, some very unfortunate usage by certain disgraced Order members. I don't know whether he mentioned my using such terms to you or Ms. Ikeda, but I thought it best to bring you here and make clean the slate in person. If I have offended you or treated you or your team in any derogatory manner, I do sincerely apologize and repent."

Matthew could not have been more caught off guard. He had expected to be called on to clarify a portion of some report at best, or chastised for some action at worst. He was decidedly uncomfortable having a senior Order member turn the tables and offer an apology to him. "No, sir, Cleric Carter hasn't mentioned anything of the sort. None of us would have assumed you meant offense, High Cleric, I'm sure."

"I'm glad you feel so, Cleric King," Postan said. "Very glad indeed." He stared into the flames for several long seconds. Matthew began to wonder if the older man had forgotten him or grown tired. He said, "Will there be anythi—"

"Do you know, in ancient times, the role of Hound was, in some ways, more important than the role of Hunter?" Postan said.

Matthew shifted. "How so, sir?"

"We now often think of the Hunter as the team lead, and in many ways that matter, that was always the way of it. The Hunter was always a Cleric with seniority, specialized training, and access to resources not granted to the general clergy. However, a team that had lost its Hound, through injury, death, whatever, was always recalled. In fact, Hunters would immediately abandon a mission if they no longer had a Hound with them. A Hunter and a Hound might finish a mission alone, or even a Hound and a Hawk, unless some lack of skill or knowledge made this impossible. But not a Hunter and a Hawk, alone. Do you know why?"

Matthew did not answer, but was listening intently.

"The Hound is the protector of the team," the High Cleric said. "He, or she, was not just a muscle-bound oaf, as you yourself are not just your strength, though I hear that is considerable. They were not merely attack hounds the Hunter could let off their leash. They guarded the Hunter and the Hawk, as I hear you recently did in rescuing Cleric Carter during his...lapse in the Klarisvan operation."

"Cleric Carter found himself in a situation not covered by our intelligence packets, sir. He is the most capable Cleric I know, and I'm proud to work with him."

"Good dog," Postan mumbled, very quietly.

"Sir?"

Postan looked up, smiling again, if only slightly. "Cleric Carter is, as you say, highly skilled and resourceful. One of our most valuable Clerics. Though he is, perhaps, a bit unorthodox?" He raised his eyebrows to Matthew.

Matthew hesitated. It was dangerous ground. Dylan was indeed very unorthodox. He only used Order hardware on the rare occasions he deemed it better than black market equipment and often supplemented intelligence gathered by Order agents with sources that he refused to name. "As far as I'm aware, sir, he directly violates no Order Pure mission precepts, and always puts the safety of his team and fellow clerics first. I am also not aware of any mention in his record of him not completing a mission to a satisfactory result."

"Your loyalty to your commanding officer is very admirable, Cleric, and it reassures me of the appropriateness of your assigned position. You guard your teammates well.

"However, the Hound, as we were discussing, had another role that, sadly, has often been overlooked, lessened, completely forgotten next to the vital role of team protection. A Hound also carefully guarded the team, and by extension, the Order Pure itself, from threats from within." He sat back in his chair and held his gaze fixed on Matthew's eyes, no longer smiling. "Cleric Carter is very important to the Order. But he is unorthodox. Sometimes, in his fervor to serve the interests of the Order, a Cleric might lead himself astray, seek methods and tools that are discouraged or forbidden for a reason. I find myself concerned for the internal wellbeing of Cleric Carter. I am calling on you, Matthew King, Cleric of the Order, to guard your team. Guard it from danger without. Guard it from wanderings within. Can you do that for me, Cleric King?"

Matthew sat by his mother's bed, holding her hand. She was sleeping, but she would wake up in a couple of hours. She took a lot of naps these days. He looked over the flowers on the windowsill. Nurses replaced them every few days. Soft music came from a small stereo beside the bed, turned down low. A doctor walking by looked in, smiled, and mouthed the words, *be back later*. Matthew took in a deep breath, held it, and let it out slowly.

The Order Home for the Impaired was good. Better than anything he could ever have afforded on his own. His mother received specialized care and comforts here she couldn't get anywhere else.

Yeah, I can, he thought. *I can protect the team. And the Order. And I can protect her.*

Chapter 7

The next three days consisted of preparedness drills in a simulated sewer environment made out of scaffolding and tarps. Dylan and Matthew ran the infiltration from four different access points, over and over. They ran drills where everything went right. Then they ran them in the dark until they could navigate the passageways with lights out and failed NVGs. Then two other OP teams, on cool down between missions, acted as hostiles and ambushed the pair as they infiltrated. With tasers. Matthew always preferred there to be acute motivation to avoid failure in training.

Ariel ran drills with them the first day, then moved into her personal lab space for two days, tweaking equipment and poring over schematics, blueprints, maps, everything she could get her hands on. She checked and double checked the back doors the Order secured into the power grid systems for Lincoln Park. She packed electronic detection equipment for three different types of supernatural energy that the team wasn't even expecting.

She was being paranoid and over cautious, and she knew it. She had almost lost her team to the unexpected. Her two "big brothers". She had somehow pulled them through it, gotten them out by luck and loopholes, but she didn't intend to take chances ever again. Her backpack was just going to have to weigh a little extra, that's all.

James, the Vampire captured a century ago and bound to the service of the Order by tattoos and spells in his own flesh, was also preparing. He was working his way through his personal collection of expensive whiskey, and wondering what it was about Dylan Carter that made people ever do anything he asked them to do. He perpetually asked for favors that were sideways and of questionable legality. James was pondered why he had even befriended the man to begin with. He remembered, guiltily, that it was Dylan who had befriended him. Dylan rarely held prejudice against the unhuman. It was humans, James knew, that had betrayed Dylan's trust first, the night they attacked his sister. Now Dylan was asking him, trusting him, to come along on a mission, to be secondary intelligence and advisor. Also, as bodyguard to Ariel, who would otherwise be left alone in a hotel room near the Elder's mansion. She would be focused on her electronics and relatively defenseless.

Several miles away, in a long vacant Lincoln Park mansion, other preparations were being made. Over the course of the week several extremely expensive cars had arrived and were parked in a climate-controlled garage behind the house. Delivery trucks, driven by dazed and dead-eyed familiars, had come and gone, leaving behind wooden crates and medical containers of the type used to transport organs. Deep underground, in a sub-basement only a select few knew how to access, the Coven of Jelena were layering several different types of magical and alchemical wards. Only a few of these were meant to protect the coven and its master from the outside world of Hunters and rivals; the rest were to protect the Vampires present from Jelena. An Elder must be respected, revered, practically worshipped, but also properly restrained.

Vuk, alchemist for the Coven, was carefully mixing a red powder with a mortar and pestle, preparing for the night-long job of painting warding symbols on the walls of the basement. He took great care that there be no waste in his work. Copper old enough not to be contaminated by radioactivity was expensive and occasionally historically important. He treated its sacrifice with great respect.

"The schedule has changed. She'll be arriving in the morning," said a voice behind him. Vuk turned to see Doina, a tablet computer in her hand. "A train transfer due to a derailment actually put her a day ahead of schedule."

"That's...not optimal," said Vuk. He looked at the walls he hadn't yet finished. "If you can get someone with any experience in alchemy down here to help me, I might be able to get it done in time."

Doina tapped her screen a few times and made some swipes. "Matvei, a junior security specialist, looks to have had mid-level training, in the early 1900s. Will that do?"

"Hardly from alchemy's heyday," Vuk said, "but yes, that should do. As long as he can keep a steady hand and copy from the texts, I can work with that. Security won't miss him?"

"No, he's only down for patrol duty tonight, I'll have the captain move someone else to his place," she said, tapping the screen again. "Done. I've messaged him, he should be here soon."

"Good," Vuk said. He slowly mixed his bowl of alchemical pigment into a large bowl filled with blood. "I feel like this was easier in the old days, Doina. We didn't have to buy houses through shell corporations, or find ways to keep them empty. We had castles with rooms kept ready for occasions like this. We didn't have to transport Elders around the world all the time to keep them off the radar. Villagers feared us and our homes and just stayed away. Now, the world is so complicated..."

"My old days didn't start as long ago as all that, Vuk. Which is why I can use a computer and a cell phone, and you can't," she said, even as she smiled affectionately.

Vuk smiled back. "And I am truly thankful you are here to handle those most difficult of devices for me," he said. The young often assumed his age meant he was ignorant of the modern world. He could use a computer just fine, much better than Doina, truth be told. Programming was not dissimilar to alchemy. He simply didn't want to have to use the machines. He didn't love them like he loved the tools of his trade: brush and ink, hammer and chisel, knife and flesh.

Doina started to respond, but her pocket chirped and buzzed. "Sorry, gotta go," she said. She tapped out a message on the screen as she turned and left.

Vuk watched her climb the stairs, then opened his ancient books to the diagrams he'd need to ward the sub-basement. He was glad his job didn't require any electronics or modern wizardry. As those things had become more necessary, the coven had felt more like a business than a family. He missed the old days, and it made him feel like an old man to think it. *Immortality*, he mused, *does not protect the soul from aging.*

"There's a problem," Matvei said into his burner phone. He was halfway down a darkened access corridor for the main basement, speaking quietly. He had a sick knot in his stomach and felt like he'd be in a cold sweat, if his body could still do that. "The schedule's been moved up, the Elder's arriving just before dawn."

"The teams are flexible, the timing isn't an issue," said a gruff voice on the other end. "The only problem will be if you can't get us in. Has that circumstance changed, Mister Volkov?"

Matvei was still unused to being addressed by his surname. He hadn't needed it since joining Jelena's coven more than seventy years ago. Saint Rollins, leader of SOJ squad seventeen, refused to call him by anything else. Matvei figured it was passive aggressive disrespect because he was a Vampire, but he didn't need the man's respect. Just his money. It would be decades yet before the coven promoted him high enough to receive a decent paycheck and he just didn't feel like waiting that long.

"No, I can still get you in," he said. "Though I might need to buy a shift off one of the other guys patrolling the tunnel to do that. I think that falls under extra expenses."

There was a pause on the line. "Very well," Rollins said. "An amount has been transferred that should prove sufficient. Coordinate with Believer Elaina and establish a rendezvous time."

"Yes sir. Got it, sir."

"And Mister Volkov? No more extra expenses. You are a convenience. It would save the Sons of James a great deal of money to simply replace you with five pounds of explosives. And one extra silver bullet."

Matvei ran his fingers through his hair. "No, yeah, I got it. We're good. No more ex—"

The line went dead. Matvei snapped the phone shut, then hurried to see the old alchemist.

Chapter 8

Dylan ran a hand over his chin and decided the stubble was too close to a beard. He didn't bother with the mirror, just picked up the same clippers he used to buzz cut his hair, took the guard off, and ran the bare blades over his face. He rarely used the mirror for much anymore. He couldn't care less whether he looked good or not.

His phone buzzed halfway through brushing his teeth. He saw Ariel's picture on the screen from the corner of his eye and, absentmindedly, put the phone on speaker. "Yeah, go ahead," he said, through toothpaste.

"Morning, boss," she said. She sounded maybe a little more awake than him. "Got developments. Field intelligence checked in with me this morning. They caught action that suggests our timeline might be wrong, so I got into some of the Coven's systems, and yup, the Elder is arriving early. Just one day early, but we've gotta go ahead and get everything tied down. We're doing this tomorrow night. Or do you think we should abort?"

"Oh, do I get a say in it?" he said. "I guess I could try making the call, being the boss and all."

"Ouch. Grumpy much? Worse morning person than me these days."

"Yeah. Sorry. Sorry. Bad nights lately. We're still a go. Let the Order know it's gonna be tomorrow. Check with King yet?"

"Just about to," she said.

"Let me know if he has any objections, otherwise let's meet back in war room seven in a couple hours. Good?"

"Good," she said, and ended the call.

"Tomlinson has my list, already packed our gear bags," Matthew said. The big man was leaning over the table, resting his hands on a map of the route they planned to take through the sewers and old access tunnels. Blueprints for the mansion were in front of everyone at the table. "I'll go check with the garage and make sure the vehicles are serviced and ready to go.

"Get a driver for me and James while you're there," Ariel said. "Apparently James can't drive."

"You can't drive?" Matthew said. "Two hundred years and you never learned to drive?"

"By the time it would have been reasonable," the Vampire said, "the Order had me under lock and key. And they aren't keen on their special assets learning skills conducive to escape or evasion."

"That's fine, just make sure it's someone who knows Lincoln Park well," Dylan said. "Hotel?"

Ariel sighed. "The Lincoln."

Dylan looked from her, to James, and back to Ariel. "The Lincoln? Don't you usually pick some hole in the wall—"

"We won't stand out at the Lincoln," Ariel said. "I have it on good authority that that one," she pointed at James, "won't dress down. Also," she said, and waved a hand toward James like a ringmaster.

He smiled, shrugged, and said, "The Order owes me a night out. It's going on their card; I'm surprised you all don't do this more often."

"Does it not bother you that we're about to kill a prominent member of your kind?" Matthew said.

The corner of James' mouth twitched. "Not much more than the putting down of a rabid dog. Which I have also done a couple of times, back in the old days, so I've got more practice than you."

"Anyway," Ariel said, "back to stuff that matters. I've already got all my gear packed. I've got routers linked to a nearby Order Wi-Fi hotspot, and I've had the room swept by a security specialist. Bianca, she's really good, even Coven level resources won't get past her."

"Bringing anything extra this time?" Dylan said.

Ariel bit her lip for a moment. "I couldn't find anything connected to Jelena to bring," she said. "From anyone. Anywhere. She's definitely swept her tracks over the years."

"They've been swept for her," James said. "She's about as old as they come, and therefore as powerful as they get. The Coven wouldn't want anything happening to her. But most importantly, they wouldn't want anyone helping her get free. You'll never find anything that helps you connect to her on a supernatural level."

"After tonight, it's not gonna matter," Matthew said. "Permission to get started, boss."

"Yeah," Dylan said. He looked at each of them in turn. "Everyone be careful on this one. Even you two, distance is no guarantee of safety," he said, gesturing to Ariel and James.

"You got us blessed yet?" Ariel said.

"Headed there next," Dylan said.

Dylan sat in a room that was filled with row upon row of wooden cabinets. His job was to meet with a Battle Priest. Almost anything the Order provided to Hunters, Dylan could find a better version on the underground market. Almost.

The priest, Masterson, appeared silently from between two of the nearer rows of cabinets. He set three round talismans on the wooden table in front of Dylan.

"Ariel Ikeda; Matthew King; Dylan Carter," he said, touching each dark talisman with thin, waxy fingers. "Mikn'e er ta'akhon ceri ni ahm'e." He looked up to Dylan. "May your lives be held."

Service Talismans were bound to each Hunter, sanctified with a drop of their own blood, and blessed in a language only spoken by battle priests. The talismans provided a level of supernatural protection few other items Dylan had ever seen could. They were extremely valuable to the Order. Only one could ever be made for a Hunter. They were brought out of their cabinets rarely, to be blessed before dangerous missions. *And yet*, Dylan mused, *this is the second time this year I've come to Masterson.*

"There is no talisman for James Wilson Clarke, the one known as Blood, as he is not human," Masterson said. "He shall have to provide for himself whatever protection he deems best for his kind."

"Yes, Brother. I understand," Dylan said. He was always respectful to the battle priests. They were Hunters who had lived long enough to retire.

Thirty minutes after sunset, an unmarked, black moving truck backed into a gate at the Coven's Lincoln Park mansion. The driver did not get out. A man and a woman approached the back of the truck from the garage and unlocked the three padlocks securing the truck's rear compartment. Inside was a large copper container, ornately worked and decorated, and taking up most of the space. It was one of only ten such alchemically and magically bonded sarcophagi ever made.

The man, who appeared to be in his late twenties, eyed the sarcophagus reverently. Fearfully. The woman, perhaps forty in appearance, looked at him. When she caught his eye, she smiled. "It's alright," she said. "It's going to be fine. She has no reason to wake right now. We're safe."

The man nodded, then reached into the truck. With one hand he dragged the copper box to the edge of the truck's bed, then placed both hands under it, pulling it almost all the way out. The woman reached a hand under the back end of the box and lifted it, carefully balanced it in her hands, and walked with the man back into the garage. They placed the sarcophagus on the freight elevator in the back of the building, then rode down with it to the sub-basement far below.

Chapter 9

"You gonna be ok out in the real world? Lot's changed this century, you might go into shock," Dylan said.

James smiled and rolled a cigarette. "Real world? I think my world a century ago was a bit more real. But yes, I think I'll be fine. I have kept up with current events, you know. I've got a computer and the internet."

"You're a step ahead of me then, I don't," Dylan said, and put a duffle bag in the back of a black SUV.

"You can be the most depressing person, you know that?" James' eyes glowed orange in the light of the cigarette cherry.

"Yeah, freakin' maudlin," Dylan said.

James considered him a moment. "Seriously though, have you been alright lately? Not to be your shrink or anything, just you seem a bit off."

"Well, ya know, I did get caught in a Demon's temple last month. Oh, and I lost a shirt at the cleaners, that's hit me real hard."

"Something in your scent, friend," James said. "I wasn't even going to say anything about it, but you've been different since that night. Not the shirt, the other. I just want to extend an offer of assistance, should you need it."

"You've just got Vampire allergies or something," Dylan said. But I appreciate the gesture. Come on, we've got work to do, go get Ikeda."

Matthew was in the driver's seat, trying to get it to comfortably accommodate his large frame. Dylan took shotgun and buckled up, setting his wide brimmed leather hat on the dash.

"Is he gonna behave?" Matthew asked.

"What, with Ikeda? Yeah, of course. Number one, she is, actually, a grown woman, you know. And B, he is, actually, a professional. If we need his expertise tonight, we're gonna need it bad, and fast. So it'll be fine."

Matthew watched the Vampire go in the rear-view mirror. "Not exactly Ikeda I was talking about, but yeah, that too, I guess. Now that you mention it." He put the vehicle in reverse. "It just makes me uncomfortable, working with...Nether. But I guess it is Order sanctioned. As long as they've got him under control."

Dylan glanced at him from the corner of his eye. "Yeah, Order sanctioned. But, ya know, James is actually a pretty good guy. Besides the biting. He's been my friend for a long time now. Might be you'd like him, if you got to know him a little."

Matthew kept his eyes focused forward. "Not really the job, boss. Getting to know vamps or whatever." After that he let it drop. Trying to check on Dylan's loyalties was making him more nervous than he thought it would. *Or maybe angry*, he thought.

"Vuk, I'm going to need you to—" Doina said.

Vuk held up a hand, keeping his attention focused on the tiny symbol he was finishing in gold paint. "Sorry," he said when he was done. "I procrastinated, saved the hardest for last. Bad habit. How can I help you, Doina?"

"No, I apologize, things are just getting a bit hectic," she said. "Listen, your info lists you as one of the most senior Coven members here, and I really need someone to come calm the younger Coven members down. Lady Jelena's sarcophagus...it's spooking some of them."

"Yes, it has that effect," he said. He noticed Doina's usually smiling mouth was anchored into a tight, straight line. She was nervous about the Elder as well. "Everything is just about done here. I'll be up in, say, twenty minutes?"

"Up?" Doina sad. "Oh, Lady Jelena is in an anteroom on this level. Ramona and David brought her down half an hour ago."

"What?" Vuk said, putting down his tools. "This close the familiars? And the blood vault? In an unsealed room?"

"I...well, it seemed respectful—"

"What does she care if she's left in the garage, she's asleep!" Vuk walked quickly toward the chamber exit. "Why do you think I've been doing down here all night? That whole wall," he said, pointing, "is to keep her from smelling blood! Which, yes, she can do through the sarcophagus, in her sleep! She was to be kept on the ground level until this room was ready to receive her. Take me to her. Now!"

The click of Doina's heels followed Vuk's grumbling out of the room. Matvei watched them leave from his perch atop a ladder, where he was working on the row of symbols that circled the room along the top of each wall. Matvei had shown interest in alchemy as a young initiate, but soon realized his skills were better suited to security patrols. He had received enough training to understand alchemical science and magic, but not enough to burn into his mind the importance of two of the discipline's most important rules: do not become distracted, and always know where your brush is. Matvei's brush was currently swirling, ever so slightly, in and out of one of the symbols in the long spell of binding he was painting. The symbol for Jelena's name was now, as far as magic was concerned, the symbol for nothing at all.

James was perfectly familiar with cars and modern travel, despite what most people thought. He'd bought some of the first models ever produced before the Order caught up to him. He could have driven them tonight if his masters trusted him not to flee. He probably would have run, he thought, if only to make them use up resources chasing him.

Instead, he was in the back seat with Ariel. He had no problem sitting next to the attractive and interesting operative, except that she wasn't talking and James was easily bored. She was focused entirely on some program on her screen, which she appeared to be writing as they traveled.

As the car stopped, Ariel closed and packed her equipment with a practiced efficiency. Laptop, cables, and an antenna all disappeared into a backpack, like a magician packing away her tricks. She stepped out of the car and stopped short, staring up at the impressive awning of the Hotel Lincoln. This was not her sort of place. She could not disappear here. At her coffee shops and tech conventions no one gave her a second glance, but here she felt like a lit beacon.

She was surprised to realize she had been staring at James for several seconds, lost in her thoughts. He was leaning against a support of the awning, smiling at her. The lamp over his shoulders made his eyes glow amber. He did fit in here, like he had been commissioned as a fixture. "Come on," he said, "nothing here bites but me." He stepped through the front doors, a tall, lean figure in waistcoat and gray trousers.

Ariel caught up just as he reached the front desk. She had been practicing saying, "We have a reservation, Nancy Smith," in her head for half the trip over. Now, resting her arms uncomfortably high on the desk, she couldn't get the desk clerk's attention. The clerk, a middle-aged man with almost no hair left, was staring at her companion, a straight line of confusion drawn between his brows. James smiled back at him for a moment with the left side of his mouth. He said, "Clarke," and smiled some more.

The older man flinched, then looked down at a screen with the guest ledger on it. "Sorry...sorry, yes, I have you here. Sir. Room 714." He handed James a key. James took it, winked at the clerk, and strolled toward the elevators. Ariel blinked at him a few times, yanked her backpack away from the reaching bellhop, and hurried down the hall.

Interlude – The Sons of James

I

1607CE, England

It wasn't hard for Gregory to tell when it was raining outside. The dungeon had no windows, and he hadn't seen the sun in weeks, but rain would seep easily through the cracks in the stone above, running down and mixing with the slow stream of fetid human waste that ran constantly through and between the cells. From where he sat he could see but a fraction of the dungeon, three cells if the mist in the hall wasn't too thick. In those cells he had counted fourteen of his brethren, Sons of James from his own and other chapters. Some of them hadn't moved in several days now.

His hunting party had been taken nearly two months ago while tracking a minor Demon through the northern forests. In hindsight he realized that underling had been bait. The ambush they found waiting for them was well organized, and of a strength suitable to taking four Hunters without much risk. Gregory managed to severely wound one of the infernal creatures, but then Marcus had fallen, and everything went to shit after that.

The Demons did nothing to conceal their course or destination from Gregory besides only traveling at night. He thought this probably kept any traveling woodsman from seeing the group.

The consideration given by his captors surprised Gregory. After the horror of the ambush, they showed no malice. Ample food and water were provided to make the trek south bearable, despite Demons requiring neither. After exiting the woods, horses were provided for the humans, though when Gregory attempted to bolt with his, the animal would not move past a walk. The tall female Demon walking next to him smiled at his attempt. He had never seen one do that, and it unnerved him terribly.

The group halted three days later at a sheer stone wall set in the steep sides of a deep ravine. A set of tall stone doors, set between a pair of basket torches, opened without sound as they approached. Past those doors, any allusions of kindness Gregory had glimpsed on the road were revealed to have been only efficiency of travel.

The beatings were precise and effective. None of the captives would be making any sort of escape attempt.

Those that died in the following weeks died at night. Gregory would wake to scuffling sounds and a darkness so thick he could taste it, feel the pressure of it in his ears. Moments later a scream would rise in a nearby cell, only to be cut short, replaced by evil, low laughter, and wet chewing. When the torches came to life hours later, there was another dead body. Most of one.

Two days ago, the Demons began emptying the cells. Gregory saw the torches gutter and dim as he watched a tall, gray veiled figure walk past. Chains clanked and men whimpered far down the hall. One long held breath later, five men shuffled by, following a silent she-Demon. The men didn't return, but the Demon did, twice a day, to lead away more Sons of James.

Gregory was ashamed at his own shock when the beast stopped in front of his cell. He had known she would come for him, yet he still felt fear, when he wanted to show defiance. When the cold shackles snapped around his wrists, his stomach lurched, and he might have spilled its contents, if he'd had anything to give.

The Demon led the men deep into the mountain, down a long corridor with ash gray walls. Gregory found he had no idea how long they walked. It felt to him as though he kept waking up from a dreamless sleep, only to find himself trudging behind the silent monster. When one of the men tried to ask the Demon where they were going, what it wanted with them, it sounded like his voice came from the bottom of a well, but with no echo. Distance, time, sound, none of it moved as it ought here.

Then there was a door before them, seemingly out of nowhere. It was a massive thing, built of dark hardwood, with images of monsters skillfully carved into it. The door seemed to have a presence all its own, as though some horrible life burned within it. Men began to weep. A puddle formed on the ground as someone lost control of his bodily functions. No one seemed to care.

The Demon reached out her hand but did not touch the door. Her fingertips splayed as though compressed against the very air just before it. She pushed for several heartbeats before the door swung inward soundlessly. Gregory wondered if there was any sense in attempting to run. Wasn't that his right as a trapped animal, however futile? He remembered the incredible length of the corridor and knew he hadn't the strength for the attempt. For the first time, he looked back the way they had come. His jaw went slack and the hammering of his heart doubled. His ears rang with the pressure of it. There, less than a score of paces away, was the doorway to the dungeon cells. Before his mind could even fully grasp his shock and fear, the chain on his wrist tugged and he stumbled through the oak doorway.

The Demon inside the cavernous room was not the same one that had led the men down the corridor. She had gone without anyone seeing or caring. The being the men faced now was taller, with a black, hooded cloak draped over his stone gray robes. The cloth of the cloak was indiscernible. It seemed to be made of the fabric of night, a complete absence of light, nothingness twisted into shape. The hood hid the Demon's face completely, but could not shield the men from the feeling of the creature's eyes upon them. One by one they each fell to their knees before it, uncommanded but inevitable. Gregory, a captain in the Sons of James, lasted the longest on his feet. Six heartbeats, by the pounding in his ears.

Interlude – The Sons of James

2

Reality shifted back into place. The Demon looked down at his former enemies, now his loyal servants. All Demons could use Worship to kill, to break the spirit, to destroy. Skill such as his, using a Demon's most powerful supernatural weapon to enslave, and leave the victim functional, useful, and even eager to obey, was something different altogether. To his knowledge less than half a dozen like unto himself existed in all the Netherworld. As the last man passed, a former captain of the Sons of James, the Demon favored him with a smile. The feeble human gazed up at him with adoring, terrified eyes, and hurried out of the chamber.

The Demon had told the men that he was an angel. That was basically true, as much as humans could understand the idea. He had told them that they would be guided by divine influence now, directly. He had reasoned with them that King James had his heart in the right place, but could never, as a mere mortal, truly comprehend the mission that now lay open before mankind. They needed someone higher to lead them. And all the while he had exerted just enough influence, just enough magical pressure, to break their minds, twist their sanity, and sink his claws deeply into their hearts. They, as the scores of men and women before them in the weeks prior, were his now.

As he sat back on his throne, he felt the presence of the female Demon come through the wall behind him. "Do you not desire at all to kill them, Brother?" she said. She inhaled slowly. "The very air is infected by their stink."

"I desire a great deal to kill them. Most of them, at least," he said. "Though there are some hearts among them so black as to need no convincing to betrayal and murder at all. I have only to point the way. I could never take the life of such an eager servant."

"As you say," she replied. Disdain for the humans burned in her voice.

"We do not play the short game, Sister. We could kill droves of the true hearted, the righteous ones, we could rely on the servitude of the dark hearts, and we could watch them eventually murder each other, beyond even our control. But with just a modicum of patience, and careful guidance, they will all of them give us the world freely."

"They do that already," she said. "They flock to our doors. They beg the Order for salvation. Except the Sons of King James. I do not understand why you nurture these aberrants, these viruses. They could fall secretly. There is patience in that also, and I would oversee it. You need not soil yourself with their presence."

"The long game, sister. The very long game. These fanatics indeed serve no real purpose now and will feel as a thorn in our flesh. But I have looked ahead. I have seen. Mankind will not always seek our protection as it does now. Magic will not frighten them forever. They will not always ask us to hunt for them. Someday we will need to reason with them as men. We will use politics and commerce, not magic and faith. What we do now is the foundation of the army we will offer to man, and they will bind themselves to us eternally to purchase it. But that time is not yet. Not for many hundreds of years. Wait with me. The long game, sister. You will see."

Chapter 10

The majority of Dylan's professional, adult life had taken place in the dark. Sewers, alleys at night, tunnels, caves, and condemned buildings. He had grown to appreciate the dark. It narrowed his focus and helped shut out the chaos of his daytime thoughts. It had been decades since the priest approached him and offered him a job hunting for the Order, promising in return the resources to hunt down his sister's killers. Dylan recognized that now as a sales pitch that would never materialize, but he had found purpose in this work nevertheless. He was helping people, and he was striking back at the monsters in the dark, even if they weren't the ones that took his sister. Every Nether he killed was someone's sister, mother, brother, or father saved.

He was in the dark now, with Matthew half a dozen paces behind him. They had used the city's sewer lines to access a series of tunnels that led directly to the Lincoln Park mansion. Every ten meters or so Dylan heard a click as Matthew fixed another signal booster to the tunnel wall, keeping the line of communication open to Ariel. With any luck there would be nothing to report except mission accomplished, but Dylan had rarely seen a mission that lucky.

Dylan had his blunderbuss slung across his back, his .357 in both hands, held low. The only thing they were likely to encounter this far out in the prohibition era tunnels was a low level guard or a rat. Neither rated the use of the expensive, experimental shells the blunderbuss fired. They'd also be likely to blind Matthew if he used one. Dylan found the tunnels had enough ambient light from up ahead to let him see, but Matthew had his NVG's down, and causing them to flair with an explosion might prove a fatal mistake.

But there weren't any guards, rats, or anything else alive, as far as Dylan could tell. The Coven seemed to have combed the tunnels thoroughly. It was beginning to make sense, but Dylan took no comfort from his realizations. The Vampires had removed any life that might tempt Jelena to break free and feed. Even insects. The Coven's obviously fearful respect for the powers of its master doubled his own. "How we doin', King?" he said.

"Everything copacetic, boss," Matthew said. "Seem extra quiet to you, though?"

"Yeah, just noticing. Not a good quiet. A little ambient noise—"

Screams from deeper in the tunnels cut him off. By Dylan's estimation they sounded human. Underneath the cries for help and wet, dying voices, he heard the whisper of knife work. He and Matthew exchanged a brief look, then took off in the direction of the voices.

"Remind me next time that complaining's a sin, 'kay?" Matthew said.

"Once again, company card," James said, sipping whiskey from the suite's minibar. "There's no harm in taking a few extra pleasures to balance the dark nature of your employment." To his surprise, Ariel only chuckled and gave a small shake of her heard, then went back to her keyboard. "So I have broken past your rebukes, then. Care for some? It's not bad," he said.

"Can't. Maybe you're unable to get tipsy, but I can, and my boys are out there. This is serious Ariel time." She pulled up a window, glanced over the information displayed there, then minimized it again. "Although, if this goes well, is there maybe, like, a to go cup or something?"

"'To go cup'?" he said. "No no, we simply cannot sin against decent alcohol like that. Tell you what, we bury the big bad Vampire, get our guys back, and head back to the Cathedral, I'll get out a bottle of absinthe I've been saving. We can celebrate in the old-fashioned way, before your boss has to lock me back in my cage."

"Doesn't that stuff give you brain abscesses or something?"

"No, not this one, this one's fine. Fairies and voices maybe, but only the normal alcohol induced brain damage." He swirled the amber liquid in his tumbler.

Ariel went back to her computer. A moment later her smile broke, and she waved James over. As he sat in a chair next to her, she switched the team comms to speaker.

"—ngaging hostiles, human. On my go," Dylan's voice said. "Go!"

As Dylan and Matthew rounded a corner in the tunnel, they saw a group of black-clad men and women, in the same basic area they had been trying to reach, but two turns away. The newcomers had been in the process of opening several antechambers in a larger room and dragging men and women out. While the victims, apparently human, cried out and begged, their assailants said nothing, unceremoniously slitting throats and leaving the dead where they fell.

"Sons of James," Matthew said quietly. Dylan's throat went dry as he tried to swallow and find his voice. The black clothing and equipment he saw hadn't changed much, if any, since that night he had witnessed the murder of his sister. In the years since he had studied the Sons of James extensively, but had rarely had any actual run-ins with them. They were notoriously hard to track down. If he could take one alive, he might be able to get some answers.

The look he saw on Matthew's face made him pause. The SOJ had a reputation. They were killers of humans. While the Order had worked for hundreds of years to protect humanity from the supernatural, Demons and other monsters, the SOJ chose to pass judgement on humans they thought had sided with monsters. Open conflict between the Order and the SOJ was rare, but always bloody. Members of the Order were taught to protect humanity at all cost. Matthew was feeling that now.

If any SOJ members were left to question at the end, that was fine, but Dylan had to take his example from Matthew here. The priority was the humans, and they had to hurry. Dylan keyed in to Ariel and told her what they were about to do over team comms. He and Matthew shared a nod. Dylan pointed to Matthew, then the left side of the room, and held up three fingers.

Three SOJ members on that side belonged to Matthew. Dylan would take the two on the right.

"Calling it in," Dylan said, then spoke quietly to Ariel through his comms mic. He looked at Matthew, and they shared a nod.

"Go!"

The SOJ were undeniably well trained. It was only too bad for them that Dylan and Matthew had been assigned to this mission. They might have had a better chance against junior Order operatives.

Dylan ducked a haymaker and heard a satisfying crack as the fist of the man he was fighting slammed into the brick wall behind him. Dylan's own fist came up short and quick into his opponent's chest, and the man went down, wheezing.

Now Dylan stepped back to the woman he had first engaged upon entering the room. She was tall and quick, and had already bloodied his nose with a left hook he hadn't quite dodged. She had a blackening eye from a clean elbow shot he had thrown. No one seemed willing to be the first to pull a firearm in the brick room and risk a ricochet.

Vuk checked the positioning of Jelena's sarcophagus once more. Six Vampires had carried it ceremoniously to the center of the room he'd warded and placed it on a raised dais. Chanters stood at the four corners of the copper box, unweaving the spells that kept the Elder in a deep sleep for a century at a time. Vuk reached out and lightly ran his fingers over the symbols that represented Jelena's name. Not for the first time, he wondered what all of this really meant anymore. The Covens kept their Elders alive now more as symbols than as rulers. If the box were empty, what would actually change?

He glanced over to Doina. She met his eye, then looked to the hallways at the back of the room. Two coven members had been sent down to lead the familiars up to the ceremony. Humans who had pledged their lives to the Coven and the Vampire religion would be given the honor of having Jelena feed on them. That had been ten minutes ago. Doina liked to keep a tight schedule, and this seemed just a bit too long for the simple task to be completed.

As she took a step toward the hall, one of the Vampires she'd sent came stumbling back into the room, bleeding from the scalp and dragging a shattered leg. "They're here!" he said.

"What? Who?" Doina said.

"Sons of James!" he said. "And someone else. Maybe Order, but I don't know. They were fighting each other! They killed the familiars!"

"You two, with me!" Vuk snapped, and walked quickly past Dione, two large security officers in tow.

"Vuk, but...the ceremony!" Dione said. "She's waking!"

"And she's going to need something to eat," Vuk called back. "If we can't save some familiars, who do you think she'll go after?"

Before Matthew could take down the last two of his opponents, a pair of Vampires walked into the room. Alliances were formed quickly, if awkwardly. For the blink of an eye everyone stopped and stared at each other. Then, one of the SOJ tried to take a swing at Matthew, but Matthew and the other SOJ had moved toward the Vampires. Dylan and the woman had both moved in unison and engaged one of the Vampires, knives out.

The woman managed a devastating kick to the leg of the Vampire, and the monster stumbled back down the hall. Rather than pursue, she immediately turned on Dylan again, and their truce was over. Before she could land an attack, Dylan wrapped his hands around the back of her neck and brought his knee up into her ribs. Her breath went out in a pained grunt as something cracked in her right side. He tried to press his advantage, but she brought her fist up into Dylan's groin, forcing him to break contact. She stepped forward into a straight kick to his chest, slamming him against the wall where they had been moments before.

Darkness pulled and tugged at her thoughts like smoky silk ropes. She could not wake, and she could not truly sleep. She was numb. It had been this way for she knew not how long. They did this to her. They forced this second death upon her time and time again. Traitorous insects.

She felt the small, candle heat of the awakening spells far in the back of her dreams. She sprang upon it like a hunting cat, hoping again to find some flaw in the magic of the containment spells that would let her live again, let her rule. Let her punish. She lay in her copper prison, and pushed hard with her mind and magic, a mother in the travails of a birth she feared might take her, again. But there was a scratch. A slight aberration in what for so many centuries had been a perfectly smooth wall of magic to contain her vast powers. She dug into the fingerhold with talons of magic and wrenched with all her might. The shell of her waking nightmares cracked like an egg.

Jelena, for the first time in a millennium, truly woke.

Vuk entered upon a scene of confusion and chaos. A third of the familiars were lying on the floor, dead, their throats cut. He could not tell which of the two groups of intruders had initiated the violence, but it didn't matter. He had to make up the difference in blood that was owed Jelena. None of them would be leaving.

SOJ Saint Rollins was short, thin, and incredibly fast. He had immediately moved to attack the bigger of the Order intruders at first contact, knowing he usually had an advantage over large, slow opponents. He regretted the decision immensely, finding from the first strike that Matthew King was far faster than such a giant should be. Every time the big man connected, Rollins stumbled back. Even through his guard, it felt like being beaten with an iron rod.

Matthew had pulled his first few strikes at the smaller man, wanting to subdue but not fatally hurt him. He had paid a price for his mercy. Everywhere on his body not firmly covered by armor was covered in knuckle sized bruises. His face was a wreck, bloodied and swelling. Both men were breathing heavily, both prosecuting their attacks with more caution.

If this didn't end soon, firearms would have to get involved. It would mean immediate retreat and a job unfinished, but neither side would offer a stalemate. Still, Rollins was surprised when Matthew reached for his gun. Not the compact, efficient 9mm strapped to his hip. Instead, what looked like a wide barreled shotgun came over the Order agent's shoulder. Entirely overkill, absolutely effective. No way to miss.

The barrel leveled with Rollins' face, and he was sure this was his last moment. Instead, he heard a bellowed, "Move!", and watched his opponent hold the gun steady without firing. He followed the command on instinct, and as he spun and rolled he saw what had been behind him. A tall, dark Vampire was holding Believer Martin above his head. A fraction of a second later, the monster dropped Martin down onto his knee, snapping his spine with a crack.

Matthew fired as soon as the line of sight was clear. The round went through the spot the Vampire's face had been, but it had dropped to its knee, and the incendiary pellet exploded against the wall behind it. The Vampire jerked to its left with supernatural speed, barely singed by the flames.

Two things happened almost at once. The woman Dylan was fighting, Believer Allison Wright, drove her knife into the top of his right lung. Then, a fiery explosion erupted over her shoulder. Dylan's head slammed back against the wall and Wright flinched away, dropping to her knees, leaving the knife in his chest. Everything human in the room was half burned and half unconscious. The Vampires all cowered away from the lingering flames and excessive light. Vuk was the first to stand back up. He shook his head, looking around to find the one that fired the shot. His eyes locked on Matthew and he advanced with a snarl. He made it a single step before his eyes went wide and his breath caught in his chest. He looked up at the ceiling. "Oh, no."

Magic is what you make it. There was weakness in the generations of Vampires and magicians Jelena woke to, each time worse than the last. They thought magic had rules, they believed it could be discovered, taught, cut up and drained of its blood. Jelena knew better, but no one asked her, no one learned from her, no one followed. They put her on a shelf like a signet ring.

She was done with it.

The flawed symbol of her name on the wall glowed, then flared bright like molten gold. Every torch, bulb, and screen in the room went dark as Jelena drained the fire from them. The next moment saw each Vampire in the room become a living, wailing torch as Jelena unleashed what she had drawn within herself.

She laughed with the joy of freedom and screamed the promise of vengeance. It was to be a long, bloody list of victims. She moved as if to fly up the stairways to the surface world, then paused, looking down through the floor. She was aware of each flaring and fading life in the chamber below, but there was one, slumped against the wall, that held a special color. It caught her curiosity. Where she stood became empty air but for the faint echo of a song, as a thin cloud of smoke fell through the cracks in the floor.

Vuk saw neither allies nor enemies, only victims, himself among them. In atavistic terror he shouted, "Run!" He flung himself towards the stairs, just as the big human with the blunderbuss pulled the trigger again. Vuk's right leg disintegrated in a wash of flames and blood. He cried out and threw a venomous glare over his shoulder, but barely slowed, dragging himself up the stairs. Whisps of smoke were leaking down through the ceiling. He had no time to punish the impudent human.

Jelena flowed into the room and wrapped herself around a young Vampire. The lights in the room dimmed as she fed. Blood puddled on the floor, and moans and choking could be heard inside the cloud of dense smoke. Then the smoke pulled in tight and coalesced into the form of a beautiful woman. Her face was strong, with prominent cheekbones and full lips. She wore a gown with a dazzling array of patterns and colors, covered by a dark robe. Her eyes were liquid smoke. Her smile was a predatory snarl.

She threw herself at the nearest living human, a Familiar who had volunteered herself as sacrifice to the Vampire cause, hoping to be chosen to ascend to their supernatural ranks. Jelena honored no such contracts and offered no favors. She fed like a starved animal, nearly chewing the woman's head off before the hydrostatic pressure in her veins had even stopped propelling blood from her wounds. Jelena's eyes roamed wildly as she bit and drank, looking for her next victim. She leapt quickly from Familiar, to Familiar, to the SOJ team member lying unconscious on the floor. Matthew and Saint Rollins both fired continuously at her, but their rounds only hit smoke, leaving spiraling holes in her body that filled in immediately.

Jelena didn't slow until she took True Believer Allison Wright by the shoulders from behind, and wrapped her jaws around either side of the soldier's neck bones. She drew the blood and spinal fluid in slowly, her eyes rolling back as she savored the taste, no longer starving. Allison was pushed up against Dylan's slumped form on her hands and knees, her face an inch from his, her mouth open in a silent, agonized scream. He watched the light fade from her tear-filled eyes.

Matthew dropped the smoking blunderbuss, its magazine spent. Rollins had fled down the passageway Matthew and Dylan had come from, leaving Wright to her fate. Matthew hadn't noticed. As Jelena tossed Wright's body away and lifted Dylan to his feet, Matthew charged, intent on crushing the Vampire's body against the opposite wall. Maybe, for someone of Matthew's size, it might have worked. Maybe against a street Vampire. Jelena was a wholly different creature, something the world hadn't dealt with for a very long time.

Jelena's right hand shot out and backhanded Matthew across his lower jaw. She hadn't looked his way, hadn't appeared to consciously notice him at all. His world filled with the cracking sound of his jawbone. He didn't feel himself hit the floor. He was unconscious before his brain even registered the pain.

Dylan wasn't exactly ready to die, but he had accepted the likelihood of the event long ago and made peace with it. Rebellious, obstinate peace, but close enough. Now he was eye level with death. The Elder held him off the floor, one handed. Through the blood, pain haze, and carnage around him, he dully mused that she was much taller than he had imagined. And she was so strong. He had seen Matthew go flying, three hundred sixty pounds of muscle and gear flying through the air like a toy. So he didn't struggle. This was inevitability incarnate, and he couldn't do anything but watch her happen.

But Jelena did not lean in to feed. Instead, she stared at him for a long time. She was absolutely motionless. Finally, she pulled him close and took in a deep breath, near his neck, taking the scent of him. She read his entire life as her senses experienced him. Blood and memory, flesh and future. She took in the pain of his losses. She tasted his very DNA, and learned things about him that science would never be able to discern. Most of all, she breathed in his magic, and she knew.

"Special," she said, and flinched at her own voice. She hadn't spoken in so long. "Special," she repeated, locking eyes with him again. "*Moja ljubav*. The world has been wasting you. Your pig masters fear you, would cast you away. But I will not. Not ever." She reached up and stroked his cheek, her razor claws leaving bloody marks down his skin. She wrapped her right arm around his waist and pulled him close, hugging him to her.

She wrenched the knife out of his chest, and Dylan found the strength to scream. "I will give you power they have forgotten to fear. And when you need me, I will always come. We must always come to aid each other, we Great Ones." Her eyes shone bright gold now. She dropped the knife and lifted her hand above her head. Outside, all the lights for blocks around dimmed and flickered. All the lights, all the small fires in the sub-basement, guttered, drained of life. In Jelena's hand, flames writhed, flowing into her obsidian claws until they were white hot.

James had been very wrong. Jelena loved fire. She brought her hand down and splayed her fingers across his chest. As Dylan shuddered, breathless, in her grasp, he felt his skin ignite under her hand. She drug her claws across his chest, twisting and dancing her fingers, writing strange symbols into his burning flesh. His throat locked, and he could neither drag in air or scream. He could not even pass out. She held him there, in the waking world. Her power held his mind vice-like, just as her arm held his body locked to hers.

Finally, she was done. The symbols on his chest smoked and glowed, then faded to black lines. She looked into his eyes and smiled. For the first time in many years of service, Dylan was terrified into hopelessness. There was love in Jelena's eyes, but an insane, alien love, inhuman. "There, my darling," she said. "You are mine. Always. The first of your kind in so long. I will never let them take you from me." With that, she lowered her lips to the stab wound in his chest, and took his lifeblood from him.

"Boss! Come in! King! One of you better answer me!" Ariel's voice trembled as she yelled into the mic. Her screens were a mess, with Matthew and Dylan's vitals all over the place, and weapon analyses running on multiple sounds of gunfire. It had been two minutes and thirty-eight seconds since Dylan had given the word to enter the room. Sixty-four seconds into the fight, which she had been confident her guys could handle, something had escalated the situation, and she wasn't entirely sure what. Then the screaming. It had been beyond horrible. Something was out of control, beyond just an encounter with the SOJ, and she couldn't raise her guys on coms. Matthew's earpiece were reading standby mode, meaning it must have gotten knocked from his ear. Dylan wouldn't respond, but she could vaguely hear someone talking through his earpiece. A woman.

There was a crackling from the speakers, then a voice. It was barely recognizable as Matthew. "'keda," he said. "Need help. Now." His voice was thick and slurred. Ariel had never heard Matthew like that before.

"King, I'm about to get Gamma in there, what's going on with you guys?"

"No, not Gamma," he said.

"They're on station for this King, just tell me where—"

"No!" he said. "Too dangerous. Ikeda, it's Jelena, she's here. Get Blood in here. Now!"

Ariel looked up at the Vampire next to her in shock. There was something like fear in his amber eyes as he stared at the screen. Then he looked at her. "James, please, my guys," she said. He gave short nod.

With frightening speed, he reached into his vest and yanked something out, putting it to his mouth. It was a flask, and he drew on it so hard and fast the steel sides caved in. He dropped it. Then he screamed. Ariel recoiled. She had never heard an animal scream in that much pain and rage before. Smoke began to curl up from his skin. His eyes locked with hers once more, and the red light in them withered her.

James shot for the window. There was a shattering sound, and his was gone. Ariel darted over and looked to the ground, but he wasn't there. Reflexively she looked up. There was a cloud of something moving away at incredible speed, and the sound of small wings.

Speaking through his shattered mouth was a pain Matthew had never known before, but he had managed it. Now he had to get up, and it was taking monumental effort. He turned to look for the Elder. To his horror, she had her jaw clamped to Dylan's chest. Dylan was dead white. Matthew yelled as loud as he could, the sound coming out as a bloody growl through his mouth and nose.

To Matthew's surprise, Jelena lowered Dylan gently to the ground, like she was putting a sleeping child to bed. She turned to look at him, her eyes distant and dreaming. Those eyes snapped into sharp focus when they met Matthew's. She smiled, and they each began to take a step toward each other.

The room filled with wind and swirling black. Matthew, still severely hurt and off balance, fell to the floor. Jelena laughed and raised both hands out to the side, as if delighted by what had interrupted them.

The cloud of wings and teeth collapsed rapidly in on itself, and James came charging out of it, red eyes glaring, fangs and claws intent on Jelena's flesh. She reached out and swatted him as she had done Matthew. There was the same sharp crack, but unlike Matthew, James stayed on his feet, and came back with a raking blow across the Elder's face. Jelena's head rocked with the blow, but the clawed fingers apparently did no damage.

Her left hand shot out in an open palm strike to James' chest, and he stumbled backwards, going down on one knee. Jelena was immediately in front of him, raining hammer blows down on him with her fist, his forearms coming up barely in time to block her. Her attack, however, was relentless, and supernaturally fast. Finally, his arms fell, and a herculean blow to his cheek knocked James to the floor.

Jelena knelt beside him. He tried to struggle away, but she simply said, "No," and he froze. He couldn't so much as breath. "Child," she said, "I should kill you for having so much as dared. Perhaps one day I shall." She looked over at Dylan. "But you are his now. His tutor. I need you to teach him what he is, and was, and shall be. Do not fail me in this, young one," she said. She looked deep into his eyes. "Or else I shall catch you, and not kill you."

She laughed suddenly, joyful and mad. She erupted into a tornado of smoke. The underground room shook, unable to hold the life and magic of her. The ceiling seemed to burst into fire, and the flames melted upward, through the bricks, until she was gone. Darkness, as it always has, returned.

Chapter 11

"Dylan, what's her address? Dylan! Where do we fi—ckson?"

"Boss, hang on!"

"Somebody open the door, I got hi—"

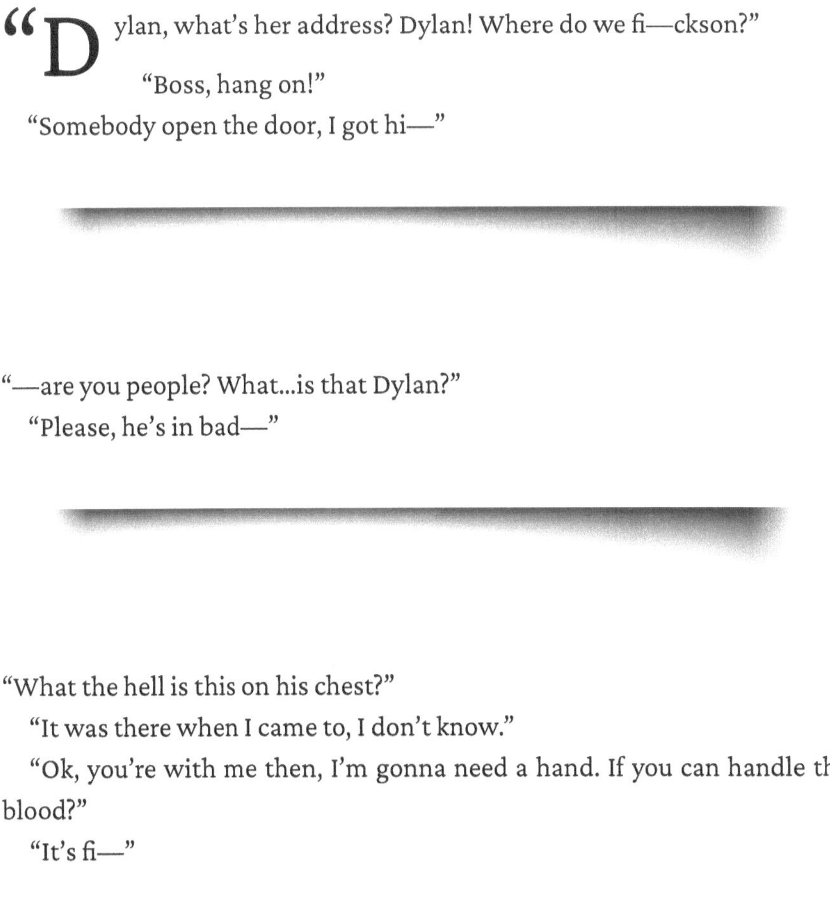

"—are you people? What…is that Dylan?"

"Please, he's in bad—"

"What the hell is this on his chest?"

"It was there when I came to, I don't know."

"Ok, you're with me then, I'm gonna need a hand. If you can handle the blood?"

"It's fi—"

Dylan had never tasted darkness before.

Chapter 12

Dylan woke standing upright in a bright room. It sounded like a hurricane was raging outside. The light shot through his eyes and deep into his skull. He winced. The room was just almost familiar, but his brain wouldn't lock any thoughts into place, and he cast his eyes around wildly.

At the end of his outstretched arm, he found his friend, James. He wore a beatific halo, made from the spiderweb cracks of the plaster behind his head. His face was calm, but his eyes glowed amber, and his breathing was a careful in and out. "You're back with us then, Dylan?" he said. Dylan tried to speak. He heard a dry snarl come from his throat. "Got him?" James said.

"I got him," Matthew's voice said from behind Dylan. Matthew grunted, and James' eyes widened, looking at him in surprise. "No, no, I got him. Just a bit more than I expected."

Dylan twisted his head around to look at the other man in the room. Matthew's huge left hand was wrapped around Dylan's wrist like welded steel, holding the arm outstretched and immobile. In Dylan's hand was a scalpel. A tray of surgical instruments lay scattered across the floor.

"Bit more than I anticipated as well, to be honest," James said. He placed his hands around the arm Dylan was using to pin him to the wall and pushed, but it didn't budge. "Don't usually see them come up like this."

A hammering sounded from the door to the room. Dylan's legs nearly gave out as the thunderous sound roared in his ears. Outside, a woman's voice yelled, "Matthew! Matthew, let me in! What's happening?"

Another woman said, "Ariel, no! It isn't safe! Give them time!"

"Why wouldn't it be safe? They're my friends!" Ariel said. Dylan recognized her voice, he knew who she was, but it didn't seem to mean anything to him at the moment. Everything was too bright and loud, and the room started to spin. There was a scuffling sound outside, then a key in the door. Ariel burst in, but stopped dead in her tracks. "Boss?" she said, eyes wide and voice trembling.

Dylan looked back to James. "It's ok, brother. I've got you. It's going to be alright," James said.

Everything went black.

When he woke this time, only James remained in the room with him. He was lying down in bed. Somehow, he knew it had only been a few minutes this time. Being asleep hadn't felt like truly being unconscious. He hadn't really lost awareness. He looked over at James.

"You get used to it," James said. "Sleep isn't really going to be the same anymore, my friend. A lot isn't going to be the same anymore."

Dylan looked around the room. He realized with a start that it was very dim and quiet. A cellar, maybe. Nothing like what it had seemed a few minutes ago. But it was the same room. Suddenly the light became intensely bright, and he threw his arms over his eyes. "What the—?" he yelled, and heard his voice echo off the concrete walls. He pressed his hands tight to his ears. "What the hell is going on, James?"

"Calm down," James said, putting a hand gently on Dylan's shoulder. "The more you can stay calm, the less it will flare like that."

Dylan tried to control his breathing. It helped, but he could still see and hear everything in the room. There were no more shadows. The roaches in the corners no longer sounded like nails on a blackboard, but he could still hear all their scrabbling legs. Realization stabbed into his gut. He looked back to James. "The Coven...I'm...they got me? I'm a...a..." Nausea welled up and threatened to spill over.

James looked back at him with pity and sadness. "You are, my friend. You are, and I'm sorry. But no, it wasn't the Coven."

He sat on the edge of the bed, by Dylan's knees, and folded his thin hands in his lap, staring down at them. When he looked up, his eyes were bright with emotion, but his face remained calm. "I should have known earlier, really. This shock, you not being prepared...I take at least partial responsibility."

"What are you talking about?" Dylan said. "If it wasn't the Coven, then why is this happening. Wait. No. No, you didn't—"

"No," James said quickly. "No, I wouldn't do that to you, Dylan. Not even to save your life. The fact is, I think this has been in process for a while, very slowly. Do you remember, before we set out for all this, do you remember I mentioned your scent had changed? That you've been acting different for a while?"

Dylan thought back. "Yeah. What does that have to do with it?"

"I couldn't figure out a good way to bring it up," James said. "And still, I should have been more direct. You smelled off somehow, Dylan, and not in any way a human would have noticed. You have for a couple of years, really, but so faintly I couldn't put my finger on it. Now I can, only far too late. I think you've been changing into...one of my kind, for quite a while now. That happens, only it's very rare."

Dylan's heart was pounding. The room was growing painfully bright again, and he pressed his palms to his forehead, trying to stem the tide of panic and confusion. "I don't understand," he said, "I've never heard of that before. People turn when they're bitten."

"You've never heard of it for good reason," James said. "I'm not meant to know either, I suppose, but as you know, I've been locked in that Cathedral a long time. Education by osmosis. People can and do change, two or three a decade, without pathogenic contact. It runs in bloodlines, I think. The Order has rigorously suppressed the knowledge."

"That's ridiculous!" Dylan growled. His eyes began to shine gold, and his nails punched through the top of the mattress as he flexed his fingers. "People would need to know, to prepare! Someone would have to find a cure!"

"There's no cure," James said. "And I thought the same, when I first learned of the phenomenon. But people have known of it, in the past. Hundreds of years ago. Think about it. The witch trials? Pitchforks and torches and all that? The masses took it upon themselves to hunt down possible bloodlines, with disastrous, murderous results. So the Order took exclusive control of the right to police the supernatural, and slowly people forgot their fear and left it to the Hunters. Mostly, anyway."

Dylan's eyes dimmed. "Mostly? No one hunts without Order authorization. You get a lot of prison time for that."

"The Sons of James."

"You mean they're hunting bloodlines? That's why they kill humans?"

"I think so," James said. He looked at Dylan, but Dylan's eyes weren't in the room anymore. He was somewhere far back in the past, and James put together the pieces he'd forgotten to consider. "Dylan...I'm sorry..."

Suddenly Dylan was up and pacing, grabbing at his hair and breathing heavily. "Twenty five years ago, when they came to our house. They took her. They were SOJ. But she wasn't changing. Wait, are you saying she was?" He looked at James sharply. "Are you saying my sister was a monster? That she was a freaking Vampire?"

"Dylan, I don't know, I don't know anything about what your sister was. They could have come for her on suspicion only, they—"

"My sister wasn't one of those things!" Dylan roared, reaching for James' neck. He stopped when he realized what he was saying. Who he was saying it to, what he was about to do. "Sorry...James, I don't mean you, I don't...I can't think straight, I know you—"

James was still sitting quietly, hands folded. "One of 'us' things, my friend," he said. "I know. I know you didn't mean me. But I am. And, Dylan, now you are too, with all the implications attached. I'm sorry."

Dylan sat on the rolling stool next to the bed and stared at his hands. They still looked like his hands. They had all the scars he'd collected over the years. But if James was right, his hands hadn't been entirely human for a while now. He hadn't been. Was he even really human when he was born? "What do I do now?" he asked.

Before James could answer, someone knocked on the door. He stood up in his quiet, graceful way, and went to open it. On the other side stood Ariel, a little timid, but determined. A memory flashed through Dylan's thoughts, of Ariel's wide eyes, of the way he had heard her heart skip several beats at the sight of him. "Oh, kid, I..." he said. "Ariel, I'm sorry, I don't know..."

She rushed forward and hugged him hard enough to hurt. He awkwardly hugged back, not sure what it meant.

"It's going to be ok," she said, sobbing a little. "You're alright, Dr. Jackson says she can take care of you, and Matthew is checking the neighborhood out, and you be more careful from now on!" She held him at arm's length. "You figure things out before you go in anymore, understand?"

"I...I think so?" he said. "You're right. It's ok, Ariel, it's gonna be fine."

"I'd like to have some say in that, if you don't mind," said a voice from the doorway. A tall, blonde woman in a pair of flannel pajamas stood there with her arms folded. "Would anyone object to the doctor examining her patient?"

James put an arm around Ariel's shoulders. "Come on then, Ariel, I saw a nice bottle of Merlot upstairs we can pilfer. Good for us both, I think." He gave Dr. Jackson a smile and led Ariel out of the room.

Dylan's eyes fidgeted around the room before coming back to Doctor Jackson.

"Hi, Coleen," he said. "I'm assuming I owe you a big apology."

"You owe me about thirty grand, considering all I had to do to stabilize you. But, as usual, you get the guardian angel discount. Plus, I don't understand half of what was wrong with you, or why you're awake and sitting up now, or just what the hell happened. If you don't mind?" She waived him off the stool and sat down, crossing her arms and legs, glaring.

"Ok, yeah. But first, everybody else ok?" he said.

"Yes, but that's not so surprising. Your Vampire friend is immortal, obviously, and Matthew is a tough son of a bitch. Ariel's half in shock though. What kind of hornet's nest did you guys get into?"

"Elder Vampire," he said. "Order sent us to kill one. I didn't even know they were real, before, and now one's had me by the throat."

Coleen arched her right eyebrow. "Really? Which one?"

"Her name's Jelena. You don't seem surprised. Know much about them?"

"I'm over a thousand years old, Dylan, I was around when Elders weren't outlawed. Saw a few of them too. But now I am surprised any of you made it out alive at all. You said her name 'is'. I take it you didn't kill her?"

"Not even close. It was a massive screw up. Sons of James showed up, started killing some nutjob humans they found in a room. We tried to save the civilians, nearly got our asses handed to us. Then some other Vampires showed up, it turned into a three-way fight, I went down...then she was there. It felt like we were all squabbling kids, and a queen just showed up. It was so weird, Coleen. Then she...she picked me up, and said something, I don't really remember."

He looked her in the eye and worked his mouth for several moments before words would come. "I think she turned me. Did she, Coleen? Could you tell that? Something was definitely wrong when I woke up."

"I talked to James about that, Dylan. We don't know. He told me what he thought about you changing the last few years, but neither of us have heard of someone coming up like you did, with strength like that. What I do know, is that you have a new set of scars on your chest, which look something like Gothic Vampiric, but not exactly. James and I, we're guessing she forged a bond of some kind with you, and accelerated your transformation. She wants you stronger for some reason. And you clearly have the potential for it. Even just at this point, I don't think there's a Vampire on the street that could match you power for power. Maybe not even some of the lower Coven members.

"But you aren't fully changed yet. We did a UV test, some enzymes, some metals. You have an allergic reaction, like a rash, but nothing dangerous. Yet." She put her hand on Dylan's. "But it's probably going to happen. Almost certainly. I think you need to spend some time talking to James, figuring out how to smooth the transition. And...I think you should work on an exit strategy from the Order. Sooner than later. They aren't going to like one of their top Hunters turning."

Dylan's head was spinning. He'd hoped that Jackson might tell him James was just shaken up, seeing things he wanted to see. Instead, she'd more than confirmed James' theories. Dylan was Vampiric, to some extent at least, and maybe always had been.

He'd spent twenty years studying and training to protect people, to keep the monsters at bay. He'd spent twenty years, in the background, studying and hunting the people who took his sister, who had shattered his young life. He had taken full advantage of Order protection and resources all that time. Now, he would be put on a target list. Maybe not immediately, maybe not for weeks, or months. But eventually.

"Well. Rats," he said. "This, uh, isn't what I had planned for the weekend."

Jackson squeezed his hand and smiled. She was used to the way he tried to deflect serious subjects like this. "Come on, let's go get you something to eat. Ben is leaving for work soon, I need to go say bye to him, then you guys can come up and get breakfast."

"Shit, Ben. What are you gonna tell him about all of us being here?"

Jackson rubbed her forehead. "First, I'm gonna try not to tell him about *all* of you. I'll tell him you came by because you, I dunno, hurt your hand and didn't want it going on a report or something. He's only gonna be half listening anyway, I'll throw medical jargon at him until he runs out the door with his coffee. Leave it to me. It'll be fine."

"Thanks, Coleen. Really. This is an awful lot for you to deal with, I know."

"Not like you haven't helped me more than your fair share, Dylan. By all rights you should have killed me as soon as you found out what I am." She smiled over her shoulder at him as she left the room. "Or should have tried, anyway."

He heard her say something to the rest of his team, then her footsteps disappeared upstairs. Left alone with his thoughts, something she'd said clicked into place. He "hadn't fed yet". That was going to happen. As far as he knew, there was no way to avoid that. There was no substitute for blood, and no Vampire had ever been able to resist the call for forever, as far as he knew. Even James fed. Dylan just didn't ask questions about it. Maybe now he had to.

What did duty say about what he should do? Was he supposed to off himself, in honor of the credo of the Order Pure? Or could he make some deal with the High Counsel, to be a Bound Element like James? He thought about James' incarceration. He was allotted a tempting array of luxuries and amenities at the Cathedral, but no freedom. He hadn't been out of Chicago in a hundred years, and rarely out of the Red Cathedral. Did the Chicago Cathedral even need two Vampires? He might end up halfway around the world.

Probably he would just end up dead, he decided. Bound Elements like Blood were not a common occurrence. At the same time, he didn't feel like doing the job for the Order either. He'd never really been big on the credo. Likely he'd make them spend a lot of resources hunting him down. He smiled at the thought.

Chapter 13

No one had really taken the last forty-eight hours well. Doctor Coleen Jackson was now sleep deprived and overworked, and hadn't even started her day shift at the clinic yet. James was restless, pacing. Ariel was a mess on so many fronts. Matthew. Dylan had expected him to react to the transformation a little more aggressively than he did. Dylan had even worried there might be a fight. Matthew had to be struggling with the same questions Dylan was, from an Order operative's perspective. Matthew, however, had hardly said anything about the situation. He'd been an unusually cheerful breakfast companion. And he had to have been faking it. Dylan just hadn't figured out why yet.

For now, all he could do was go home and rest. Ariel had been able to put together a basic message and log to the Order saying everything had gone down the drain, without actually mentioning anything about Jelena's attack. Most of the blame had been shifted to the surprise appearance of the SOJ, and that the team would be going dark for a while to make sure they weren't followed, compromised, or hunted by Vampires. James was to be in Dylan's "custody".

Now he and James were taking the winding stairs up to Dylan's low rent apartment. He'd specifically picked a spot in the worst neighborhood he could find. He'd also developed a reputation as someone not to be bothered. The high crime and dangerous streets were a natural barrier between him and those that might come looking for him. Even monsters know not to get involved in back alleys and gang wars.

As Dylan walked through the front door, James suddenly stiffened. "Dylan, watch—" he said.

A figure sat in the dark, in one of the chairs by the window. "Cleric Dylan Car—" he said.

Dylan drew his revolver. He pulled the trigger at the same moment the stranger fired his own weapon.

Part Two

Clockwork Heart Publishing

Interlude – The Order Pure

1743CE, Carpathian Mountains, Northern Romania

"For the Pure! For the Living and Worthy!"

Captain Glostner was a large man, with a full beard and a bald scalp. His armor was a gift from the Council of the Order Pure. Lions and dragons warred across the breastplate. The steel reenforced collar was studded with glass ampules for garlic oil or quicksilver, should any fell creature come close enough to try for his throat. The hand and a half sword in his right hand and copper etched shield on his left arm made that scenario exceedingly unlikely.

Behind him, twenty-five Living Knights urged their horses forward. Each horse was blind from birth. Each soldier's sword blade was laced with spells in silver inlay, and their shields were rowan wood. Only the strongest and bravest could ascend to the ranks of the Living Knights. Of all the companies, Glostner thought his the best.

Yet, none of them would dare move forward without the cloaked trio a hundred paces ahead leading the way. Hunter, Hawk, and Hound. Each reeked of magic, alchemy, violence. Madness. Who could judge them for it, considering the lifetime of nightmares that was their lot? So long had they toiled in dark places, that the Hunter could now barely tolerate the light.

Today their holy mission was to free a village from the curse of lycanthropy, by command and in the name of the Order Pure. The village of Dranwyn was deep in the valleys and forests of the Carpathian Mountains and contact with the residents was rare at any time. However, three tax cycles had passed without tithe and the Order had sent scouts to investigate. Then more scouts. Too many to attribute their loss to predators or exposure. Of the final scouting party, two members returned. They were grievously wounded, near mad, and screamed tales of werewolves as they entered the Black Cathedral on a rainy November morning. They were disposed of as humanely as possible and their remains purified.

Glostner sniffed the cold air. Snow, pines, smoke. Blood. Rotting meat and decay. He kept a steel hard face for the sake of his men, but he had never gotten used to the scents of evil. He reached up and touched the blessed parchment affixed with a wax seal to his breastplate. Carrying these blessings always helped remind him where he stood, that he was a wall between the monsters and the innocent. He looked over his shoulder to the prison wagon at the rear of the company. "Bring 'em up!" he called.

Moments later a trio of soldiers marched past him, dragging behind them a pair of shambling, ragged prisoners. Sorcerer hopefuls. Eldritch scum. Gloster's lieutenant, Hawkins, spat on the ground behind them as they were led to the village gates, where they were handed off to the Hunter. If the three soldiers made it back to formation a little faster than they made it to the gates, no one judged them harshly for it.

Glostner had been on half a dozen of these village cleansings, but this part always puzzled him. He watched as the Hunter pulled a prisoner close and whispered into his ear for long seconds. Then the prisoner went slack, his eyes vacant. The process was repeated on his comrade. Glostner had no idea what was said. The one time he'd asked a Hunter, the look he'd gotten had been bone chilling. "Not words for the likes of you," was the response. He'd felt uncharacteristic shame at the chastisement, and never asked again.

Without prompt, the prisoners walked through the gates and into the deserted shell of Dranwyn. *No*, Glostner thought as he watched the men shamble forward. *Not deserted. Not near so much as would be best.* He look back to the Order clerics, but they had disappeared. Magic was behind that, certain. But magic on his side, civilization's side, and therefore, right.

Captain Glostner had perfected his timing several missions prior. Nothing stirred in the village, yet, but he felt the tension of the creatures within. The beasts had noticed the bait. He waved forward with a hand and lieutenant Hawkins called, "Draw arms! Advance!".

Beyond the gates, the prisoners stood, trembling. Then a flash of gray fur. One man, crawling on hands and knees, remained. Glostner's company broke into a gallop. There would be no attempt to save the man. He was just bait. Reaching him in time to kill that which sought to kill him, however, was important. Glostner saw the second charging werewolf from the corner of his eye and adjusted to intercept. His horse's shoulder slammed into the creature just as it reached the remaining prisoner. Poisoned spikes attached to the horse's armor pierced and cut gashes in the wolf, and it fell screaming to the ground.

Other wolves had come out, charging at his men. Silvered swords rose and fell, and horses kicked out with silver shod hooves. Still, several soldiers were taken from their saddles, flashing teeth and fur there and gone in an instant. It was a double sorrow for the Living Knights. Even if they found one of these brothers alive later, he would have to be killed and his corpse purified with fire. For now, heartlessness and slaughter. Mourning later.

The population of Dranwyn was ninety-eight souls, by the last census. Within a quarter hour, sixty wolves lay dead in the bloody mud. Inside the cottages and huts, those yet appearing as human were hunted down and killed with quick mercy. Except the children. Always the Order demanded the right to try and prevent the curse from taking hold in the children. All those twelve and under would be taken back to the Cathedral.

After the killing was done, Glostner went to the village square, a modest stone pavilion set aside for little more than watering horses, where he found the Hunter, Hawk, and Hound. Hawk and Hound stood with heads bowed, hands held forward in prayer. The Hunter lay dead, next to the body of a massive, red furred werewolf. The leader of the pack. Originator of the curse. Something that looked like a small scythe with a silver blade was stuck in its throat. The Hunter was wounded in almost the same place, raking claw marks exposing bone and muscle.

Glostner barely took note of the strange weapon and he could no longer be shocked by battlefield gore. What held him rooted to the cobbles, his mouth parting but words refusing to come, was the Hunter's face. His eyes. His teeth. Curved, slender fangs where there should have been small canines. Red sclera and amber irises. Glostner had not seen many Vampires, but few had been enough.

"Our eyes play strange tricks, do they not, Captain?" Glostner looked up to see the Hound facing him. Only the lower half of his face was visible from the cowl of his cloak. "We would be wise to forget the deceptions of our eyes. Don't you think?" he said.

Glostner looked back at the bodies, then sharply up again at the pair of clerics. He nodded, and walked away, numb and terrified at once. He tried to forget so many lies. The fangs. The evil Vampiric eyes. The clean paws of the werewolf, and the small drop of blood falling from the claws on the Hound's silver gauntlet.

At the Black Cathedral, High Cleric Mauntes watched from an alcove as a Sister inspected a group of children. Captain Glostner and his Living Knights had rescued nine poor, orphaned unfortunates from that dreadful village of monsters. The sight made him smile. As he smiled, the children shivered, without knowing why.

Except one boy, perhaps ten years old, standing just so slightly apart from the group. He turned and looked to the alcove. Pleased, Mauntes emerged from the shadows and walked to him. The boy looked up into the cleric's eyes, the boy's flecked with gold, the tall cleric's swirling with gray.

"Such a tragedy," Mauntes said. "That evil should fall on the home of one so young and full of promise. Your family, cursed and damned. Yet such evil as this and worse runs rampant and nigh unchecked under dark skies." The boy blinked, tears forming in his eyes. He dropped his head. His fists clenched.

Mauntes laid on a hand atop the boy's head. "Would you like the chance to fight that evil, and avenge your family?"

Chapter 14

Dylan woke to the sound of profuse German swearing. James was standing over him, a small derringer in hand, which he had pointed toward the stranger in the chair. Dylan had been shot before, but based on past experience, this pain seemed excessive. The hole in the right side of his forehead radiated waves of jolting pain. Then the pain doubled, and he arched his back, screaming. Two excruciating seconds later, there was a metallic ping on the tile next to him, and the pain vanished. He looked down and saw what looked like a .22 caliber bullet, with strange symbols etched into it.

"Nasty piece of work. Glad your body ejected it. I wasn't looking forward to digging around in your brain to get it out." James glanced down at him. "You haven't exactly been the nicest patient these last few days."

"What…" said Dylan, touching the shrinking hole in his forehead. "Who…all the fucks! What's going on?"

"Visitor from the Cathedral, I believe," James said. "That's the who. He's coming around, so we'll get the rest of your answers from him."

Now that Dylan was fully conscious, he recognized the cursing man in the chair. The Inquisitor. A man who, like James, was essentially a prisoner of the Order, held in captivity for his talents. Not exactly torture, not really execution. Rather, he had a willingness and ability to find truths, to dig out truths that people sometimes didn't even realize they held. By reputation he was vile, terrifying.

Dylan saw that he leaned back in the chair at an awkward angle. Only his lips moved as he continued cursing, as though everything else was paralyzed. After a few moments there was a squelching sound and a snap as the man lifted his head. Blood clung in tendrils stretching from back of the chair to his head. The Inquisitor's neckbones snapped back into place, and his body twitched to life. A hole in the dead center of his forehead closed over, leaving a smudge of blood behind.

"Not as expected," the Inquisitor said. "I'm not disappointed, mind you. This bodes exceptionally well for my plans, but I was not prepared to get shot in the head today." He pulled a handkerchief from his suit's breast pocket and dabbed at the blood running down his face. He looked at the smudged silk in disgust and threw it over his shoulder. "I have a much cheaper outfit for getting bloody, you see."

Dylan looked up at James, who still held the derringer rock steady, pointed at the Order official. He pointed at James, then the Inquisitor. His finger wavered between the two for a moment, then back to James.

"Cleric Carter, I came to—" the Inquisitor began.

"Shh-shh-shh," Dylan said gently, placing a finger from his free hand over his lips. "I'm processing a lot of questions right now. Shush. James. Dear friend. Why...ok, no, hang on, I've got this. Yeah. Why haven't you shot this freak again?"

"Wouldn't do any good, I suspect," James said, "but I am prepared to ruin his day, if he gets excitable again." He lowered the barrel of his gun until it pointed at the Inquisitor's crotch. The Inquisitor arched his eyebrows and gave a "fair enough" head waggle.

"Ok, that should have been obvious, I guess. You then," Dylan said, getting to his feet. He pointed at the man in the chair. "Why are you in my apartment?" His eyes widened a fraction, and he cocked his head, listening. "Why aren't my alarms ringing?"

"As to the latter, your security was good, very good, really, but I've been slowly disabling it for days now. I'm in your apartment because I'd like to make a proposal to you." The Inquisitor's German accent had leveled out from a sharp, swearing burr, to a background hum. He sat comfortably, as if at a business meeting they had all agreed to.

"Not interested, I'm not the marrying type," Dylan said. "You're the Order's Inquisitor, right?" He turned to James. "Ok, so we're not actually allowed to kill him. Again. I've got thumb screws in the-"

"Stop being a fool, Cleric Carter," said the Inquisitor, "I'm not here to hide secrets from you or to hurt you. Yes, I know, the bullet in your head, you're fine. Don't be a baby." The Inquisitor looked him up and down. "As to that, I had expected you to be down a little longer than you were. We'll have to get to the bottom of that, but honestly, I am most pleased. Cleric Carter, in brief, I need you to rob someone for me. Someone unusually dangerous. I believe that is your specialty? Interactions with dangerous individuals"

"What? No. You don't give me orders, I get those from Postan."

"Not when it is Postan who is the target."

Dylan's jaw slowly dropped. "You...you're trying to ask me to steal from the High Cleric? Right, same Postan?" He turned to James. "We don't know another Postan, do we?"

"Not on this continent," James said. He lowered his gun.

"I should report you for even saying that," Dylan said. "Actually, given that you're obviously some spooky ass immortal, I think I'm actually allowed to kill you for it. I mean, I'm allowed to try another way to kill you, since obviously this doesn't work," he said, holstering his pistol and drawing his knife.

"Cleric Carter, I understand you're lying and dissembling out habit, self-preservation, and good common sense, even. But besides the fact that I shot you and you seem remarkably well recovered, your D7 report indicates a clear familial history of Vampirism. It's in your genes and your soul. That is hardly the part that interests me. It's the apparent strength of your particular curse. I've waited a very long time for someone like you to enter the services of the Order."

Dylan's eyes narrowed. "Since when do I have a D7 report? And why would you have access to it?" Department Seven was an intelligence sector charged with compiling reports of observational and statistical data on enemy targets. As far as Dylan knew, only enemy targets. Hunters were allowed free access to those reports, but since they often contained sensitive and private data, no one else should legally have been able to access them.

"This is going to be a rough night for you, Cleric, and you're going to have to let go of a lot of assumptions. You have a D7 report because you are a carrier of the genes for Vampirism. Well, to be more accurate, you have a report because you are Nether, not just because you are a Vampire. Half the members of the Hunting Clergy have a report, Dylan, because half of the Hunters are Nether, of some form or another. Vampire, werewolf, djinn, sirens, and some exceedingly rare beings, from time to time."

Dylan turned to James. He didn't look shocked. He didn't even look amused. If anything, he looked almost relieved. The Inquisitor's ridiculous pronouncement hadn't surprised him at all.

"No," Dylan said, staring at him. "Really?" James turned to look at him, and gave a shrug.

"I never had proof," James said, "but almost as good as. Over the decades I noticed one after the other beginning to turn. Then they'd disappear. Death while on a hunt, usually. One honest to goodness mugging gone wrong, which may have even been real, I don't know."

"And you never told anyone?" Dylan said. "Never reported it to the heads of the Order?"

"Oh, I did, Dylan. That's how I learned they were the ones orchestrating the whole process. I was silenced. Aggressively." James winced, then met Dylan's eyes again. "Besides, my friend, not every Hunter I've worked with has been as willing to trust the house Vampire as you've been."

He looked back to the Inquisitor. "If I've guessed right, you're not going to like much your guest here has to say for probably the next hour. But I think we both need to hear him out."

The Inquisitor smiled. It was horrible.

Dylan didn't like any of it. The Inquisitor started at the very beginning, all the way back to the first reports of Nether beings in ancient times. He explained how superstitions and primitive magic had been employed by family units and tribes to fend off as many hostile supernatural beings as they could, with limited success. This wasn't enough once people began to form villages and small cities. Early governments began to form sanctioned hunting groups. Most of the time these were little more than angry mobs with signet rings or royal seals on documents they couldn't read.

Then came the years of Awakening, when anointed priests of the Order Pure were given instruction by dreams and miracles on all the ways to guard humanity from evil forces. The Order codified official practices, and eventually banned the formation of independent Hunter orders. According to the history books, what followed was centuries of peace and safety.

"All of this you know, of course," the Inquisitor said. "Any good middle-schooler should be able to tell you nearly as much."

"But you're gonna tell me it's a lie," Dylan said. "Which part?"

"Nearly all of it, in fact," the Inquisitor said. "From the very first werewolf attack. Or Vampire, ghoul, whatever happened. That's not recorded anywhere. What is true is this: the monsters of the Nether were not the first danger to humankind. They were not even the first recorded terror. The histories I've managed to scrape together, even you would not be able to access, Cleric. They aren't for us."

Chapter 15

Ariel Ikeda didn't have to think about what she was typing. Her mind was in a dozen different, fractured places, so she just let her fingers work without her. She'd never really had to try with computers. The lines of structure in a circuit and code on a screen were places she fit. Sometimes her would-be teachers would ask her to explain how she'd made a system do this or that, and she'd struggled, not because she didn't know, but because it was like trying to explain how to walk.

She let her loneliness and confusion pour through her fingertips, and they gave her what she needed without the need to define it. She spent six minutes coding an encryption algorithm, one that in no way resembled, and was an order of magnitude more complex than, the systems used by the Order Pure. Two more minutes to access a partition in a server owned by a Belgian food processing corporation, upload a portion of her program, and let it begin routing her connection through several hundred other servers. When that finished, she secured her new backdoor into Matthew King's cell phone. For two more minutes she sat staring at the return key, not able to find an explanation for the call she wanted to make as easily as she had prepared the security necessary to make it. At last she pressed the key, hoping maybe he could explain it to her.

Ten blocks away, in a small apartment within the Cathedral complex, Matthew King sat with most of the lights turned off and a plate of spaghetti getting cold on the table beside his recliner. His phone rang twice before his eyes came back into focus. He pulled it out of his pocket, looked at the caller ID, then slid the green icon on his screen and held it up to his ear.

"Hey, Ikeda. Didn't we agree not to use these for a couple of days? Until the boss could figure things out?"

"Take the phone off your ear, dummy. This is a video call."

He looked at the screen in surprise, then sat back, smiling at the annoyed look on Ariel's face. "You know, I think this is the first time I've ever gotten a video call."

"Don't get used to it. I just wanted to ask you about...karate."

"You mean Muay Thai? I do Muay Thai."

"Whatever," she said. "I just wanna know how to punch Dylan really hard next time I see him." Her keyboard clicked rapidly in the background.

Matthew understood now. Dylan had made her mad by getting hurt. Again. Little sis always tried to keep the boys in line. "A noble pursuit," he said. "Wanna tell me more about it?"

"Whatever," she said. "We can talk about it if you want." Furious typing.

Matthew sighed and leaned back. "Actually, yeah, I kinda do," he said. "Had some things on my mind lately. About Carter."

"Do you think he's not really ok?" Ariel said, instantly sounding worried. Matthew regretted using such a serious tone.

"No, no, Ikeda, I'm sure he's fine. That doc friend of his checked him out, he's ok. But, I mean. He is changed. That vamp, the Elder. She did something to him."

"Yeah," Ariel said. "That was...that was really scary. I mean, is Dylan a Vampire now? Did he get turned? I've never heard of a Hunter getting turned. Killed by vamps, yeah. But what does the Order do with someone that's been turned?"

Matthew thought for a moment. "Nothing comfortable, I'm sure," he said. "If they find out. When they find out. Ikeda. We might have to report this. Eventually."

"Turn Dylan in?" she said. "Like, betray him?"

"If we go to the right people, and don't wait too long, maybe they have a way to help him. I don't think he's fully turned. Blood didn't seem to think so either. Maybe Postan can help."

"Crusty old geezer," Ariel muttered.

"Don't like him much, huh?"

"He always looks at me funny," she said. "Like I'm sick or something, and he doesn't wanna catch it."

"Yeah, I get that," Matthew said. "Hey. Don't worry about Carter too much, ok? He's tough, he's smart, and most importantly, he's got us. It'll be ok. Sorry I scared you. Didn't mean to do that."

"It's ok. I just got kinda lonely over here. You're right though. He's a big, smart, tough idiot. Our idiot. I'm gonna see if the Order has anything on Hunter's getting turned, or if there's a treatment."

"Unofficial channels?" Matthew asked. After a few moments of silence, he put the phone down. The screen was dark. Ariel came and went as she pleased and he didn't take it personally.

All these unofficial channels are finally catching up to Dylan, he thought. *Gonna take us all down if we're not careful.* He glanced over to the untouched spaghetti. A picture of his mother sat beside the plate on the table. He didn't notice the coldness of the food as he sat in the dim light of his thoughts and ate.

Ariel sat in the light from her monitor, staring ahead, somewhere through the screen. Lines of code raced across, without error, without hesitation, as she hunted through the Order's archives.

Despite being able to follow so many paths of information on her screens, she didn't notice the silence of her keyboard, or the stillness of her fingers.

Chapter 16

Through the night Dylan had learned that the accepted history, that monsters had arisen from the darkness and Demons had invaded and attacked a world already weakened by the supernatural, was false. The Inquisitor had explained how angels had fallen, become Demons, and hidden in the shadows on earth, weak and afraid. They'd hunted humans, picking off the weak and lonely. And they had stained humanity, actually creating Nether creatures just by being present, like radiation. As the Demons grew stronger through the centuries, they began to attack more openly, increasingly bold in their power.

Then a division had arisen in the ranks. The more feral Demons wanted to rule the world through violence and fear. But a small sect, the thinkers, the planners, wanted to work from a place of safety and power. Even in those days, special humans, gifted men and women, could occasionally manage to fight a Demon on equal terms and, sometimes, win. The humans would continue to grow stronger. Brute force was no guarantee of supremacy for the Demons. So, this more civilized sect broke off from the pack and called themselves the Order Pure.

They studied the heroes of the age: the monster Hunters, the Demon slayers, and the dragon killers. Few ever survived long, dying young and taking wings as legends. The few that did live into their middle years always disappeared, fading into obscurity. Through a careful hunting program of their own, the Order found them. Vampire lords. Alpha werewolves. Creatures of immense power and terror that had no names. A plan took shape.

Heroes were nothing more than the most powerful of monsters, touched by the corrupting influence of fallen angels, who had not yet taken their final shape. The power, the curse, seemed to run in bloodlines for these unfortunates. If they managed to reproduce before transforming, then another hero would manifest in their lineage within a few generations. The Order began to protect these bloodlines, guide them. Watch them. When a promising candidate arose, some tragedy would befall their parents and siblings, and the young hero would be recruited to the Order. Now the Demons of the Order had their own fighting force. Fiercely loyal for their salvation. Natural born protectors. Vicious in their hatred of the monsters that had taken their families.

The Order gifted these Hunters with training, magic weapons, knowledge, and authority. When Hunters strong enough were found, the Order unleashed them on the wild Demon lords that opposed them. Victory was costly, but what of it? Always there were more Hunters to be found.

Soon, the Order was on equal footing with all major political powers. Cathedrals were built across Europe and Asia. Campaigns of outward expansion were undertaken, bringing the Peace of the Order to distant lands.

The New World. The peoples living there had inhabited the land for over ten thousand years. They had their own monsters, their own protectors. They had their own relationships with the spirit world, both the negative and the positive. These practices did not align well with the beliefs taught by the Order Pure. Perhaps most importantly, though, the people of the New World had vast natural resources. The Order commissioned exploration teams and colony architects. They brought a bloody and brutal Peace to the inhabitants of the New World.

Present day. Chicago. The Red Cathedral was now the center of power for the Order in the northern New World. In fact, only the original Black Cathedral in London wielded more influence. All of it, if the man called Inquisitor was to be believed, held in the coffers of a cabal of Fallen Angels.

When the Inquisitor finished, Dylan folded his hands and settled more deeply into his chair. "I'm gonna look into all this myself, obviously," Dylan said. "Fallen Angels, alternative histories. See if I can find some geneticist in the underground, because goodness knows the underground is renowned for its degree earning inhabitants. But most of all, you. I'm gonna start in the dictionary under 'creepy fucker', then go all the way through the information community. How about a D7 report? What am I gonna find in yours? Maybe it's in your better interests to disclose any ulterior motives before I find them."

"By all means, Cleric, be as meticulous as you like. As to my motives, they are entirely self-centered. I have enjoyed a long and not uncomfortable tenure at the Order, but experience tells me there is change coming, and I feel it is time to move on."

"So why bother with us? You seem like a capable individual. You shouldn't need my help to put a few extra holes in the right heads."

The Inquisitor folded his hands on his lap. "You're going to have to come to a concrete understanding on at least one fact about me, Dylan. I am just a man. I have no D7 report, because I am not a being influenced by the Nether. I have no special physical strengths, no particular affinity for magic, no—"

"Nope, bullshit detector is way off the scales," Dylan said. "Killed you. With a not inconsequential piece of lead. Yet here you sit, breathing my premium air, in my formerly favorite chair, trying to sell me...what are you trying to sell me?"

"Freedom, Dylan, before it is too late. Make no mistake, I would not help you if I didn't need your help. I would dissect you. I would shelve all your parts, and keep alive the most interesting ones. I would do the same to your whole team. Not him," he waved to James, who scowled. "I already have too many of him on the shelf."

The Inquisitor leaned back and stared at the ceiling. After a few seconds he said, "You know, they used to tell stories about me. They said I had sinned and couldn't enter heaven. They said I had tricked the devil, so he wouldn't welcome me into hell. I wouldn't know. I never get that far, either way. The truth is, Death will not speak to me. Certainly will not take me. Death only ever said one thing to me, then nothing more, ever. 'Soulless.' Just that."

He looked Dylan in the eye. "So far as I know, I am the only human ever born without a soul. There is nothing for the Reaper to take. I come back from the dark. Every time. It has given me a certain insight into the workings of mortality, as what you might call an outside observer. It makes me very valuable to the Order. A few hundred years ago they went to great lengths to acquire and bind me."

He sighed. "I cannot fight them. Not the Demons. I am nothing in power compared to them. But they could kill me over and over, were I to cross them. Therefore, Dylan, you. I have waited a long time for a Hunter with the strength you've shown, but more than that, your circumstances. They sent you to die by Klarisvan's hand. You were victorious, but not unscathed. You were exposed to the blood of a feral Demon lord. You ingested it. And it has made you an unpredictable element."

"What? You got Demon blood in your mouth?" James said, staring wide eyed at Dylan.

"Yeah? I mean, not on purpose. And I spit it out."

"My sources say you did not, and they were quite sure. Not all of it."

"You must be mistaken," James said. "That would have killed him. Nothing drinks from a Demon, not even a Vampire. It would have burned him from the inside."

"You are correct, for almost every observed incident, Mr. Clarke," Inquisitor said. "The pestilent influence that Fallen exert on the world, which eventually creates beings such as yourself, is far too potent if taken directly. Some mortals have tried to harness its power, to disastrous ends. Yet, on rare occasions, a Vampire, a werewolf, sometimes even a ghoul, is born that can not only tolerate, but be strengthened by exposure to the pure Fallen essence. By my estimation, had the Order sent Dylan to Klarisvan a year or two earlier, they might have succeeded in eliminating him. My private observations of your friend indicated he held promise. I altered certain reports in your files and gave you the chance to fight for your life on better footing. I could not have foreseen your enhancement, but all the better."

"Sources," Dylan said, still glaring at Inquisitor. "Only two other people had any idea what happened in that room. Neither would willingly betray me. You need to explain what you've done. Succinctly."

The Inquisitor's smile held far too much evil pleasure. "No, Cleric Carter, you need not doubt your team. Succinctly, then. Sheila Donovan. She told me."

"The woman? I gave her to the medical wing. She was catatonic. She wouldn't know anything. Why would you have her?"

"It is my job, Dylan," the Inquisitor said, low and malevolent. "Everyone sees more than they think. And I know where to look. I'm very good at taking things apart." He shrugged. "Putting them back together, not so much."

A red light began to glow in Dylan's eyes.

"Dylan," James said. "Order official. Can't touch him."

"He's just as bad as every other monster I've ever taken down." Dylan said. "It's either here or sometime when he's not looking. But I will tear him apart."

"Perhaps," said Inquisitor, "but not today. We need each other. The Order won't fail in its designs a second time. The end is coming for you, and perhaps for us all. I have security bypasses already in place everywhere in the Red

Cathedral, and I can arrange for all of your Service Talismans to be gathered in one place, safely away from meddlesome Battle Priests. That is my payment for your services. The lives of your team. I am not bound by a pact with a Service Talisman. Instead, a very special scroll is used to bind me to the Order. It is kept in the Demon Postan's personal chambers, of this I am certain. Deliver it to me and the talismans will be delivered to you. You tell me when you plan to retrieve my scroll and I will give you forty-eight hours to meet me somewhere, a place of your choosing, to trade."

"And if I don't? Want to trade, succeed, survive, et cetera?" said Dylan.

"Then I use the Talismans and my connections to an underground practitioner of the dark arts to burn you all to ashes. You will not succeed in escaping the condemnation of the Order without me. Others have tried, and I have learned from their mistakes."

"Ariel…" James said. He lifted his eyes to Dylan's. "And Matthew."

Dylan looked back to the Inquisitor. "What's this change that you think is coming? Maybe we're in trouble ourselves, I dunno yet, but why the rush for you?"

The Inquisitor sighed. "The Sons of James. They add an entirely new layer to the puzzle, one that I only discovered recently, well, in the last fifty years, anyway. Previously the Order took advantage of the religious zeal of the peoples it ruled over. That zeal, I'm sure you're aware, has been eroding for the better part of the last century. It was a good plan while it lasted, but the fear of magic and spirits holds little sway with the populace now when examined under the light of science.

"Postan set plans in motion long, long ago for such an eventuality. The Sons of James may have started out as a real rebellion, an attempt to combat the power of the Order and the forces of the Nether, consisting solely of pure blood humans. It was quite impressive. It was not nearly enough. Within only decades their ranks were infiltrated, their commanders captured and subjected to the power the Fallen call Worship. They were sent back as wolves in sheep's clothing, so to speak. The SOJ believes it opposes both the Order and the Nether, not realizing they are one and the same, or that the SOJ ultimately answers to and is guided by the secret Fallen of the Order.

"They are the Order's secondary force, more secular in nature, capable of being wielded as a military power. I believe the Order will soon cast off the guise of religion, and use the SOJ to claim political domination. We do not have a place in that Order, Cleric Carter. We will be seen as remnants of the old ways. Moreover, your kind, the Hunters begot of Nether forces, have always posed a significant threat. The SOJ will be a safer alternative."

Interlude – The Ouruqan

Year of the Fifty-Third Star (Ouruqan Calendar), Central Africa

Adegoke watched the intruders from halfway across the plain as they marched through the heat haze. Filthy creatures. A great horde of monsters born from nightmares. The Fallen Angel had marched its army across Egypt and into the heart of Africa, to claim what it did not own. Bold and arrogant. This was the second attempt they had made on his tribe. It would be their second failure.

The light was fading. The last sweat of the hot day was evaporating from his huge arms and chest. He stood with his arms folded, breathing calmly, waiting. The Nether monsters posed no real threat. The Fallen, though. That would need to be dealt with swiftly, or it would be a long night.

"Volunteers?" he said, without turning around. A chorus of voices rose up behind him, every warrior seeing their chance for glory. He smiled. His people had not faltered when the Rain God came up from the south to conquer. They had not scattered when the Kijivu came down from the heavens. They did not fear this beast.

"Nkemdilim!" he said. Cheers. His most fierce warrior. A message to send to future Fallen with ambitions. Africa was not their home. The Ouruqan were subject to no one.

A tall woman moved silently to stand beside Adegoke. She was heavily muscled, with hair down to her waist, bound in dozens of thin braids. Her right eye was cunning and cold. Her left was milk white, with a scar running through it from eyebrow to the corner of her mouth. Her gaze locked on the Fallen, and she handed her spear to her chief. She growled low and quiet in her throat and charged. Nothing on the plains was faster than Nkemdilim. The Fallen angel watched from inside his stone-gray hood and crouched to fight.

Nkemdilim was a breath away when she disappeared into the grass, just for the blink of an eye, but it was enough. The Fallen faltered in his stance, trying to locate the warrior. He wasn't ready when she burst out of the grass to his left and slammed into him, the sound like a tree exploding from a lightning strike.

She had taken the Fallen by surprise, but his confidence wasn't shaken. He allowed the tackle to carry him onto his back, bearing her down beneath him as he rolled, ending above her on his outstretched left arm. He took her by the throat in his other hand and drew her up like a knocked arrow. Again and again he slammed her against the earth, until the dust rose thick around them and hid them from sight.

A sound like the snapping of Elephant's tusk. The Fallen stood in the clearing dust, his left arm broken, swinging by a strand of muscle and tendon. What little cry of pain or outrage escaped his lips had to struggle past Nkemdilim's teeth, buried deep in the Fallen's throat. Her feet were planted firmly on the ground, her height equal to the beast. Slowly, she was forcing him over backwards, her arms wrapped in a crushing embrace around his lower back. The sound of the Fallen's vertebrae grinding rolled across the plane, and the creatures of the Nether flinched away.

Nkemdilim tore her mouth free with most of the Fallen's neck still in her jaws. She let go of him with her arms, and snapped her head forward, her forehead colliding with the bridge of his nose. He slammed into the ground like a bone cast down by the goddess of the Hunt.

The warrior turned her gaze to the unnatural army of Nether. Werewolves, ghouls, and the undead. Filthy. Weak.

Prey.

She raised her hand in the air. With a whistle her spear flew across the grasses, thrown by Adegoke. She snatched it from the sky without looking away from the enemy and charged the beasts. Behind her, the tribe thundered forward. More than three hundred Ouruqan warriors.

It was a short night.

Chapter 17

"Ikeda, can I have some of this juice?" Matthew asked. He was bent low, almost squatting on the floor, buried head and shoulders in Ariel's refrigerator.

"Got it just for you this morning," she said. "Cups in the left-hand cab—…or just, you know, take the jug," she said. He smiled at her as he walked back to the living room, a quarter of the three-liter jug already drunk down.

Dylan assessed them out of habit, barely conscious of the act anymore. Matthew in a Hawaiian shirt and jeans, two knives concealed under the shirt, a snub revolver in an ankle holster. Ariel, surprisingly, had her 9mm semi-automatic tucked into her lower back, in her own apartment. She wasn't taking any chances these days.

Dylan had changed a lot in the week since the failed mission against the Elder Vampire, Jelena. Though not yet accustomed to the changes, he at least accepted them. He found himself much stronger than he had ever been before. How strong, he didn't know. Other changes were easier to gauge and more foreign to him. He could see at night. He could smell everything, hear everything. His mental clarity was beyond anything he had ever felt.

Yet even with these newfound strengths, he found himself going around more heavily armed and warded than ever before.

"So he was just sitting in your chair? Kinda cocky, isn't he?" Matthew said. Dylan started and looked up, reverie broken.

"Yeah, well. Clearly he can back it up, to some extent anyway. We both showed a winning hand of Russian roulette, so I guess you call it a draw."

"Obviously he was lying about being human," Matthew said. "What did you find on him?"

"Exactly what he said we'd find," James said.

"No D7 report in the Order servers," Ariel said.

"And nothing in the underground's archives about some immortal going by 'Inquisitor, The,' or anything like that," Dylan said. "I did pick up his last known alias before the Order got him, from a family of shadow lurkers who live under Merrionette Park. In 1857 he was calling himself Barnard August. From there it was a trip through the public records, then an online search of England's public records, and Germany, and so on."

"Finally got a cross between one of his old names and locales in a lore book in the Harold Washington Library," said James. "Not as reliable as a vetted Order Narrative, but as good as we're going to get. It told of a man who'd been to trial a dozen times, in the 12th century, and executed a dozen times. He'd wake up moments after being hung or burned or having his throat cut, laughing. Local clergy tried charms and wards on him, to no effect. Then one night, he was just gone. To be honest, I think the local magistrate was relieved he'd apparently left that part of the country and didn't pursue."

"Guy's obviously a monster, though. You don't just pop back to life like that..." Matthew trailed off, seeing Dylan staring at him. "Sorry, boss, I know you're not—"

"Maybe I am. I don't know right now. It's ok, King. This is way beyond weird, and weird is our job. But D7 is thorough. They'd have made a file, a note, something, if he was Nether. I don't know about his story, about Death wanting nothing to do with him, but whatever else, he's human."

"So, we trust him, then?" Ariel said.

"I do want to say something, actually, on that," James said. "I may be a bit biased, being a monster myself," he said, looking to Matthew, and then back to the room, "but there are worse things than being a monster. Our Inquisitor may be just a man, but he is, I warn you, evil. The things he was tried for...they were human crimes, and of the worst sort. Whatever else he may be, we need to remember, he is not our friend."

"As for the intel he's given us, that checks out, so far," Dylan said. "I'm out of time, I have to go back to the Cathedral and file some kind of formal report. While I'm there I'll see about checking on the Order security measures he told me and James about, and see if I can verify that he's actually done anything to mitigate them."

"You gonna need me to come help, boss?" Ariel said. She didn't look excited by the notion of going back.

"It's ok, Ikeda, I can handle this much. Been watching you work, after all," he said, smiling.

After a minute of silence Matthew said, "How are you feelin', Carter? Did you go back to normal, or what?"

"Don't call him normal, you'll make him feel weird," Ariel said.

"I didn't go back to anything, man," Dylan said. "If anything, I've gotten weirder. I think this is my new normal."

"I mean, I gotta ask then," Matthew said, squeezing the words out of a tense throat, "about feeding."

Dylan noticed Matthew's hand had twitched. Barely a fraction of an inch, toward one of his knives. Matthew probably hadn't even realized he'd done it. On one level, Dylan was pleased, seeing good instincts at work in a member of his team. Still, it hurt.

"No," Dylan said. "No feeding. No thirst or hunger."

"Is that a 'yet' on the end there, boss?" Ariel said.

"Maybe," Dylan said, reluctantly.

"And what do you think, Blood?" Matthew asked, looking at him. So far he refused to call the Vampire by his true name. "How long does our boy have before we have to find an alternative solution?"

James crossed his arms and leaned back against the wall. "To be honest, I'm not sure. He and I have been monitoring his changes, and he's not progressing normally, at least not in any way I've ever seen. Most fresh Vampires are starved twenty-four hours a day. Sometimes they're kept in pens and fed at reasonable intervals, if they're fortunate enough to have an older Vampire looking after them. If I'd met him on the street just today, I'd have told you he's at least a couple of hundred years old. He's very settled into his transformation. If he were that old, he could choose to feed whenever he wanted, for strength or magic or just the raw hell of it. But he wouldn't necessarily need to feed more than once a year or so. I've got to assume that's what's going on. He's skipped a big part of his Vampiric youth."

"Don't talk about him like that, like it's permanent," Matthew said. "I still don't buy this whole D7 thing the Inquisitor says the Order has on all of us. Maybe he caught some Vampire virus down in the tunnels, something some blood sucker alchemist came up with. Maybe we need to go back down with a team and find it so we can stop it before they let it loose on people, I don't know. But Carter isn't a monster. None of us are, except you."

"Matthew!" Ariel said.

"It's alright," James said, but his eyes glowed faintly amber.

"Let's all chill," Dylan said, toneless and cold as iron. He was looking at Matthew. "No one really knows what's going on yet. Maybe I'm a monster. Maybe always have been. Maybe we're all special some way and we need to figure that out. The one thing I require be understood now, with complete clarity, is that we are a team. All of us. We have all saved each other's lives at one point or another. Your lives come first to me, before anything else. I need all of you to exercise the same mindset with each other." Dylan's eyes did not glow. They sucked all the brightness out of the room. Shadows swirled around in them like smoke. "We're all good with that, right?"

Everyone nodded, but Dylan kept his eyes on Matthew until he said, "Yeah, boss. We're good."

"Great!" Dylan said. Immediately all the frost went out of him. "I need pizza. I can have pizza, right?" he said, looking at James.

"What? Um, yeah, pretty much whatever you want, I guess."

"You don't know what you can eat? Have you not eaten this week?" Ariel asked in horror.

"Maybe not? I've had a lot on my mind."

"I told you to take care of him!" Airel said, walking past James and punching his arm.

"I am! I just don't think about food much!" he said, following her into the kitchen.

The room was quiet without Ariel and James in it. For a while Matthew and Dylan each held their end of the silence, staring off into nothing. Matthew was thinking about leaving when Dylan said, "I'm scared, King."

Matthew looked up, his stern features softening.

"It's too big, any way it goes," Dylan said. He was still staring into the middle distance, deep into his thoughts. "And I think it's true. And I don't want it to be. I really didn't think about food all this week. The whole time I was running around the Underground asking questions and looking for people, it just didn't cross my mind. I didn't even realize it until just now. Things like that keep happening. Realizing I haven't turned on the lights in a room at night, but I can still see. Weird stuff."

"Gotta be some kind of treatment, man, something," Matthew said, "Something back at the Order medical unit, or maybe Postan—"

"I don't think so," Dylan said. "You ever heard of a team bringing a Vampire in alive? Besides James, I mean? It's not what the Order does. I've never heard of anyone doing it. I think, whatever this is, we have to work with it ourselves." He looked up at Matthew, his features aged with strain. "I need to ask a favor of you."

"Yeah, boss, anything," Matthew said, leaning forward.

"Not as your boss," Dylan said. "As a friend. If you see anything happening...like, me not being me anymore. Me about to go down the dark road. Me about to hurt our friends," he said, glancing toward the other room. James and Ariel were laughing about something. "Not in front of her, man. But you gotta take care of it. She can't be a part of it, she's better than us, and she doesn't deserve that. You understand?"

After a moment Matthew nodded, keeping his eyes locked on Dylan's. "Yeah, man," he said. "I got you."

"Want something to drink? You said Vampires could have whatever, so, red wine?" Ariel said.

"No, thank you, I'm fine. Frozen pizza rolls? That doesn't count as food even in my world," James said.

"No, it's perfect, Dylan loves them, he never actually advanced mentally past fourteen. What about Fruit punch? Tomato juice?"

"No, I—wait, are you offering me exclusively red drinks?"

"Maybe. Ketchup?"

James laughed. "I'll take a rain check on the red wine then."

"Oo, someone thinks he gets to come over next time it's raining," Ariel said, smiling as she put a plate a plate heaped with pizza rolls in the microwave.

They listened to the microwave in a comfortable silence. Finally James said, "Dylan isn't a monster, you know. I've known a lot of monsters, human and Nether. He's just a good man. Not to make it a put down, he just can't compete with what I've seen on the evil scale. With things I've done."

"I wouldn't care if he was a monster," Ariel said. "I don't really know anymore what makes a monster. I was never very black and white to begin with. If he is a monster, he's our monster."

James folded his arms, staring off into space. "You know, I'm not one of the good guys, Ariel. I've lived on the other side of the line. I would be still, if the Order hadn't caught and kept me. And I can't say I'm thankful to them for that. I'm going to help you all because you're the first friends I've had in a very long time, longer than I've been undead. But I'm not like Dylan. I never was a good man. When this is over, if you don't want to see me again—"

"We're all monsters in this together, James. You don't get to run off after. You're all my boys. My monsters."

The microwave dinged. James reached in to grab the plate, then yanked back a burned finger with a growl of pain. Ariel giggled at him and he turned to glare at her. She laughed louder and said, "Hah! Purple means embarrassed! Right?"

"What?" he said, sticking his finger in his mouth.

"You're eyes. They glowed purple for a second, and I think you're embarrassed. I'm cracking the code!" she said and punched his arm again. "So what kind of Nether do you think I am? My D7 didn't really say anything, just the day I was found and my statistical info.

"I really don't know," James said, rubbing his arm. "The only things I've ever heard said about you have to do with how good you are with computers. Oh, and that you're an exceptional boxer."

"Really? Who says that?"

"Dylan, usually while holding something cold to his face. I can see why, too," he said, smiling as he stretched his arm.

"Maybe I'm just normal, after all," Ariel said, a hint of disappointment in her voice.

"Oh, no, I don't think that could ever be said of Ariel Ikeda," James said, and winked.

"Pizza!" Ariel called loudly, blushing and rushing from the room.

"You know, in my day, when pizza was first invented, it was something special. This," James said, eying a roll, "may not even be food."

"This is the pinnacle of the culinary arts and you're in denial," Dylan said, taking the roll from his friend's hand and eating it.

"I mean, I don't think vamps and I share much in the way of food preference, but we might agree tonight," Matthew said. He chewed his seventh pizza roll loudly.

"You're welcome and all," Ariel said. "Not like I bought these special last night at the food mart around the corner because I knew you guys would be coming over and I'd have to feed you something in bulk."

"Oddly specific," Dylan said, on his twelfth roll.

"Sorry, Ikeda, just playing," Matthew said. "Ok, so let's pretend this D7 stuff isn't some big misunderstanding and that the Inquisitor isn't a creepy con man."

"No, he definitely is," James said, "but proceed."

"What's my report say? Just for fun. Gotta be some kind of were-something, or, like, I dunno, thunder god?" Matthew said, flexing his bicep.

"Ouruqan," Ariel said through a mouthful, "whatever that is, it didn't elaborate."

Dylan suddenly choked. James froze. Matthew emanated sickened shock and anger. "What. The hell. Did you just say?" he said.

"Is that bad?" Ariel said, looking around, confused. "I don't know what that is."

"She didn't mean anything, King," Dylan said. "You know she's been sheltered, and people don't even talk about that anymore. It's not even her saying it, man, it's the D7."

"No, see, this is where stuff starts to break down," Matthew said, rising to his feet. "This is something that lying Inquisitor snuck in, some fucked up racist joke or something. No, this is all bullshit, because I'm not some heretic Orc. Are you saying you think I'm some animal, Carter? That...woah, no no no, that my family are animals? That my mother is some kind of half-breed Orc?"

"Matthew, wait," James said, his palms held forward, trying to calm Matthew. "It's not like that. A long time ago—"

James's head whipped back so hard when Matthew struck him that it cracked the wall. He slumped down to the floor, barely conscious.

"Hey!" Ariel shouted.

"Shut up," Matthew said quietly, breathing hard. "Everyone shut up. We're not doing this." He looked around, trying to say more, and failing. Dylan stood by the couch, tensed to move if Matthew lashed out again. Angry and confused, Matthew turned and stalked out the door.

Chapter 18

Ariel knelt by James and took his face in her hands. "You ok?" she said.

"Been a bloody long time since anyone put me down like that," James said, slurring.

"Can someone please tell me what's going on?" Ariel said. "The report just said Ouruqan, whatever that is. It didn't say Orc anywhere, and besides, those are just boogeymen! They aren't real."

"You're not wrong," James said, his jawing popping loudly as he shoved it back into its socket. "But neither is Matthew. The Ouruqan were real. But the Order created the Orcs in the hearts of people, to Demonize and vilify the Ouruqan. That made the Orcs real, to the masses, anyway. To Matthew, that lie is very true."

"I think you're gonna have to back up a little for me. We're not all old men with long memories," she said, sitting on the floor in front of him.

"I guess 'orc' has lost some meaning since you were born," Dylan said, still staring at the door. "Information age, maybe. When I was growing up, some people still believed they were real. It was still a slur, something you just did not call another person. Well...something decent people didn't say, anyway."

"Much more common in my day," James said, leaning his head back against the wall. "Still vile. A century before me, though, people died just for being accused. At the behest of the Order. I noticed the decline in the usage, and hoped those days were far behind us."

"So were orcs really real then?" Ariel asked.

"No, not as you think of it," James said, "And not as Matthew thinks of it. The Ouruqan were a race of people who lived in Africa, people blessed with many gifts. As I've heard it, they were great philosophers and artists. They were also exceptional fighters. They believed their ancestors gave them strength and speed, and that the longer your bloodline, the stronger you were.

They may have been right. Stories say they were the only beings on earth that could face a Fallen Angel one on one, hand to hand. We call the Fallen Angels 'Demons' now," he said, seeing the question on Ariel's face.

"The Ouruqan wouldn't submit to Order rule. When the Order realized they couldn't be conquered with force either, they turned to propaganda. Africa was still a fairly secluded continent then and the Ouruqan had always kept to themselves, even among Africans. Few Europeans or Asians had ever even heard of them. It wasn't difficult for the Order to arrange for a few explorers to come back with tales of monsters worse than werewolves and Vampires. Orcs, as they called them, were malicious animals with no relation to humans at all, no former lives to lend any honor or respect to who they might once have been before being turned. The few Ouruqan they managed to capture and bring back to London were either incredibly old or young, and even then it would take a small army to bring them down. Once captured, they were tortured and mutilated, physically and magically, weakened to the point they could barely stand. They made them look as much like the nightmare they wove as they could. Then they'd set them up for execution by the public. Get people's hands bloody. Force them to commit, or die with the 'orc' as a sympathizer.

"It worked, and it stuck fast. For centuries people propagated the idea of the filthy orc. A lot of innocent Africans died for it. A lot of people of any skin color, really, but especially non-Europeans. The Ouruqan were strong, but to take on the whole world? Nor did they want to go to war, with anyone. It wasn't in their nature. So they hid ever deeper in the vast forests and mountains of Africa. No one's heard from them in a long, long time."

"People knew this, and still followed the Order?" Ariel said. "That Demons are Fallen Angels, Fallen Angels are the Order, and the Order tried to orchestrate a genocide?"

"The Order hands out food to the poor," Dylan said. "The Order buries your dead. The Order kills monsters, and the High Clerics aren't Demons. Everyone's seen the Clergy, met with Clerics, gone to a Cathedral. What James just said, well, that was all just some ridiculous propaganda thought up by anti-Order zealots. Almost no one ever believed it. And no one now believes orcs were ever really a thing."

"Did you believe it?" Ariel asked. "Either of you? Any of it?"

The two men looked at each other. "I think a lot of us didn't want to think about it at all," Dylan said. "People sort of stopped being so attached to the Order around the time I came along. I mean, a lot of people don't even believe the things we hunt are real. And that's encouraged, helps 'control panic,' or whatever."

"I was never an adherent to the Order even when I was human," James said. "I'd sit in bars with other likeminded friends and chant any anti-Order story with them that was going around at the time. But I can't say I really believed anyone had ever been persecuted by the Order either. We were just young and stupid, rebellious, with our eyes wide closed." He shook his head. "Took a hundred years of immortality and another century of captivity to get my head on straight, make me start thinking. And what we've all been digging into for the last week...yeah, it ties a lot of pieces together. Makes a lot of sense."

"I gotta go after him," Ariel said, reaching for her jacket. "I gotta tell him I didn't know."

Dylan laid a hand on her shoulder. "He knows, Ikeda. I don't think it's about you. You know how important the Order is in his life. It's literally keeping his mom alive. He stands to lose more than all of us if the Order's been lying all this time. I'll go talk to him, it's my responsibility to make this alright."

He grabbed his heavy coat and wide brimmed hat off the couch. "You have your key, James? I might be out a while."

"Yeah, sure. I'll see you in the morning."

"I'm planning on us heading back to the Cathedral tomorrow. Get this ball rolling."

"Wanna help me start some cover IDs for all of us before you go?" Arial said to James.

"Absolutely. I've got plenty of dead friends from a long time ago that we can recycle," James said, dragging a chair over to her desk.

"Let me know how the big guy's doin'," Ariel called over her shoulder. "And tell him...I love him."

"Will do," Dylan said, and left.

Chapter 19

Six stories beneath the city of Chicago, in an offshoot of an abandoned sewer tunnel known by the Underground locals as "Hunt's Lane," Tobias Monk was taking inventory. He was what passed for a librarian in the society of beings who lived beneath the human world. Among illegal creatures and cast-off lives, he was a man who couldn't let go of his belief that society, any society, needed access to books, to repositories of knowledge. He provided this as a service, free of charge, to his otherworldly neighbors. He had done so ever since a growing aversion to sunlight and a series of undeniable physical changes had forced his family to disown and abandon him, leaving him to fend for himself on the streets and live under them.

He was reshelving several volumes that his friend, Dylan Carter, had recently requested. Strange, old volumes, mostly full of legend and speculation, as far as Tobias could tell. An odd mixture of texts. Not so odd as Dylan himself. Tobias smiled thinking about the strange Hunter, who constantly went out of his way to help many different residents of the Underground. Anyone with half an attention span could tell the man was no zealot, that he was barely even an adherent to the tenants of the organization he worked for. Old myths and fairy tales were hardly scratching the surface for someone like Dylan.

The last book Tobias was replacing on the shelves was a copy of court records from the sixteenth century. Unedited, unauthorized court records. It was exceedingly rare, fragile from centuries of improper handling and hasty concealment. When he dropped it, the bottom of the spine hit the floor sharply, causing the front cover and dozens of pages to rip away from their binding. He would have mourned the damage, if he'd had any life left in him. He hadn't heard the black-clad figure slip into his shop, nor seen the blackened blade. He'd felt the knife strike home, between the ribs on the left side of his back, but only as a solid blow, like a club. He was dead before he ever registered he was in trouble.

Kazia Isingale hid in a dumpster behind a boarded-up TV repair shop. She'd been running frantically down back streets and through old buildings for too long, well past her endurance limits. She just needed a minute to breathe. She needed to think of a place these people wouldn't follow her or wouldn't think to look for her. Something. Maybe someone to take her in. Boss Gabbon was a bad man, but he didn't appreciate top worlders messing in Underground affairs. If she could get on the L train, maybe she could make it to his station before they found her again.

Kazia was a Whisper. She made her way in life listening to the Ether, picking out people's secrets and selling them to whoever paid the right price. She figured someone had now paid the right price to have her silenced. She briefly wondered if it was because of Dylan. He always asked for weird stuff, but he never asked for Order secrets. Until two days ago. Maybe she'd gone a step too far, taking his coin for that job. Maybe, if she survived this, she'd add Order business to her list of off-limits services.

There was a loud metallic slam as something hit the inside of the dumpster next to her. A second later she realized it was a gas grenade, spewing out an obnoxious cloud of sensory irritants. Getting out and running was a bad choice. Staying put and choking was worse. She jumped out and ran with all she had left in her.

Boss Gabbon might have admired the efficiency of Kazia's death, if he'd been there to see it. There was no malice, threatening, or cruelty. The black-clad man simply stepped out of the alley ahead of Kazia and slammed an open palm into the center of her chest. Her forward momentum versus his control and timing. She lost, ribs and sternum cracking, and she toppled back, her head striking the sidewalk. She was not conscious when he reached down and snapped her neck.

The man looked down the sidewalk to the woman who had tossed the grenade into the dumpster. He stood straight and nodded. They both walked back into their alleyways and disappeared.

Kate Benson was asleep when the SOJ operative plunged a silver spike into her heart. It was his way of being merciful.

Chapter 20

"I understand your concern, my son," High Cleric Postan said. "Alas, I have seen situations such as this before. I worried, but in truth I never really expected this of a Hunter of Cleric Carter's standing." He sipped wine from a cup carved out of dark gray stone. "And to learn that one such as our Inquisitor is encouraging this poison in his mind. Most disappointing," he growled.

"So, these D7 reports don't exist then, your Holiness?" Matthew asked.

"Of course not, Cleric," Postan said. He set his cup on a table and turned from the fire to face Matthew. "You should esteem yourself more highly than that. I do not say that Ms. Ikeda found nothing in her searches, but whatever she saw must have been placed there by zealots of some terrorist group, perhaps even by our wayward Inquisitor. And to think they would attempt to cast such a disparaging light on you, one of our finest Hunters. Well, it only shows how important you truly are, for someone to try so hard to bring you so low. An orc, indeed. Vile aspersions to cast against one so faithful."

"Thank you for your confidence in me, your Holiness," Matthew said. "Is there maybe some way to bring the team back into the Order's good graces? I don't think Clerics Carter and Ikeda are acting out of pure malice. They've been deceived. Surely that holds some weight in their defense?"

Postan rubbed his hands together in front of the fire, his dry skin rasping like an insect's wings. "The Order Pure extends safety and hope to all who will accept. I'm sure Cleric Ikeda can be made to appreciate the truth of her circumstances. She is young, intelligent, and of no little value to our work. But as for Dylan Carter," he said, his brow furrowing as he sat back in his chair, "Cleric King, I had you watching him for a reason, and I have to believe you can understand why now. He has always been unorthodox. Effective, but self-willed, even reckless, though I'm sorry to say it. Now you say some physical change has come upon him, something of the Nether."

"He is...sick. A disease or plague he came in contact with during our last mission, I believe. I hope, at least. Something that maybe the medical division could treat?"

"There have been times of disease brought on by Nether creatures," Postan mused. "Although I'm not convinced in this case. Yet, you would still wish so much to save your friend? After he was willing to entertain these wild notions?"

"As you say, your Holiness, the Order exists to give hope. I still hope for him. He has his own methods, but he also has a good heart," Matthew said.

"As you say," Postan said, his tone low and doubtful. "I will have word sent to Dr. Mikkelson. He may have some ideas. I caution against over much hope though, my son. If there is no treatment or if Cleric Carter proves a danger in the interim to the public, then steps will have to be taken to stop him. Do you understand?"

"Yes, High Cleric. I do," Matthew said, looking at the floor and nodding.

"And if it should be determined that you are best qualified to enact these measures against your team leader? Your friend?"

"I will do what is necessary to safeguard the Order and those under its protection," Matthew said, his eyes hard.

"To say you play a dangerous game doesn't quite cut the skin, Postan."

"And yet none has ever been so well positioned for success in such an endeavor as I, Kinyr," Postan said. He still sat in his chair, though he no longer looked like the ancient High Cleric that Matthew would have recognized. He had slipped his ring of office onto the middle finger of his left hand. In so doing, he had removed himself from the realities of the world by just a hair's breadth, so that his true form could show. His stone-gray robes flowed over his seated form, shifting constantly in a wind that could be heard but not felt.

His face was transformed from dry and dying skin to a parchment mockery of flesh.

Kinyr walked across the room from a hidden alcove and sat in the chair next to Postan's. Her robes were infinite layers of dusted cobwebs, and her face was the dull glow of a dying ember. Her black eyes studied Postan for long moments. "These creatures? They're dangerous. If it knew, it could kill you in your own chambers and none of us could do anything about it. Yet you sit there, unguarded, drinking and talking with it."

"No Fallen has ever had a pet Ouruqan before," Postan said, amusement coloring his voice. "I have in my collection a Vampire and an immortal. What a menagerie it will be when I can boast an Orc as well."

"You play the game too lightly," Kinyr said. "You endanger us all. If you must do this, at least collar it soon. I shudder to see it walking the halls of the Cathedral like this." She stared into the fire, tapping a long finger on the arm of her chair. "You should dispose of the immortal. His threats are not to be taken lightly. You know this."

"The Inquisitor? Dispose of him?" Postan laughed. "I honestly wouldn't know how. Bury him in the ice at the bottom of the world, perhaps, but I still wouldn't wager against him." He took a long drink of something that was not quite wine, cradling the stone cup in his hands. "Besides, he's played this hand before. It's entertaining, but futile. I doubt he expects success this time either."

Chapter 21

"Poor Matthew," said Dr. Coleen Jackson. "I don't envy you, Dylan. Trying to escape the Order; that's like trying to outrun civilization."

Dylan switched his cell phone to the other ear. Apparently even burgeoning Vampires could get sore ears from a phone. "I mean, yeah, that's exactly what it is. Which is what I've been helping Underworlders do for years. Including good doctors of the Lycan-ish variety."

Coleen heard the smile in his voice and smiled with him. "I know, Dylan. And I'll always be grateful for the life you helped me get. But that's just it, Dylan. I have a life. A career. I have Ben. Maybe that sounds selfish, but what am I supposed to do, just give him up? He'd never understand if he found out what I am."

"I want you to be selfish about all that, Coleen. I don't want you to feel like you owe me anything, ever. Hell, you've literally held me together with wire and tape before, the balance is all on me. I just had to ask."

Coleen rubbed her forehead in the dark of her kitchen. Ben snored peacefully two rooms away. She loved that awful sound these days and her eyes stung with tears at the idea of ever losing any of this life. "You know I'll always be here for you and the team, Dylan. But I can't get that exposed. I'm sorry."

"It's all good, Coleen," he said, and meant it.

"You'll keep in touch, let me know everyone's ok? Please?"

"Absolutely, doc."

"Stay safe, Dylan."

"You can't tell me what to do," he said, and she heard him chuckling as the line clicked dead. She put her phone down on the table and leaned back in her chair.

He'd said that to her years ago, when he was just a bottom rank Hunter and she was a med student with a secret. She'd been walking home from an evening class, when a group of street vamps and ghouls had attacked her from an alley. She was fine. Even without transforming, she could have handled them.

Dylan hadn't known that. He had been at a hole in the wall diner that night, same neighborhood, and was walking back to a bus stop. He'd seen what was happening and rushed in like a man who hated plans. His rescue attempt went as expected. He got his ass kicked.

She'd managed to help him limp back to her apartment, patched him up, and let him sleep off an awful headache. She was out getting food for them when he woke up. It didn't take much looking around for him to figure out what she was. She wasn't as good at hiding in those days, and he was smart. And even back then, he couldn't follow the rules. He couldn't repay her kindness with a bullet. So he'd become her friend instead.

She'd sent him home with proper medical instructions and good advice. "You can't tell me what to do," he'd said, and smiled like he thought he was Casanova.

No, Dylan, I suppose I can't, she thought, staring up into the night. *I don't guess anyone ever will be able to.*

Dylan put the phone in a pocket inside his coat. He'd actually hoped Coleen would refuse. He'd asked for her help because he had to, for his team. The truth of it was, they were as likely to die trying to get away from the Order as to succeed. Maybe more so. The Order certainly had the equipment and personnel to end their lives, no matter what kind of special talents he and his friends had.

His head suddenly jerked to the right with a powerful reflexive action. In almost the same instant a brick exploded in the wall of the building ahead of him, and Dylan realized he had literally dodged a bullet. He whirled and saw a group of three men following him several blocks back. One of them was hastily racking the bolt on a rifle with a very impressive looking suppressor and mouthing the word "shit".

Dylan ran down the nearest alley, heading quickly for the dark end of it. He hadn't been expecting trouble tonight and was trying not to focus too hard on who it might be. Questions would be answered later.

To his surprise he found two other assailants at the end of the alley. A woman shot her leg out from where she was hiding behind a dumpster, trying to trip him. He jumped over it, only to be clotheslined mid-air by a tall man unfolding himself from behind a short stack of pallets. They were using actual Vampire hunting technique. Put the target into a position that only individuals with superhuman reflexes could avoid, and then shoot or strike where the target is most likely to dodge to, without bothering to aim. And it had worked.

Ariel's fuzzy slippers made scuffing sounds on the carpet as she walked to the apartment door. The doorbell rang a second time as she reached for the latch. "Help you?" she said through the narrow crack she opened.

"Delivery, just need a signature," said a young man on the other side. His face was tired, but smiling, alive with good customer service.

"Not really expecting anything," Ariel said.

"Just the delivery guy, ma'am, if you could sign."

A voice behind him said, "Never seen a delivery person with that model tucked in their belt." The young man whirled, pistol in hand before the package he had been holding hit the floor. James caught his wrist with one hand, pistol pointed rock steady the wrong way. The Vampire snapped his head forward, connecting with the assailant's nose. Ariel grabbed his shirt collar and yanked him through the open door, slamming him to the ground.

James cried out in the hall, hands over his eyes. "SOJ! He's covered in silver gel!" He tore his hands away, revealing eyes both glowing red and burning from the supernatural irritant.

Ariel aimed a kick at the operative's ribs but jerked back with a sharp cry when her ankle connected with the man's drawn knife instead. She fell to the floor and rolled away. Instead of following, the man reversed the grip on the knife, rolling onto his back and pointing the blade up. James landed squarely on top of it, driving it deep into his right lung. "Bloodsucks," the man said, wrenching the knife around, "Never any restraint. Your own fault, man."

"Open," murmured the woman kneeling at the back door of Coleen Jackson's house. Her two teammates moved silently past her into a mudroom. The house was pitch black, all the curtains drawn. Still, they kept their NVGs on minimum UV output. Dr Jackson was a confirmed Nether, but with unverified ancestry or aberration levels. Her range of vision was unknown. Caution could not be over applied.

The team moved through the kitchen and rounded the corner into the living room. True Believer Justine, the woman who'd picked the locks, was about to declare the room clear, when her weak UV lamp touched the stairs. They were at the far end of the room, and at the edge of the NVG's illumination area. Through them she could just make out the form of a woman standing on the bottom step, bathrobe open, naked underneath. And a sword. Dr Coleen Jackson grasped an ancient Merovingian ring-sword comfortably in her right hand, a gift from a teacher now long dead.

"Shit," Justine said.

Dylan rolled hard to his left, dodging the stake he hadn't yet seen but knew must be coming. Basic anti-Vampire combat techniques were hundreds of years old and varied little between Order and SOJ strike teams. The silver spike buried inches deep in the asphalt where Dylan had been. He threw a sharp backhand that struck a glancing blow on the man's jaw, then rolled over his left shoulder and came up on his knees. Just in time to see the muzzle flash as a round exited the female operative's pistol.

Ariel tried to control her breathing, stood, looked around to find her lost sidearm. She didn't remember having dropped it, and scanned the room wildly for it. Before she could spot it, the false deliveryman threw James off to the side. He stood and took a fast step toward Ariel, then brought his knee up to her ribs. She half twisted away from the blow, but she was already backed against a wall, and the impact took a lot of breath out of her. He pinned her against the wall with a forearm to her throat and smiled. "Don't look like any Nether I ever saw," he said. "Don't matter, though. Gotta do what I gotta do, babe."

He was not expecting the strong right hook Ariel directed to his left ear. He fell away, grabbing at his ringing ear, and came back with murderous intent. Ariel looked terrified. But she wasn't looking at him, and that brought the operative up short.

"You're the talkative one in your circle, aren't you?" Something in the quality of the air changed, became less breathable. Shadows grew in the corners and reached out like smoke. "So fucking chatty."

The operative whirled. The Vampire should have been immobilized by the organ damage the knife had done. Instead, he saw James standing, bleeding profusely from the chest. The dark pits of his eyes were filled with the same smoke that reached out from the edges of the operative's vision. The operative lunged, the knife leading. James was on his throat faster than mortal eyes could follow.

True Believer Justine fired her weapon at Coleen. Coleen simply leaned out of the way, dodging the round as if it were a thrown toy. In the next instant she'd closed the space between herself and the operative, burying half her sword in the woman's right shoulder. Coleen tore the blade across Justine's body, severing her scream at the windpipe, and pulled the sword free. She caught the next operative by his NVGs as he was rounding the corner, yanked his head forward to expose the back of his neck, and cleanly beheaded him.

Her backhand return swing was meant to decapitate the final man as well, but it rang hard against the spine of a large combat knife. He lashed out with his left hand, catching Coleen behind the ear. She stumbled into the middle of the living room, head ringing, and felt the burn of silver on her skin where she'd been struck. The man was wearing coated brass knuckles. No novice then.

The ringing quickly subsided, and she waded back in, the sword now in a two hand grip. She didn't waste energy or opportunity on showmanship, no spinning, no posing. Her cuts were efficient, her parries minimalist. So were the final operative's. He weaved and dodged, retorted with short stabs and jabs. Neither combatant gained much on the other, until the operative made a swipe at Coleen's forearm, cutting a burning line down the outside. She twisted reflexively to protect the injury and he began pummeling her with the brass knuckled hand. Ribs, cheek bone, and shoulder socket were crushed under his heavy blows. Finally, as her sword dropped, he brought the knife up in a swinging uppercut into her stomach.

Coleen staggered back and fell against the wall, sliding down to the floor, breathless. The operative hesitated, watching to see if he'd done enough to kill the Lycan. It was a bad practice, that hesitation, but life had let him get away with it before. He had not been facing creatures from bloodlines as strong as Dr Coleen Jackon's before.

Her breath came back in a powerful gasp. In one fluid motion she stood, dropping her robe behind her as she rose. Her transformation was so fast it sounded like a tree breaking over in a storm. In the two steps it took to reach Saint Cary Brewer, she went from a woman to a berserker werewolf. She wrapped her arms around him, crushing his spine, and lifting him off the floor. He stabbed over and over, but it only made the beast flinch. The silver coated brass knuckles couldn't penetrate her thick fur. He screamed in frustration and terror. She silenced him with her terrible fangs.

Lately Dylan was observing too much of his life only in retrospect.

He was standing at the opening of the alley, on the sidewalk, hands in his pockets, staring back into the darkness he'd been fighting in moments ago. He had to concentrate hard to remember how he'd gotten out, why he wasn't dead, or even hurt. He remembered the muzzle flash of the woman's gun. He remembered how slowly the bullet had moved as it spiraled out of the barrel.

Blank.

The woman was dead, smashed back hard against the brick wall. He was pulling away from her, kicking the man with the stake into the other wall. The depth of the boot print in the man's chest implied he was dead before the bricks caught up to the back of his skull.

Blank.

So many bullets from the mouth of the alley.

Blank.

Three men, torn to pieces, blood on Dylan's hands.

Then he was standing where he was now. Slowly, he pulled his shaking hands out of his pockets. They were still covered in blood and bits of worse things. For a moment he wondered if he might have fed on it, licked it off like a hungry dog. He didn't think so. Still, as he looked at the drying red on his fingers, he began to feel...

He shoved them forcefully back into his coat pockets. *Ah. That's why those were in there.* Looking down he saw that he hadn't escaped injury after all. The coat was full of holes across his abdomen and thighs. Small holes in front. Bigger, he was sure, in the back.

As he stood there, feeling more unsure of himself than he had since that day in his sister's apartment so long ago, his phone rang. Somehow, in his coat's inner pocket, it had escaped disaster. He pulled it out, looked at the screen, and answered. "Ariel, I—"

"Dylan, I need you. James is hurt."

In the half dark, Coleen felt tears sting the corners of her now human eyes. Her husband, Ben, looked down at her from the top of the stairs, horror written on his face.

Chapter 22

Dylan hadn't made it far from Ariel's apartment before the attack and was back at her door in under ten minutes. He found himself wondering for an instant if he should knock or just bust the door down, when it opened, a very pale Ariel Ikeda standing on the other side. "Security cams," she explained, "Get in here."

The awful smell hit Dylan first. Something had been burnt, badly. Maybe was still burning. Next he saw how dark it actually was in the room. He could see just fine, but he noticed how all the colors were switched to the ones his new night vision used. Ariel was shuffling awkwardly to the far corner of the room, a hand held out to feel for furniture and other obstacles.

"James?" she said, almost a whisper. "Sweetie? Dylan's here. I got him, just like you asked."

A bundle of dark shadows whimpered and growled low in the corner of the room. No, not shadows. Smoke. Tendrils of heavy, sooty smoke clumped on the crouching form there and slowly fell to the floor, forming unnatural, writhing pools.

"Dylan...help me..."

The voice was graveyard wind and Dylan felt the pull of powerful magic laced into it like fine wires. He glanced at Ariel and saw that her eyes had gone blank and unfocussed, the pupils huge. Right now, she would have done anything James told her to do. Likely several people on the street were affected almost as severely. Dylan carried items meant to nullify hypnotic magic, and his new physiology seemed to have a certain amount of natural defense against it, but still, the call was sharp and imposing.

Kneeling beside his friend, Dylan noticed ghosts of ember glow moving along the Vampire's tattoos. The ones the Order had given him to restrain him. "Did he feed?" he said, looking at Ariel. He finally noticed the robe, and had a thought that made him feel equal parts guilty and anxious. "Wait, are you ok? Was it you? Ariel, did he feed from you? Ariel!"

Ariel shook her head sharply, then pulled the robe tighter around herself, protectively. "No…no, we were attacked. The Sons of James. One. James got stabbed, then he…" She trailed off and began looking around the apartment, even in the dark, trying not to see the scene play out in her mind again.

Suddenly James whirled from the corner and lunged, but whether at Ariel or himself, Dylan didn't know. He caught James by the wrists, both men still on their knees, struggling hard. James was strong in an otherworldly way, much more so than Dylan expected, and he felt his own newly enhanced body protest the stresses being placed on his joints and muscles. Worse was when he realized James was trying to hold himself back.

"The spike, Dylan," James said. He was gaining the upper hand, pushing Dylan back. "That's why I wanted you! The spike!"

Dylan understood then. One of his favorite tools was a sixteenth century silver spike, the length of his hand, with a holder for small quartz crystals at the blunt end. He knew what James wanted him to do with it but wasn't sure how to disentangle himself long enough to use it. James solved the problem for him.

With phenomenal power, James twisted his right hand in a half circle, breaking Dylan's grip and taking hold of his wrist. There was a sound like cracking stone and Dylan's hand hung useless from his arm. James shoved past and lunged for Ariel. Before she had time to draw breath to scream, Dylan whipped the spike from its belt sheath with his good hand and slammed it into James' back. James spun and slammed his hand through Dylan's ribcage, reaching for his heart.

The quartz crystal in the spike exploded.

Chapter 23

"**Y**our phone rang. I answered it."

Dylan was vividly aware of the long process of opening his eyes. It seemed to be the only thing he had strength or will left to do for several moments.

Finally he said, "What?"

"You wanted to know why she was here."

His fuzzy thoughts registered the speaker as Ariel. But he didn't remember having asked a question.

"Why who?" he said.

He saw Ariel look from him to someone on the opposite side of...couch. He was on a couch. With great strength and bravery, he swiveled his eyes to his left and saw a tall blonde woman standing over him. "Hey, guy," she said. There were tears in the corners of her eyes.

"Jackson," Dylan said. The situation was becoming exhausting. "Who's hurt?"

"I can't with these guys right now," Ariel said, her voice dripping with frustration. "I'll be on the balcony."

Dylan watched her leave the frame of his vision and decided not to try turning his head. Tomorrow, probably. Unless today was tomorrow? What had today been?

"You're hurt. Again," Coleen Jackson said. "Pretty bad this time, if I'm honest. Also James, also pretty bad, but not as bad as you. And that guy's dead," she said, pointing toward the kitchen. Dylan took her word for it.

"Who got us?" Dylan asked. He was finally aware enough to realize how bad breathing hurt. He couldn't decide if he wanted to keep doing it.

"I think the dead guy got Ariel on the ankle, James got the dead guy on the throat, then you got James in the back, and he got you in the chest." Coleen gestured down Dylan's body and he managed to tilt his head up enough to see that he was shirtless, his chest mummified with gauze and tape.

"What the..." he said. Snippets of memory began to come back. Blurry, then faster and clearer. "Oh, shit," he said. "But James is alive, right?"

"Hurt, but alive," Coleen said. "I'm not actually sure you could have killed him in the state he was in, but maybe. I don't know. That Vampire stuff is all weird," she said, waving the subject off with her hand.

Dylan tried to sit up, then fell gracelessly back to the couch. "I remember what I did to him," he said, "but what the hell did he do to me? I got shot in the head a few days ago and it didn't hurt this bad."

"He went for your heart," she said, her tone grave. "Nicked it, actually, with a claw. You're a very lucky Vampire, Dylan. Afraid that's why it hurts so much, the heart's a Vampire's real weak spot, and it's gonna hurt for a while. Brains, even solid rock one's like yours, are easier for you to heal than a heart injury."

"Noted," Dylan said.

"What does this do?" Coleen asked, holding out the silver spike he had used on James. She held it gingerly, wrapped in a paper towel. "I pulled this out of his back. The silver had burned the skin a little around the entry point, but it wasn't deep enough to have hurt him as badly as he seems to be."

Dylan reached for the weapon. He was surprised and pleased to see that his left hand functioned more or less normally again. "It's a Sicilian Stake," he said, turning it slowly between his fingers. "Used to use them to incapacitate Nethers in the Renaissance, so they could be brought in for questioning. It's kind of like a magic heatsink, sucks most of the power of out Nethers in a heartbeat." He furrowed his brows, looking at the empty socket on the blunt end of the spike. "Ought to be a crystal right here. You put in a gemstone, and it pulls the magic into the crystal. Did you find one somewhere? I usually use quartz."

"No, not really," Coleen said. "But there is a little sand or something in the carpet where you two ended up."

Dylan whistled low and quiet between his teeth. "Shattered quartz?" he said. "Quartz isn't the very best, but it usually holds most anything we run into. He must have been having a hell of a bad time."

"Still am," a voice croaked across the room. James was standing in the door to Ariel's bedroom, leaning raggedly against the doorframe. "A lot better thanks to you, though."

"Why do you get the bedroom?" Dylan turned to Coleen. "Why am I on the couch and he gets the bed?"

"I'm prettier," James said, then he coughed. He examined Dylan for several seconds, wincing. "I'm sorry I did that," he said, "truly, I'm so sorry. I didn't mean to..." He trailed off, looking guilty.

"I know, man. I mean, you owe me a really strong drink, but yeah, that wasn't you." Dylan managed to sit up enough to look at the corpse of the SOJ operative. It was withered and ghost white, drained completely dry. "Did feeding make you get like that?"

"No, not entirely. More these wretched tattoos," James said. His eyes pulsed amber, weakly, then went out like spent candles. "They're meant to burn the blood away, so I can't overpower the Order and escape. But I'd had a lot of blood, to try to fix this," he said, gesturing at the blood stains on his shirt and ribs. "And, well...I was pissed at him."

"So why was he here?" said Ariel. She was technically back inside the apartment, standing just inside the doorway to the balcony, arms crossed tightly in front of her. She took a reflexive step away when James tried to stand up straighter. "I'm aware the SOJ and Order have friction, but I didn't think we were actively hunting each other now."

"Wasn't just you," Dylan said. He carefully put his feet on the floor. There were no comfortable positions left to him. "I got jumped on the way home. Five of them. They were equipped for Vampires."

"They thought I'd be with you, then?" James said.

"Maybe, but they came at me like I was a vamp too. So they have really recent intel on us, and accurate, too, I'd guess." He looked around the room, realizing who was missing. "Any word from Matthew?"

"Took an hour, but I finally got him on the phone," Ariel said. "He's ok, nobody bothered him. He was at the Cathedral, so I guess they didn't want to risk hitting him there. He's taking extra precautions and he's alerted the Order guard."

"So now the safest place for us to be, is with the institution we're trying to escape. Lovely," James said.

"Coleen, there's a good chance the SOJ know about you, about you helping us," Dylan said. "You and Ben should get out of town for a while. Maybe out of country. Take a vacation."

Coleen folded her arms. "Oh, they know. The Cathedral too." Her chin dropped to her chest. "Ben called them. The Order. Told them himself. After he saw…me. The real me. The Sons also paid me a visit tonight."

"Oh, Coleen," Ariel said. "I…that's why you called Dylan. I didn't even ask. I'm sorry, I wasn't thinking."

"It's ok. Worked out for the best," Coleen said.

Dylan sat with his head hanging, pinching the bridge of his nose, thinking. "I used to have a nice, normal, monster hunting life," he said. "How did it come to this?"

After a few moments he raised his head. "I think we might be thoroughly screwed," he said. "We can't stay on the street, the SOJ is still hunting us. If the Order hasn't connected us to Coleen yet, it will soon. An intern could do that much. And James and I messed each other up good. Not really a great start to a fight with supposed Demon forces."

"There's still me and Matthew," Ariel said.

"And me," Coleen said. "I'm with you guys. I can't go home anymore and now I've got two agencies after me."

"Maybe Matthew and I can get the talismans," Ariel said, "Especially with Coleen helping us?"

"Tempting," Dylan said, "But we're gonna need you doing your cyber warfare thing with the techs at the Order. You need to erase as much of us as you can from their system and run counter security and intel once King and I go in for the Inquisitor's binding scroll."

"And I should be getting Matthew's mother out," Coleen said. She folded her arms, thinking. "I'm going to need a map of the medical wing. And maybe an ID, some scrubs."

"I can print an ID for you," Ariel said. "I've got all the stuff for that here."

"James, the tattoos. You said the Inquisitor had an idea for neutralizing them?" Dylan said.

"Yes, something like that," James said.

"Something he could be ready with fast?"

"I believe so. He seemed…eager to help."

Dylan nodded, staring into the middle distance. Finally he said, "I really didn't want to rush this. But I think we've drawn all the cards we're gonna get." He looked at his friends. "We'll go for the scroll tomorrow night."

The Inquisitor was reading a crumbling anatomy book when his cell phone buzzed One of his phones anyway, he had a dozen of them in a secure lockbox hidden in his tools. Only Cleric Carter knew the number to this one, and he would be texting only for one reason. The Inquisitor fished it out of his pocket and unlocked the screen.

'*Tomorrow night.*'

'*So soon? Patience, Cleric Carter, there is time yet*' he replied.

'*Not anymore, there's not. Can you be ready or no?*'

The Inquisitor frowned at the phone, curious about the rush. '*I can,*' he typed, and pressed the send icon. He waited several minutes for a response, but there was none.

Part Three

Clockwork Heart Publishing

Chapter 24

Matthew King sat in his apartment in the Red Cathedral. He twirled a knife absently between his fingers. The attacks on his teammates had him seriously disturbed. He could understand the Sons of James coming after Carter. They had somehow found out about his infection, his transformation into a monster. Matthew would have hunted down the SOJ bastards responsible if they had managed to kill Carter. But that account was squared.

He couldn't wrap his mind around the angle with Ikeda. She was just an Order tech nerd. Attacking her was a bare declaration of war with the Order. The SOJ were fanatical, but not stupid.

Unless.

Matthew spun the knife back and forth, letting it flow with the speed of his thoughts. Ikeda had mentioned that Vampire, Blood, was there. She'd said James, but as far as Matthew was concerned, that name was voided when the man became a monster. A Nether. Filth that should have been left in its cage at the Cathedral. What if he'd cut a deal, made an exchange for help from the SOJ in escaping the Order? Everything had gone downhill since the operation at the Coven meeting. Blood had been a key informant on that. Or saboteur.

Blood had attacked Carter. Nearly killed him. Sure, he appeared to have saved Ikeda, but what if that had just been a plan gone wrong? Or maybe he'd wanted the kill for himself, couldn't stand to see a human agent taking it from him. In the heat of the moment, Ikeda might not have realized what was happening. Now the Vampire was trying to salvage his alliances. Matthew was going to have to factor the Vampire's capture into his plans to arrest Carter. Maybe more than capture.

Carter. He had finally gone way too far, played too free with the rules. Sometimes even friends have to face consequences, if they're determined to try the bounds of their loyalties, and Carter had done that.

The knife reversed in Matthew's hand, began a different series of move-ments.

The Inquisitor could shed a lot of light on all of this. If he could be found. Matthew had ventured down into that rat's tunnels, hoping to hammer some answers out of him.

The lab was empty. Several items seemed to be missing. The Inquisitor had run. He had to still be somewhere within the Cathedral, by his own admission he was bound to it. That didn't really help much. There were literally hun-dreds of years of corridors and tunnels underneath the Cathedral, kilometer upon kilometer of hiding space. No one knew them all, no map covered more than a fraction of them. Many of those maps contradicted each other. No, Matthew would not be finding the Inquisitor.

He didn't have to, he decided. By running, the Inquisitor had confirmed a very important detail. The timeline. The Order's personal Inquisitor couldn't just run away and hope to be forgotten. He wouldn't run unless he expected to be freed.

Carter would be coming in soon. He had to. Nowhere in Chicago was safe for him now. The SOJ had already Demonstrated its determination. He be-lieved the Order had a vendetta against him. Misguided as that was, it would drive Carter to action, and fast. Tomorrow, maybe.

Matthew had to be prepared to take his friend into custody. Tomorrow.

He looked at the framed picture of his mother on the desk. The knife in his hands stilled. He wished he could ask her what to do. She didn't wake up much these days. She might not have long left. He thought about the injustice of it. Nether monsters, killers, abominations. They almost always got some kind of life extension along with their unholy powers. Some, like Blood, might live forever.

The knife began to twirl again.

Yet a good woman, who had raised him alone, who had worked two jobs, and who had still had time for charity work with Order programs, got put down not halfway through life. Bedridden all these years. Laid low by a Nether.

Matthew paid no attention to the pain in his hand as the knife slipped, the razor-sharp blade cutting deep. He did not hear it clatter to the floor. And as so often happened when he got hurt, he wouldn't let himself think about why the cut was gone an hour later.

Chapter 25

"I grant you no sympathies for setbacks caused by using mortals," Kinyr said. A cold wind of annoyance stirred the air in the chamber, but she paid it no mind. "I was against the taming of the Sons from the beginning, if you remember."

"They have served faithfully for a thousand years," Postan said, looking into the fire. It was his habitual response when Kinyr brought up the Sons of James. He usually let her opinions on the subject slide away like water on oiled glass. Today he was dangerously close to agreeing with her.

"They are resourceful, I understand that, old friend. And they breed like rats. You'll never run out of them. But why? Why keep vermin when the glory of the Fallen is at your fingertips?"

The flames on the hearth began to wither under the Elder Demon's gaze. His dissatisfaction with the night's events had been growing for hours. Finally, he took a deep breath, and allowed the fireplace to roar to life again. "Because you do not understand politics or civilization, Kinyr. You never bothered to understand the vermin and how they move through their lives. I do."

He stood and great wings unfurled behind him. Long, ragged, red spattered feathers constantly tore away from them, pulled by an unfelt wind, and faded out of sight into the Ether. Few of the Fallen had managed to retain their wings and he usually kept these sigils of his strength hidden, to preserve the power of their impact on his subordinates. Kinyr, it seemed, needed to be reminded.

The only sign she gave of her fealty was an ice-cold silence. Good enough.

"Change is a foreign concept to our kind, Kinyr. Even for me, it is difficult to grasp. When we lost our Grace, was that not enough? Change vast enough to consume eons in the comprehension? I am as you in this."

He slowly circled his chambers as he spoke, touching books, instruments, weapons, almost every object he passed, with dry, papery fingertips.

"These 'rats', they change every day," he said, half to himself. "Entire lives spin about hourly on circumstance and whim. It is...maddening."

He stopped walking and stood before Kinyr. "Yet strong enough are the currents of their combined lives that even our ships must give way, if only just. We ride such a current now. The masses do not flock to the protection of the Cathedrals as they once did. The teachings of the Order do not guide lives to compliance. Against all evidence of senses and dreams, the people lose their belief in magic. They will not long serve our purposes through the Order as once they did."

"Then you admit that the endeavor was doomed to begin with," she said. There was a hint of defiance in her countenance, but then, few Fallen had ever fully embraced the civilizing influence of the Order as the Five Elders had. Inwardly Postan laughed. So much more like mankind than they could ever believe, the lower Fallen.

"I admit no such thing," Postan said calmly. "For the humans we have been a guiding light through millions of their small eternities, and in exchange, they have given us the world, fought and killed to hand it to us, begged us to receive their offering. They have brought us magics, powers, servants of chaos, and left us to do with them as we will. Is not this better than the struggle of open conflict? Than the deaths of Brothers and Sisters, already so unjustly denied the cosmos in the Falling?"

Kinyr was looking deep within. At least she was trying to understand. Human lifetimes were as hard for Fallen to comprehend as eternity was for a mortal. Human motivation often seemed nothing more than madness to her. Yet Postan spoke a truth. Humans had rarely slain an Order allied Fallen. There had been some sense in the creation of the Order Pure.

"And now you say that all of this is to change yet again?" she asked. "That we are to abandon the Order?"

"Oh, no, not abandon," Postan said. "Not for many years yet, at least. But while it still has some strength left to it, we must spend its influence wisely. Invest it in another body."

Kinyr pinched the bridge of her nose. "Please speak plainly, Postan, you know I despise mortal economics," she said. "Even for them, it is a waste of imagination."

"As you say. We must empower the Sons, in a political and military sense. We must legitimize them, bring them to light and claim them as allied with the Order. A partnership. Peace struck from the stone after so many generations."

Kinyr sat deep in thought, sipping from a stone goblet. "I can see the possibilities," she said at length. "Provided your systems of control are more firmly built than those employed with certain of your Hunters."

"Isn't he a fascinating thorn in the side?" Postan said, a half-smile on his face. "After the Inquisitor recovers from his punishments, I'm going to have him dissect Cleric Carter. I want to know why he advanced so quickly. There may yet be some advantage to the process, if it can be duplicated." Postan frowned. "Provided we can find the Inquisitor bastard," he said, to no one in particular.

Kinyr had never thrown her hands up in disgust before. It was much too human a gesture. Yet they twitched now, almost rising. "You simply cannot leave the fire to burn, can you?" she said. "Always more, always other ventures, other schemes. One would almost think you a mortal." She tossed the remaining liquid from her cup into the fireplace, where it burned a deep green. "Careful you do not drag us all into the flames with you."

Postan sat, content to let Kinyr's wrath burn away in the flames. After several minutes he heard her mutter, "He is a fascinating subject." He arched an eyebrow as he looked at her.

Kinyr noticed the gesture and shifted in her chair. "His transformation," she said. "Never seen anything quite like it. How do you suppose he's taking it?"

Postan laughed once, without mirth. "With arrogance and without caution, if I know Cleric Carter."

Kinyr thought about that. She didn't agree, but kept her assessment to herself. *You don't know him as well as you think, then. That might be your undoing, oh Arrogance incarnate.* "As you say, High Cleric."

Interlude - Kinyr

One year ago, The Red Cathedral

Chronicler Miranda could feel it in her bones. Or perhaps her stomach. There was a dread stench to the air, an oppressiveness. Trouble was coming. It broke her train of thought, and she had to trace her pencil back to the beginning of the paragraph she was working on to remember what she had been cataloging. No good. She couldn't get it back. She closed the book, laid the pencil carefully alongside it, and watched the door.

Dylan Carter had the unmitigated gall to smile and wave when he walked in. Miranda only folded her arms and waited, almost patiently, as he strolled around the Order Museum anteroom, hands in pockets, like an innocent little boy. She arched an eyebrow as he feigned particular interest in an eighteenth-century cane sword in a glass display.

"This new?" he said, looking at Miranda while pointing at the case.

"No more so than last time you asked," she said, taking off her black rimmed glasses and placing them on her ledger. "Cleric Carter, where is it?"

Dylan meandered toward the Chronicler's desk, stopping once to look at a display of ancient quills. "Sorry, what now? Where's what?"

Miranda pinched the bridge of her nose, then almost ran a hand through her dark hair, before remembering it was tied in a tight bun today. "Why do you always think I have time for you? Can't you just get to the point?"

"As a matter of fact, that is the point," Dylan said, putting on his most charming smile. "Do you have time for me today? Tonight, that is? What time do you get off?"

Miranda was an attractive woman in her mid-thirties, tall, with her mother's dark brown skin and her father's hazel eyes. She knew Dylan was attracted to her, and she couldn't deny that he had a certain primitive handsomeness. They often flirted in passing. Except when he came in like he did today. Acting innocent. Dylan Carter was never innocent, and never less so than when he pretended to be.

"You mean when do I clock out so you can sneak whatever it is back into its case?" she said, looking around. "Must be something small, none of the larger artifacts is missing."

Dylan actually managed to look minimally ashamed. "Honestly, I was going to bring it back sooner, I just forgot about it after I put it in a pocket."

"You weren't supposed to have had 'it' at all, whatever 'it' is," she said. She planted a stern fingertip on the desk. "Right here. Now."

Dylan rummaged in an inner coat pocket, frowned, and switched pockets. His face brightened as he produced a small gold pocket watch, placing it carefully at the tip of Miranda's black polished nail.

Her eyes widened. She turned to look at a case against the wall and gave a small gasp. "You stole Beethoven's pocket watch? What on earth for? It's barely magical!"

"Ok, first," he said, resting his elbows on the desk and leaning in conspiratorially, "I didn't steal it, it's right there. Or I didn't steal it for long, at least. And B, it's only not very magical by itself, but if I told you what things you have to combine it with to amp up the magic, you'd say you wish I hadn't told you. So, you're welcome, I'm not telling you."

"But what for, Dylan?" Miranda said, rushing the watch back to its case.

"I used to it to drive a werewolf slightly crazy. He couldn't figure out where the music was coming from. Really got him to drop his guard."

She came back and sat heavily on her tall stool, staring daggers at the smiling Hunter. "Someday you're going to die carrying something from this Museum on your person and it's going to be a true tragedy," she said.

"Aw, I didn't know you were so concerned, Miranda. We really do need to arrange a dinner soon," he said, turning and strolling out the door.

Miranda was just beginning to blush when the display of enchanted quills caught her eye. The red one, the one that belonged to Alexander Dumas, was gone. She thought about running after Dylan, about having security stop him, about reporting him to the senior Clergy. Then she opened her ledger and resumed cataloging.

If Dylan Carter had some use for the artifact, it was against the enemies of the Order. She'd give him a week to return it.

Checking her watch, she realized Dylan had almost made her late for a meeting with Postan. She turned and unlocked a door that was marked "Employees Only." The all too human subterfuge was hardly necessary. The door was warded so heavily against curious eyes that even Hunters didn't take note of it.

The room beyond was unnaturally dark. Dark enough to smell and taste it. As she stepped through, the flesh that was Miranda fell away like sand, and the glowing face of Kinyr shone forth.

Chapter 26

"What's the play, boss?" asked SOJ operative Saint Lindon.

Matthew didn't feel like the boss. Of the eight people gathered in the war room, only half were Order operatives. Clerics Anne Simmons and Maxwell Smith he had worked with before. Junior Cleric Kevin Hawkins was a talented young Hunter, positioned to get a full team by the end of the year.

The other four people were the problem. Matthew ground his teeth as he regarded them. All SOJ. All Saints. All forced into his arrest team by Postan's personal aide. He had said, "The Order of the Sons of James have offered their services in apprehending the criminal, Cleric Dylan Carter. His attacks on both the SOJ and the Order Pure have made him a clear threat to the well-being of the city of Chicago and a common enemy. Integrate them fully into the teams you assign to arrest Cleric Carter."

Matthew absolutely did not like it. This was an Order affair. The brawl under the mansion, as far as he was concerned, had been justified. The attacks on Dylan by the SOJ in the past week were now being treated like approved actions by the Order. All in all, it did not feel like he had any real say in how things went from here on out. But he followed orders.

"Our primary concern will be the two entryways leading down from the hallways on the east and west sides of the Cathedral basilica. Cleric Carter is most likely to use these to access the level that the High Cleric's chambers are located in."

"He's gonna use the front door?" said Saint Hernandez. "Why, is he stupid?"

"He is not, and he'll only give you one chance to forget that," said Matthew. "But he doesn't like games. He doesn't have patience for them. He knows we'll have equal security on all other passageways into the Cathedral. Those passageways are longer, more narrow, and make his particular style of fighting more difficult. So he'll take the front door."

"What are these other passages?" said Saint Lindon. Of the four SOJ, Matthew decided he was the most capable. He was actually taking things seriously.

"Purpose built tunnels on the intercardinal points of the compass," said Matthew.

"What're those?" said Saint Bills.

Lindon rolled his eyes and looked at him. "Points between north, south, east, and west. You shake my confidence, Bills." He turned back to Matthew. "Continue, Cleric."

"These tunnels were put in place in the seventeenth century, as a way to launch clandestine missions, and bring prisoners into the Cathedral, without public knowledge. Security mostly consists of several sets of heavy iron bar doorways. The keys are kept in a vault in the Armorer's office. D7 has already reviewed security logs and declared him uncompromised, so the keys aren't a concern, and nothing supernatural is tearing those doors off their hinges. If one of Cleric Carter's team were ambitious enough to bring a cutting torch, however, the tunnels could become a problem."

Over the next hour, callsigns and communication protocols were established, and a chain of command. Matthew was lead, but decided to put Lindon in place as his second, as a show of good faith to the SOJ. Everyone was supplied with a detailed digital map of the pertinent areas of the Cathedral that could be displayed on a smartphone.

"What if one of'em heads into a spot not on this map?" Hernandez asked.

"Then you go get a candy bar while we take care of it," Matthew said. "We need to be clear. The Cathedral is still the sole responsibility of the Order. High Cleric Postan appreciates your offer of assistance, but you do not have free roam of the Cathedral. Any curious wandering will be treated as a high-level threat. Lethal force is not out of the question. And while we're on that," he said, picking a case up from the floor and setting it on the table, "only nonlethal force is authorized against Cleric Carter and his compatriots, unless specifically ordered by me in the moment. You'll each be equipped with a weapon designed by Order Armorer Tomlinson, called a Nether Stunner." He pulled what looked like a heavy pump action shotgun from the case and put it on the table between everyone.

Bills whistled. "Bet that can put a hole straight through an ox."

"The best this could do is piss one off really bad," said Matthew. "But against Nether, it's like getting hit in the head with a baseball bat, minus the brain damage. It fires an electrified cartridge of primarily colloidal silver, with small amounts of other elements mixed in. It's very short range, about three feet, and you shouldn't fire more than two cartridges in a short span to avoid excessive aerosol saturation. After that, switch the weapon to energy only mode, and trigger pulls will energize remaining particulate around the target, stunning them and neutralizing their supernatural abilities."

"Does he always talk like this?" Bills said. "Can someone put it into plain English?"

"He said boom stick go zap, don't lick the tip," Cleric Simmons said, and popped her bubblegum. "Do you need me to break out the crayons, or...?"

"Do we get to familiarize ourselves with these weapons, Cleric King?" Lindon said.

"Tomlinson has agreed to allow limited use of his range and facilities. You'll all be granted temporary pass cards," Matthew said. Lindon nodded, satisfied.

After the meeting was over, the SOJ operatives left, following Cleric Smith to the Armorer's cage to get outfitted. Cleric Hawkins went as well, intending to get a refresher on how the stunner worked.

Matthew sat down heavily, and Cleric Simmons put a hand on his shoulder. "You're doing fine," she said.

"I don't wanna be doing this at all," he said. "Being good at something doesn't mean I enjoy it. Pray the SOJ guys disrespect Tomlinson. We'll have our house back in under an hour and most of that will be cleaning up the mess."

Chapter 27

"**W**ait."

Dylan reached down slowly and placed a piece of pizza crust on the ground four inches in front of a massive rat. The rodent and the Vampire stared at each other for long seconds.

"Ta—"

The rat lunged and ran off with the crust. *Jumped the gun again. Still*, Dylan mused, *progress.*

"You gonna start a rat circus, Mister C?" said a young man entering the alley. He had been dribbling a basketball on the sidewalk as he approached but cradled it protectively as he entered the filth of the alley.

"Shaun, finally. If you took any longer, I'd have had him walking on his hind legs for pepperoni."

Shaun Henry was one of Dylan's few friends in the neighborhood. Nineteen and bound for better things than Dylan could have aspired to, they had bonded over a shared love of the corner pizza store, Johnnie's. The young man shrugged and smiled, tossing the basketball hand to hand. "Sorry, man, I ran into Lisa."

"Oh yeah? Get her number this time?"

"You know I'm workin' on it, man. Gotta play it slow."

Dylan smiled and held out his pizza box to Shaun. "What happened at my place?"

Shaun grabbed the largest piece left and took a bite. "Nothing," he mumbled through a mouthful. "Nobody there. Nobody answered, anyway."

Dylan should have felt relieved, but he didn't. He had staked out his apartment for hours, from before dawn to midmorning. He'd been sure the SOJ would have people there waiting for him, if not the Order. He saw nothing.

Not on his cameras, which he accessed with his smartphone, but those could have been hacked. Not in the faces on the street. Just regulars.

Eventually he'd decided to track Shaun down and ask him to go knock on the door. If anyone answered, he was supposed to say he was looking for Terrance, or Linda, dealer's choice.

"You in pretty deep, mister C?" said Shaun, concern furrowing his young brow. "Worse than usual, I mean? Do you need help?"

Dylan looked up, met Shaun's eyes. He was nervous, but serious. He'd help if Dylan asked.

"I appreciate it, Shaun. It's ok, I'm fine. Just got nervous about something." He held out the pizza. "Here, take the rest of this. Thanks for checking on my place."

Shaun took the box, doubt on his features. "Alright, C. If you need me, I can get my brother, he'll help too."

"Alright, I'll remember. For now, I just need you to get Lisa's number. That's your assignment, and you're already late. Turn it in this weekend."

Shaun smiled, lopsided, and raised the pizza box in salute as he turned and walked away.

Dylan had his revolver in hand as he walked down the hall to his door. Despite all his watching, now that he was here, he could tell something was wrong. He had smelled blood from the moment he stepped inside the building. It made his skin burn and his heart race. Hungry. His reaction worried him almost as much as what he might find behind his front door.

He slid his key in the deadbolt and turned. It was already unlocked. Assuming the other, secret locks were opened too, he grabbed the handle and went in, smooth and fast, gun raised.

The woman in his chair was wearing an expensive business suit and minimalist jewelry. Her long black hair fell over one shoulder. Her smile was predatory and fearless. Jelena.

People had to stop sitting in his favorite chair when he was gone.

"I killed a guy for sitting there last week," Dylan said.

"I killed a man while sitting here this past night," she said, and licked an imaginary drop of blood from here lips.

"Fair enough," Dylan said. He looked at the pistol, and back to the Elder. "This isn't gonna do me any good, is it?"

"You don't need it anyway, *moja ljubav*. I wouldn't hurt you."

Dylan slid the pistol into its holster. There was a man standing in a far corner, just inside Dylan's peripheral vision. Dylan saw him wince at what Jelena said. "Who's this guy?"

"He is good with these things," Jelena said, waiving vaguely in the direction of Dylan's security cameras. "I told him to make them blind. Did he do a good job? Did you see me?"

Dylan looked at the tall, thin black man. Too thin, even for a Vampire. Vuk, the Coven alchemist. His left arm had no hand, and he cradled it instinctively against his body.

"He did good."

"Excellent. Maybe I'll let him have his other hand back." She smiled warmly at Vuk. "Maybe not. We'll see how I feel later." She looked Dylan up and down, slowly. "How are you feeling, darling? Your heart, it doesn't sound so good."

"Been better. And I'm not your darling, or your lee-yoo-bov, or whatever you called me. So, respectfully, you need to get the fuck out. I have stuff I need to get done, and this is eating up time."

"Respectfully..." Jelena said, growling the word out slowly. "No, but you will learn respect, eventually. Many will. I've got a lot to get done too, *ljubav*, but I took time out of my busy schedule for you." She picked up a bloody pack of cigarettes from the table and put one between her lips. She pulled deeply on it, and the unlit tip began to glow orange. "I love these," she said, smoke puffing out with each word. "Makes humans' blood taste terrible, but for Vampires, is fine. Want one?"

"I quit. What do you want with me?" He thought back to the night in the tunnels under the Coven mansion, how Jelena had drug burning claws across his chest. "You do something to me that night. Besides turn me?"

Jelena laughed, a sharp, short bark. "I didn't turn you, dear one, you were already there, just on the edge. I only helped you along. You didn't think you were hot shit all by yourself, did you? Come, Dylan, you've seen young Vampires in the streets. They can barely speak. Oh, you're special, but you'd have been little better than them when the hunger clawed up your throat. I saved you decades of pain and suffering, centuries even. And I did a little more, yes. You bear my sigil now, soul and body. No other Elder will move against you. And you cannot move against me. But you don't want to, do you, *ljubav*?" she said, smiling, soulless.

"Bullshit," said Dylan. He saw her face light up. The denial had sounded hollow even to his own ears. He was trying hard to hate her. Hard to work up the desire to hunt her. He was struggling too much with other desires he felt building toward her. The longer he was in her presence, the more he wanted her. He felt owned by her, and he was beginning to like the feeling. Vuk, standing in the corner, in the darkness, was a thorn in his side. Sick jealousy was building in Dylan at the other man's relationship with Jelena, monstrous as she was.

"You are in trouble, yes, Dylan Carter?" Jelena said.

"What?" he said, shaking his head. He realized he was trembling and fought to regain control of himself. "What kind of trouble do you think I'm in?"

"Those Fallen Angel monsters at the Order have finally betrayed you," she said. "It's what they do. It's what they did to me, to my kind, to everything that walks this earth touched by their magic. You, and all of your friends. The Ouruqan, the Vampire, and the Fae."

"Do you know you're a very confusing lady?" Dylan said. He sat down on the couch across from her. "There's no such thing as Fae. That one's fake. So now you're trying to trick me."

"Oh, no, she's the most real of all of you," Jelena said, still smiling, but more serious than she had been yet. "The only magic natural to this world. Even the Ouruqan started somewhere else, though so long ago even I don't know where. But the girl," she said, leaning back, "she is so very special. You're very lucky to have one of those."

"Lies mean we're done," Dylan said. "It's a rule of mine. Leave. Now."

"The Elder never lies," Vuk said, stepping forward.

"Oh, fuck off, I do so," Jelena said, waving a hand at him. "These Coven Vampires, they think we're gods or something. They make us sound no fun at all. But I'm not lying, Dylan," she said, the smile gone. "Not about this. If I'd had a Fae at my side long ago, like you have now...I want you to take care of her, so she can take care of you. You are very important to me.

"Why?" Dylan said.

"Your bloodline. It's very old. Very strong. You will be my consort one day," she said, without a hint of modesty.

"Do I get a say in that?" he said.

"You'll say yes. You know you already want to. But not yet, *ljubav*. You have a lot of growing up to do first. For a start, your magic is terrible."

"Hey, I only buy from the most reputable scumbags," Dylan said.

"No, not the trinkets. Your Vampire heritage. You don't even use it, well, not on purpose, it seems. I'd have given you a few decades to grow, but you're going to need it a lot sooner than that."

"I don't need your help," Dylan said. "I'm not even sure I'd be in this mess if it wasn't for you, at least not this deep."

"Careful, dear one," said Jelena. "I'm about to save your life. Again. Show a little gratitude." She rose and walked toward him. He rose on instinct to meet her, though he still couldn't bear the idea of drawing his gun again.

She was every bit as tall as Dylan. She closed the distance until their bodies were touching. She reached up to gently place her hands on either side of his face, her smile wicked. "First I have to let you die a few times, though," she said, and kissed him, full and deep.

Chapter 28

D ylan's eyes opened to a forest, ancient and dark. Night. Strange fires danced through the branches in the distance, and he could hear shouting. Chanting.

"My home, long ago," Jelena said behind him. He turned to look at her and was surprised to see tears in the corners of her eyes. "The singing over there. We were performing a feast ritual." She waved the thought away and looked at him. "But that isn't important right now. I took you into this dream so you could feel your magic."

"Dream? As in, we're both asleep?"

"No, we're just in a dream. Dreams are other places, other worlds. Humans go there most easily when asleep, but you are not human, *ljubav*, so I took you here with me. Magic works more easily in dreams, works as it is supposed to."

"You brought me here to teach me spells? I tried learning magic when the Order recruited me, it didn't go so great."

"Do not insult me with talk of Order magic," she snapped. "Spells and incantations and alchemy, all are reins and bits in the mouth of a horse that should be let free. They are for the weak and the afraid, those without true strength. Know this, Dylan Carter, when you face the Demon Postan, he will not use spells. He will move with magic unharnessed, shaped by his will and his thoughts. If you do not do the same, you will die, and if you die that way, I am better off without you."

"Well, I mean, I certainly wouldn't want to inconvenience you with my death," Dylan said. "Ok, fine. I'm in wizard school. Show me how to do magic."

Jelena laughed. "Oh, you're not ready to learn what I have to teach. You won't be for centuries."

"Ok, then how—"

"Vuk is going to kill you," she said, turning to walk away. "When you can defeat him and his spells and his alchemy with real magic, I'll let you go."

"Wait, no, hold on. This sounds like a really bad—"

A dark, iron-hard hand reached around from behind Dylan and ripped his throat out.

Dylan woke lying on his back, staring up into a sky full of branches and moonlight.

"She won't let me at your heart," said a voice to his right. Dylan turned his head slowly to see Vuk standing next to him. Here, in the dream-memory, he looked like a complete version of himself. Both hands, his body strengthened and restored, and full of confidence. "You'd be gone forever if she had allowed that. Still. I'm going to tear you apart, over and over. And when she sees how weak you really are, she'll do away with you herself, and take me as consort."

A heavy boot connected with Dylan's skull, and the world went black again.

"You think your life got bad when you received the blessing of the Elder?" Vuk said, pinning Dylan to a tree with a long, sharpened branch. "My family, my Coven, fell apart. Died. Almost all of them. I don't know where the ones who escaped are. But then she took me in, spared me, gave me a new life. Now I protect her."

Blackness.

Dylan had a long-standing, healthy aversion to death. As that sensation became numb in him, his annoyance with Vuk grew. The man whined constantly. Every time Dylan woke up, Vuk was praising the glory of the Elder, damning Dylan for being her favorite, calling Dylan weak and pitiful. Even called him human once. Dylan was surprised to find that insulting.

He couldn't deny that Vuk was incredibly fast and strong. Dylan felt a childish sense of pride the first time he managed to land a blow on the other Vampire. Until he realized he'd interrupted what for Vuk had been a game, entertainment, catharsis. Now Vuk was angry.

Vuk's skill with alchemy vastly surpassed his physical strength. His creativity may have been shackled to spellwork but he had not been idle in devising interesting methods of torture and execution over the centuries. At any given resurrection Dylan might find himself on fire, frozen to the ground facedown, or crucified inside a tree, arms and legs stretched into the wood of the living branches. Sometimes his eyes ran from their sockets in streams of liquid mercury. Once, his teeth exploded, tearing his lower jaw and half his throat away.

There was no counting how many times Vuk destroyed him. There were no days to mark time by, only one long, endless, ancient night. The chanting Vampires beyond the trees became a pounding chorus in Dylan's head. The moonlight and the firelight traded places more than once, burning stars above and pale ghost-fog under the branches.

Somewhere in his increasingly addled thoughts, Dylan realized it wouldn't have done him any good if he had known any spells or alchemy. He couldn't think clearly enough to remember how he even got into that forest anymore, or why Vuk was hunting him. More and more he moved through the trees like an animal, hiding in branches and holes.

Then something came awake inside him. Something new. This new self saw the world differently. Wanted to be the Hunter, not the hunted. Was always hungry. Loved the dark and the small lights. And it seemed to draw strength from the bright moon above.

He was staring up at that wonderful silver orb the last time Vuk found him, next to a massive, ancient oak. Vuk had spent the time between Dylan's resurrections carving alchemical patterns into small stones he could carry in his pockets. He had three in his hand now, arranged in order. He was preparing to melt the calcium in Dylan's bones.

Dylan hadn't heard the Vampire make a sound, had not yet turned around to see him smiling in the dark of the forest. Still, he knew Vuk was there. He could feel him, the pressure his existence exerted on reality, just as he could feel the shape of every tree and stone and hill. He just wasn't paying attention to Vuk. He was busy, watching storms of magical energy dance and fight and make love around the moon.

Vuk spoke into his fist, and the stones warmed, releasing energies bound within, channeling magic carried on the Vampire's breath. An invisible wave, crackling in the Ethereal plane and fractal in its geometry, sped across the distance between the two men.

Dylan felt that, too. His instinctual, Vampire self was curious. He watched, with the suite of senses awake within, as roiling destruction came on. He pitied it. It writhed and screamed with the same voice as the magics in the sky. It wasn't whole. Cut and bound askew. Vuk thought it was a spell of destruction. For eons it had been so much more. It was a thought torn from the mind of magic, a splinter of a self-aware dream.

Dylan turned and held out a hand. He let the wave of malice flow through his fingers like liquid silk, let it have what it needed to break its bonds. What it did after, where it went, that was its own business.

He thrust his grasping hand forward and—

Grabbed the back of Vuk's neck. He had decided not to be where he was before. Now he was here, behind his prey. Ready to end him.

To Vuk's eye, Dylan had disappeared, moved with an impossible speed. Vuk was blessed with his own instincts, but more importantly, centuries of experience. Surprised as he was, his body reacted to the feeling of claws on the sides of his neck. He jerked away, colliding into a nearby tree.

He stood and straightened his robes, regaining a measure of his composure. There had been a grand finale planned, something to make Dylan regret his immortality, his ability to regenerate. Something that would put pain into his flesh for all eternity. It would do well enough now.

Vuk produced a delicate statue made of forest materials from a pocket and held it up for Dylan to examine. It was a perfect facsimile of Dylan. "You and I are alike in ways I will not readily admit outside of this dream, Order dog," Vuk said. "I, too, will play with forbidden magics from time to time. Only I know what I'm doing with them."

Vuk brought the simulacrum up to his forehead and began to whisper in a language that made his mouth hurt.

Dylan felt the effects immediately. His skin began to writhe like a snake wrapped around him, a separate creature full of malice and hunger. Fire erupted in his veins, and a deep groan passed his teeth.

"Hello, baby brother."

Dylan was staring down at his open, empty hands. The same long fingers and wide palms. His hands had always been a little too big. Now, though, they looked thin and awkward. Soft. Younger.

He looked around and recognized his sister's room from almost thirty years ago. For so long now he could only remember the damage, the broken glass and splintered wood, and men in black surrounding something that almost looked like Linda. This room was clean, whole. He was sitting on the floor. So was she. His sister. Whole. Just like she'd been before that last night.

"They'll be here in a few minutes," she said. "Memory dream. Inside this other dream thing. I don't really know how it all works."

"Comes from the moon," he said, looking at the night out the window. His sister looked at him quizzically. "Magic," he said. Then, "Never mind. Why am I dreaming this? This isn't a good time to be talking to myself. Not that I'm not happy to see you, but I'm kinda busy. I think I'm getting my ass kicked."

"Yeah, you are," she said, frowning, "But not by flea market Dracula out there. I've been watching. Everything's kind of just happening to you. That's not you. Not the you I know, anyway."

"What? I'm a rebel without a cause, sis. A thorn in the side of the establishment."

"No, you're a pain in their ass, it isn't the same thing. The Order says go, you go kill. Jelena says put your gun down, you heel. That Inquisitor creep got in your house, and left without a scrape."

"Scraped his brains off the wall," Dylan said.

"You've been like this since this night," Linda said, looking around. "My brother used to save kids from bullies on the playground. You got straight A's even when your teachers thought you were a slacker. We were talking about checking out colleges in a year. But you didn't need me for all that, Dylan. I love you, but what happened?"

Dylan flinched from the question, but he thought about it. "I guess...I wasn't such hot stuff after all," he said. "Maybe I just got lucky for a long time. But when those men, the SOJ, broke in and just...took you. There wasn't a thing I could do about it, not a freakin' thing. I guess that's it, Linda. It's hard to stand up anymore. So I just make myself a pain in the ass. That's pretty easy to do."

"Yeah," she said. "I get it. I might have done the same thing if these guys had come for you." The next moment the lights went out. Not just Linda's room, but the street lights outside too. The whole block. To Dylan's immense discomfort, Linda smiled, showing fangs in the dark. "And I can't tell you to stop it, because, you know, everyone's telling you what to do. Maybe you could do me a favor, though?"

Dylan was looking around wildly, caught in the emotions of the memory. They were coming for his sister again. The night that ruined his life, all over again. "What?" he said. "What favor?"

"Stop holding back," Linda said, rising, facing the door. "For your own sake. Last thing. You aren't talking to yourself. Come find me."

The bedroom door exploded inward, splintered wood flying through the air.

Dylan's .357 revolver was in his hand, cutting an upward arc toward his enemy's face. All the power and pain Vuk had filled him with, all the loss the SOJ inflicted on him when they took Linda, all his resentment at the control imposed by the Order and now Jelena, ran down his arm like lit gunpowder. The hammer fell with thunder-bolt energy. A lance of fire shot from the barrel, igniting the air as it closed the distance between Dylan and Vuk at the speed of thought. The simulacrum, pressed to Vuk's forehead, exploded as the shot connected.

Dylan opened his eyes to Jelena, drawing back from their kiss. She smiled, bloody and predatory. Her face became a mask of shock as Dylan's hand shot up between them, closing around her throat in an embrace that would have torn the head from a lesser creature. He lifted her to his full reach off the floor and brought her back down in a splintering crash onto the table behind him. He slammed his knee into her chest as he knelt on top of her, drawing his knife in an underhand grip. He saw something in Jelena's eyes that no one had seen in hundreds of years. Fear.

Dylan's vision went dark, and he heard himself crash to the floor. He stayed conscious, if barely. The Elder struggled out of his grip underneath him. He forced himself to one knee and shook his head to clear it. His sight came back in conflicting combinations of ultraviolet, infrared, and normal spectrum as he fought down a wave of nausea.

He raised the knife between himself and the Elder, who had fled to the other side of the room. Jelena's mouth hung open. "Impressive, *ljubav*," she said. "Disrespectful, but well done. You shouldn't exert so without feeding. I sustained your strength in the dream, but in this world, I'm afraid you'll find yourself quite tired."

"Screw you, and get out," Dylan said, fighting to keep his head up.

Jelena took a step toward him, but stopped as the blade began to glow, Dylan's eyes going black. "No more foreplay today, Jelena. I'm busy. Leave."

Jelena grabbed Vuk by the collar where he lay on the floor. Dylan didn't know if Vuk was unconscious or dead, and he didn't care. The Elder drug him to the door, then smiled at Dylan once more. "Very impressive, *ljubav*. We'll be together again soon."

Chapter 29

The printing shop on St Michael's Court had an attic. It was accessible only by a ladder, hidden behind a false wall, in the back of a closet, in the back of the building, in the upstairs residential area. John Clemins had decided long ago that no one needed access to his attic.

He was amazed to find the building completely undamaged. It had been a decidedly long time since he'd had access to the premises to maintain and secure them. Nearly a hundred years, in fact. Even the spare key in the loose brick underneath the rear rain gutter was still there. He sighed with relief at finding it. The original key was who knew where now.

Clemins now lay curled in the darkness of the attic just absorbing the quiet and the cold. He laughed again at the name. It had been a nod to one of his favorite writers at the time he bought the building, a comedic author of Mississippi River adventures and paradoxical fairy tales. James W. Clarke had not used the name in forever. Perhaps long enough that he could recycle it, when this was all over.

He groaned and rolled from his back onto his side, heedless of the carpet of dust he was lying in. He'd never had back pain in life, hadn't lived long enough as a mortal for it to set in before his progenitor had taken him. He wondered if this was what it was like. A massive bruise had formed around the puncture wound from Dylan's blessed spike. James had known what the spike was for, but not how thoroughly it would do its work.

He'd limped away from Ariel's residence just before dawn, leaving himself bare minutes to get inside his old shop and climb to the windowless attic before the sun bathed the world in fiery pain. He'd spent the ensuing hours wondering how he was going to heal in time to be of any help to Dylan, when he couldn't even feed.

He dwelt obsessively on the thought, without solution. To let the fruitless query slip his hold would allow the images of a terrified Ariel to fix in his mind's eye again. He hated this part. The revealing of his true self. The fear in the eyes of his friends. The loss of someone who had, against his better judgement, become special to him. He'd sworn he wouldn't allow it again. *The vows of fools are comedy for the gods*, he thought.

Ariel stared blankly at her screens, doing nothing. Not coding, not researching. Usually, she could put her mind to half a dozen lines of thought at once and still do better work than all her peers. She couldn't summon the energy now. Her entire world had fallen apart, then walked out the door, one person at a time.

"I hope you don't mind. I found this in the kitchen cabinet," Coleen Jackson said, placing a steaming cup of tea on the desk by Ariel's keyboard.

"I honestly have no idea how old that stuff is," Ariel said, then took an experimental sip. "Nah, we're good, it's still drinkable."

Jackson pulled a chair close and sat. Even dressed in worn jeans and a rock band T-shirt, she still would have looked like the most capable, mature person in any room. Ariel envied that. Right now, she didn't even feel her twenty-three years.

"Did you sleep at all?" Jackson said.

"I don't know. Sort of, I guess. In bits. Five to seven felt shorter than two to four."

"I think you ought to lay down a while."

"Doctor's orders?" Ariel said, smiling at Jackson.

"Amazing auntie's orders. I hereby adopt you as one of my nieces. But I do have something in my kit bag that could help you rest," Jackson said.

"Maybe in a little while," Ariel said. She reached out to her keyboard and toyed idly with a system setting, before reverting it back to its original state. "I kinda wanna ask something," she said, "but I don't wanna sound rude or insensitive or anything."

"It's fine, honey," Jackson said, "ask away."

"Did you always know that you were…you know, different?"

"Different than what?" Jackson said gently, trying to draw out Ariel's thoughts.

"Than other humans," Ariel said.

"Well," Jackson said, "first off, I was never human. Not homo-sapiens, anyway. I was born into a long family line of Lycans. Secondly, it was never hidden from me. I've known ever since I could know things. So I've never felt different. I'm just the same as the rest of my family."

"Oh," Ariel said.

"Not what you were expecting."

"Just sounds kinda nice, I guess. To always know who you are."

"Yeah, it is," Jackson said. "I understand you never really had that?"

"No," Ariel said. She scratched at the lint on her mousepad. "Never had a family. Never knew who I was as a human. Now I find out I'm not even that. I just want to figure out how to feel. About not being human anymore, you know?"

Jackson rested her elbows on her knees, clasping her hands in front of her and looking the younger woman in the eyes. "You know, the funny thing is, I was raised to think humans were the weird ones. We looked down on them a little. We considered the Order a threat. We didn't marry outside the established family bloodlines. Most of those marriages were arranged."

"Doesn't sound cool."

"Yeah, that's how I felt. But I was going to go along with it. I for sure wasn't going to marry a human."

"But isn't Ben…"

"He is. And that wasn't smiled on. I never would have considered it, except for the influence of a friend I made."

"Dylan." Ariel said.

"Dylan," Jackson agreed. "I mean, yeah, little bit of a rocky start, but here's the thing: despite calling himself a Hunter, despite working for the Order, what came most naturally to him in the end, was to see me as a person. That's what he sees in me. And in Matthew, in James. And in you." She placed her hand on Ariel's arm. "That's why I married Ben. Dylan taught me to see the person. That's what you are, first and foremost, always. To him, and me. That's the other thing he gave me, and I think you feel the same."

"Yeah. You're right." Ariel said. There were small tears in her eyes, but she was smiling. "He's family."

"We're family," Jackson said.

Chapter 30

Matthew's parcel locker was vibrating. He'd been staring at it for five minutes. He knew what it was, or at least he was pretty sure. No need for the bomb squad. He just didn't want to deal with what was inside.

It hadn't been easy, accepting that he was going to arrest Dylan. It hadn't been easy to accept that his team was essentially dismantled. Least easy of all was avoiding thinking about the possibility that Ariel, Dylan, and even himself might not be human.

He felt human enough. He was a big guy, so he was strong, but so was everyone he'd played football with in high school. He hadn't even been the strongest. Most importantly, there was no way he was going to entertain the idea that his mother was some orc descendant.

Ariel was gifted, but not magic or anything. And her file, if you wanted to call it that, hadn't even listed what sort of Nether she was supposed to be. No, Ariel was just a gifted kid. He had to get her away from Dylan and the bloodsucker before they really messed with her sense of identity.

Now Dylan, yes, something was wrong with him. Maybe he'd been born wrong and the Order was just discovering it. More likely, it was all about that night trying to take down the Coven. Dylan was just infected. Maybe he could be cured. But if he couldn't be, Matthew wanted to be there for him. As his friend. To end his suffering. He owed Dylan that.

As to the matter of James Wilson Clarke, the Order was likely to put him down. If they didn't sanction it, Matthew would find a way for the Vampire to accidentally get caught out in the sun.

Matthew leaned his forehead against the buzzing locker. Dylan had somehow arranged to have a burner phone delivered to Matthew's Order address. On it would be some message about when everything was going down and how. Matthew couldn't deal with the burden of needing to reply, of trying to fake camaraderie with his team leader anymore. Let them just come. They had to. They couldn't live normal lives without taking the Service Talismans they'd used to bind themselves to the Order. And Matthew couldn't make his team any readier.

He turned and walked away, leaving the phone to die of a low battery in his locker.

"Dylan says we're ready to go in tonight," Ariel said, looking at her computer monitor. She had routed the burner phone Dylan had given her through her PC, like she did with every communication device she had. "What do you need from me to get Matthew's mom out safely?"

"I mean, what sort of things can you get me? Short of putting me into the Order's medical systems?" Jackson said.

Ariel smiled. "I already did that. Your ID card printed an hour ago. But, like, what medical equipment do you need to pull off a disguise? Or tactical equipment? Gear to hack a PIN pad or anything? I've never actually been in the medical wing, I don't know what it looks like over there or how you need to act."

"You just made me a doctor in the system? Well, that's pretty nearly it, I guess. I have my own scrubs and kit with me."

Texting was always going to feel a little weird for James. He was still slightly in awe of radio, let alone cell phones. He looked at the screen telling him Dylan would be infiltrating the Red Cathedral in thirteen hours. He found himself wondering what would come next. Not next in Dylan's mission. Dylan would get in and find what he was after, and nothing was going to stop him.

No, James was thinking about what wonders the future might hold. He remembered paying a man in pennies for the privilege of sending a telegraph message all the way across a fairground, to a woman whose affection enthralled him as much as modern marvels. She confirmed shortly thereafter that she had indeed received his telegraph and sent a reply, it was no trick. Now she was long buried somewhere and James was holding a burner phone with a message on it. Literally meant to be trashed after use.

That sense of wonder had kept him alive for centuries now, through all the loss. Always there was some new wonder to behold. It fueled him now, even knowing what tonight held for him. Pain, danger, loss.

What would come next?

Dylan had always believed a person could get used to anything.

He'd told himself for years now that he was used to the preparations that he had made in his home, preparations to wipe the building off the map if the need to disappear ever came around. He'd gotten used to the idea that such a situation might someday occur. Maybe he'd even been hoping for it, he realized.

He stood in front of the gas stove in his kitchen. He enjoyed cooking, he was good at it. Yet only one burner worked on the range top, the front right one. He didn't have a lot of visitors. Maybe if he'd had friends over, they might have commented that he ought to have the range repaired, or the entire unit replaced. He wouldn't have. He was used to this stove.

He had no more time for reflection. He had a large duffel slung over his shoulder, packed stiff with books, weapons, and magical items, far more than he'd realized he owned. Surprisingly few clothes. The fire alarm had been ringing for three minutes, ever since he'd walked out in the hallway and pulled the lever. The building only had two other residents anyway and he'd already checked that they were gone, but the alarm made sure the place was empty.

He put an unlit cigarette between his lips and flicked a match with his thumb. After two puffs, he set the cigarette by the back left burner and pushed the corresponding knob three times. Sixty seconds.

The ensuing explosion was later attributed to a leaking gas line. A badly leaking line.

Dylan had designed it all to look exactly so, and only so.

Postan was sure Cleric Carter knew someone was always watching his apartment building. He was a fool if he didn't know that.

When the woman, a useful human agent, had called in frantically reporting that Cleric Carter's entire building had just exploded, he'd calmly thanked her, and hung the phone back on its receiver. It was time.

He had intended to have the changing Cleric killed all those weeks ago in the same way he'd been having Hunters who'd been touched by the Nether killed off for centuries. Not always with such extreme prejudice as having another Demon do the killing, but Klarisvan had old sins to pay off. Killing Cleric Carter would have cleared the debt. That events had taken such an unexpected turn, in so many ways that his compatriots considered to be complications and failures, was terribly exciting. Things were now in motion that would finally drag his narrow-minded Sisters and Brothers kicking and screaming into the modern age, and for their own good. In time, they would praise him for his foresight.

The Demon Lord Postan sat by the eternal flames of his hearth and smiled, cold and malicious.

Chapter 31

Harold Tomlinson had been armorer for the Order Pure at the Red Cathedral for longer than Dylan had been a cleric. Supposedly he had once been a cleric himself, before being injured badly on a mission. He was a mortal human, at least as far as Dylan had been able to find out. Underworld Nether didn't seem to like to talk about the man.

The thing Dylan was most certain of was that Tomlinson deserved better than Dylan was about to give him. He was going to incapacitate the old man, rob him, and in the process humiliate him. It couldn't be helped. Security would be in place in all the known Hunter's Tunnels and in the Basilica above.

Dylan only knew about the Armorer's Way because Tomlinson had told him once, had trusted him with the knowledge. He'd said it wasn't a secret he shared lightly. "Only for when it all hits the fan, you hear me?" Tomlinson had said. Now Dylan would betray him, for the greater good.

The wall at the end of the tunnel didn't have a door. The stones were made to slide sideways, once unlocked. Dylan reached into a pocket in his long duster coat and brought out a small wooden box. It contained a rabbit's foot, charmed to open the door to the Armorer's Way. *Ironic, that you'd only need it when your luck's gone bad,* Dylan thought.

It was pitch black in the tunnel, but Dylan's new sense of vision wasn't hindered. He walked up to the portal and waved the foot in front of it a few times. When Tomlinson had shown him how to open the passageway from the other side, it had only taken a couple of passes.

Nothing happened. Dylan tried again. Maybe he had broken it somehow? Could that happen? What had he stored it next to that might have leached magic?

"What are you doing in my tunnels, Cleric?" said a voice behind him.

At least, Dylan thought it was behind him. When he whirled around, reaching out with an open palm strike to incapacitate whoever it was, he found only air.

Tomlinson's knuckle found Dylan's cheek, just above his upper gumline. An electric pain shot through Dylan's face and neck and he flinched away from it, hard. He tried to swing an elbow to the rear and catch Tomlinson's head. The strike went over the old man, who came out of a crouch, hooked a leg behind Dylan's knee, and struck him in the chest. Tomlinson's knee was in Dylan's stomach when he hit the floor. A polished wooden stake was in Tomlinson's hand, putting uncomfortable pressure on the area over Dylan's heart. "I didn't think it was that complicated of a question," he said.

"Need weapons, old man," Dylan said, wheezing. "Figured I'd go for the best."

"I always did think you were smart," Tomlinson said. "Only problem is, I arm Hunters. Why should I arm a Vampire?"

"What makes you think—"

"Rabbit's foot only works for humans, or at least humans who haven't gone through the change yet."

"Ah," Dylan said. "Might have mentioned that."

"Asked you another question, son. You need to get in the habit of answering."

"SOJ's after us. Order's turned on us. Need to get my team out. Need to get something out of Postan's chamber for trade." He thought it prudent to leave out the part the Inquisitor was to play, for now.

Tomlinson nodded. "My knee hurts. I need to keep holding this on you?" he said, waggling the stake.

"No, sir," Dylan said. "I'll behave."

"You will," Tomlinson said, getting up stiffly. "Come inside."

The air inside the armory smelled like gun oil and leather. Underneath Dylan could sense the magic stored in the room, something he'd never been able to feel so acutely before. Overlaying everything was a sense of strangers, a scent and a feeling. "Who was here?" he asked Tomlinson.

"SOJ," the old man said. He perched up on his stool inside his cage. "Lot of unexpected visitors today."

"What did they want?"

"The fuck you think they wanted? Same thing everyone who comes down here wants. Same thing you want. Only I saved the special toys for you."

"The Order is working with the SOJ?" Dylan asked. He had come prepared to deal with people he'd called friends for years. The SOJ threw an unexpected and dangerous element into his plans.

"You're gonna have to ask your buddy King about that," Tomlinson said. "They were answering to him."

"Impossible," Dylan said.

"I'm not concerned with the possible. I only worry about reality, and they called him sir. He had credentials with him authorizing those bozos to get gear, so I armed them up. Hopefully they'll shoot themselves in the foot and save me the trouble later. Now, what about you? If you used that tunnel, think the Order betrayed you, and the SOJ are here, then the fan is just buried in shit."

"You might not want answers to that, sir. Might even be safer the less you know."

"Safer?" Tomlinson said. "You think you're keeping me safe? You think I sit in this cage for protection? Son. If you need help, you need to let me know what's going on. It's not gonna be worse than anything I've seen before."

Dylan started to evade the question again, but his eyes locked on the old man's. He might not ever see him again after this. He was owed answers out of respect. He deserved to get to prepare himself for any fallout of Dylan's actions over the next hour. "What if I told you Order leadership wasn't what we thought it was?"

"What if I thought it was a bunch of Demon bastards set on ruling the world?"

Dylan threw his hat on the floor. "Does everyone but me know? Do I get to surprise no one?"

"Plenty of Hunters out there in the halls who don't know, and almost none of the general populace. Knock yourself out spreading the word, if you think you can handle the fallout," Tomlinson said. "Those who know usually have the good sense to avoid making waves. I'm pleased to find that you have no good sense. Means I finally get to save one of you." He got up and walked to a locked safe directly behind his desk. "You'll be wanting the big gun."

Dylan straightened his hat and put it back on his head. "You should come with us," he said. "We'll get you out too."

"How am I gonna help the others who find out if I leave?" Tomlinson said. "You're not the only Hunter walking around with a key to that tunnel. I'm just waiting to see if they figure out they need it before it's too late."

The gun safe he'd been unlocking finally clicked. To Dylan's surprise, it only held a handful of weapons, less than a quarter of its full capacity. Dylan's eye immediately went to three identical revolvers lined up on the top shelf.

"So, last time you came to me Demon hunting, I sent you out with the .454," Tomlinson said. "That's about as much as most Hunters can handle on a close quarters mission." He reached up and hefted one of the heavy pistols, quickly looking it over. It was matte black, with an empty rail along the barrel. He handed it to Dylan, then reached back into the safe, coming out with half a dozen speed loaders full of a cartridge nearly the size of Dylan's thumb. "I ordered these revolvers from a friend of mine up in the Appalachians, a retired gunsmith. They're chambered for .500s, with reinforced barrels and grips. Some backwoods mountain magic etched into the steel, stuff the Order doesn't like to see running around free. McKinney's work don't fail." He looked Dylan up and down. "Seems to me you can probably handle this cannon now."

"Maybe if you give me a protein shake and a month to work out," Dylan said. Holding the gun, he felt the sheer bulk of it. "You saved these for Hunters that survived the change to Nether. You actually prepared for this day."

Tomlinson looked at him, through him, his eyes far away. "I've been preparing to amend my wrongs," he said. He limped back to his stool and climbed onto it.

"Wrongs?"

"Son…a long time ago, I was one of the best the Order had, in Chicago, anyway. And best here means best in the New World. One day, my team was assigned something unusual. A Demon. Hadn't been one this side of the Atlantic in decades. But we were the best. We went out, tracked it, killed it. My team lead, cleric named Jacobs, he put a round in its skull. He was so fast. Never seen his like." Tomlinson reached under the counter next to him and pulled a bottle of whiskey and a glass from a hidden shelf. "Don't tell," he said, pouring a glass. He took a sip and winced. He seemed to age by degrees as he told his story.

"For some reason, the upper Clergy didn't seem too thrilled we'd done what we were told. No commendations, promotions, bonuses, not even a thank you. Whatever. Not why we do the job, but still. Then a couple weeks later, I get called in to talk to the High Cleric. Hands me a folder from the D7, says they have evidence Jacobs has been contaminated, infected. Nether influence. They task me with hunting him down."

He drained his glass and poured another. "I was...I was a bit of a zealot in those days. I spent a day or two struggling over it, but I did my job. I hunted down my team leader. Not exactly my friend, mind you, it was more business for us than it is for you and your team, I can tell that. But when I put him down...Carter, the last light in his eyes, it wasn't Nether. Not really human, but not a monster. It was just Jacobs. I didn't save the city from a monster. I murdered a man."

He set the glass down and rubbed his right leg. "That's how I got this. He jacked me up good before I got him. The Order patched me up best they could, with what they had to work with back then, but I wasn't fit to hunt anymore. So they gave me this cage," he said, looking around. "Less reward, more enclosure. Prison, maybe. But I knew, after Jacobs. It was a splinter in my mind. I started digging as I could. Learned a lot. Found out about the Hunters, how some are Nether touched. Found out about the High Clergy too. I couldn't have taken them on, even whole. I'm only human. So I started looking for those about to change, and prepared to help them. But none ever made it this far. I've been waiting a long time for you, son. You might be our one chance to start making a change here."

Dylan turned the hand cannon over a few times, examining it. "I understand," he said. He flipped the cylinder open and closed, tested the weight of the hammer. "I think I ought to test fire this," he said.

"If you didn't, I'd know I failed you as a teacher," Tomlinson said.

Twenty meters down a stone hallway was the firing range. Once there, Dylan pulled a speed loader from his pocket and fitted the rounds into the pistol's chamber. Tomlinson pushed a button, and a paper target slid out of the ceiling. Dylan took a two-handed grip, braced himself, and fired.

The ceiling would never screw with him again.

"What was that?" Tomlinson said.

"Kicks like a mule," Dylan said, embarrassed.

"Well, get it under control. I gave that to you because you're not human anymore, so stop shooting it like a human."

Dylan thought for a moment, then held the gun out one-handed.

Bang.

High and right of the head painted on the target.

He let strength bleed into his arm that didn't come from his muscles.

Bang.

Center of the forehead.

"Magic is what you make of it," she said.

BANG.

BANG.

Two shots in less than a second, through the same hole in the forehead. The last shot was filled with Dylan's magic and set the target on fire.

"Ah, shit!" Tomlinson said, grabbing a fire extinguisher and half jogging down the lane.

Dylan looked down at the weapon. It no longer felt heavy. It felt alive. It felt like it belonged to him, like it knew him.

"Yeah," he said. "I can work with this.

Minutes later he was back in the cage, filling a satchel with ammunition, grenades, knives, whatever Tomlinson had squirreled away through tricky inventory. The new gun hung on his right thigh. His own bowie knife hung off his left. Tomlinson had taken a look at it and given it his full approval.

Dylan's thoughts churned as he worked, until the question was finally ready to be spoken. "So," he said. "King."

"Yeah?" Tomlinson said, sipping his whiskey more slowly now.

"Came in with the SOJ. Stocked up on weapons. Guess I'm his Jacobs, right?"

Tomlinson stared down into his glass, looking for answers. "King is one of the best men I've ever met," he said, low and slow. "He's devout. But he isn't like I was. He isn't a zealot. This isn't a job. You aren't just a target. If he's coming after you, they had to have worked on him awful hard to get him there. I don't know if you can turn him around. But he isn't the same as me, Carter." A tear ran down the old man's cheek and he didn't bother wiping it away.

Chapter 32

James woke at sundown. He rolled over slowly on the floor, swearing for several long seconds before he remembered why he felt this bad. Dylan's little medieval toothpick. He groaned and got to his knees. His own idiot idea to use it. Well, it was what it was. Now time for the hard part.

An hour later he was in the west Hunter Tunnel, shambling toward the Cathedral. He had copied the key to the gate fifty years ago. Tomlinson's predecessor had been easier to trick than the current Armorer. James left the key in the iron gate's lock when he shambled through. However tonight turned out, he wasn't going to need it again.

His job was to make it to the Inquisitor's chambers. He and the Inquisitor hadn't talked much about what would need to be done to free James from the spells binding him to the Order's service. James had a pretty good idea what it might entail. Half a dozen times he stopped and asked himself if he really wanted to go through with it. Half a dozen times he saw the faces of his friends, who were now fighting for their own freedom. If he stayed, even if the Order didn't destroy him, he'd be used against them, one way or another. So he kept going.

James' world had been a symphony of sight and sound, scent and sensation, for over two hundred years. Now his body and mind were dulled, barely more than mortal. It would pass, he knew. He'd get his strength back when he was free. His thoughts were focused on that goal when a bright electric explosion engulfed him.

He hit the floor amid a blinding torrent of red pain. His body would not respond in any familiar way. Before he even managed to roll onto his back, he felt silver studded clubs slam into his ribs. One slammed into his leg, breaking the femur. The assault lasted only seconds. It was enough.

"You really walked right into that," said an unfamiliar voice. "Thought you'd be a lot more trouble, how Cleric King talked about you."

The words registered sluggishly in James's mind. He tried to focus his eyes on his assailants, but the world kept spinning in and out of focus. SOJ uniforms. Tomlinson's Nether Stunner guns. An ambush.

"Not crazy about taking orders from some Cathedral lackey, but he said take it slow with you, and that sounds fine to me."

A line of bright fire erupted in James's stomach. A silver bladed knife. He realized they intended to torture him to death, and at Matthew's direction. His mind tried to find an avenue of escape, a way to warn Dylan, Ariel. His body tried to fight, like a wounded animal. A glancing blow against someone's body armor was all he could manage.

A shadow moved in the periphery of his failing vision.

"You are lost, gentlemen. These are my halls. And I do not appreciate visitors," said a familiar, German accented voice.

The two SOJ operatives weren't novices. They hadn't seen the figure approaching, but their reactions showed the quickness of training and experience. They spun toward the voice, hands going to holstered weapons, drawing, firing.

The Inquisitor moved as if he'd fought every fight, seen every gambit, committed to memory every series of attack and parry. He held a long, thin rapier in one hand, the other hand tucked comfortably behind his back. The tip of his blade met each pistol an instant before the muzzles flashed, gently bumping the weapons off target. Between trigger pulls, he lashed out, seemingly doing little more than nicking his opponents. Yet within five quick, ringing gunshots, the SOJ operatives slumped to their knees, streaming blood, pistols falling from slack hands. The Inquisitor stepped over one, ignoring his moans of pain. The other he stabbed through the heart, before turning to James.

"Sorry about that, my friend," Inquisitor said. "I can't say they were unexpected, but they were most unwelcome."

"Could have fucking warned me," James said through gritted teeth.

"Where is the fun in that?" the Inquisitor said, smiling. He sheathed the rapier and reached down to grab James by the collar. He dragged him across the floor with surprising strength, ignoring his cries of agony. "Don't worry, Vampire," he said, bending down to take the remaining SOJ member by the collar with his other hand. "We'll get you a snack, and you'll be feeling much better."

Whistling tunelessly, he dragged both men around a corner, into the darker corridors leading to the auxiliary lab he had set up deep within the Cathedral's forgotten tunnels.

Chapter 33

D r. Jackson was surprised at how cold the halls of the medical wing felt to her. Logically she knew they were the same temperature as those of any hospital where she had worked. But the feeling of cold and too bright lights, the sharp scent of antiseptic, was familiar. It didn't take long to place the memory. Her residency, as a medical student right out of university. She'd felt out of place for weeks, like she didn't belong and it had made every sensation foreign and intense. She was out of place now for the first time in a while. She held no actual authority here. These were not her friends and colleagues. She was, in fact, here to rob them of a patient they may well have sincerely cared about.

Her guarded upbringing frequently warred with her doctor's mindset in her life. Anyone could be an attacker. Anyone could be a person who genuinely meant to do no harm. She had to shove both voices down. She could only care for one person today. She had to find Matthew's mother.

It was taking longer than expected. Finding the elder care branch hadn't been difficult, there were signs pointing to it everywhere. Once there, though, she couldn't find a Mrs. Rhonda King. There was no way Dylan was wrong about Matthew's mother being here. He'd visited her several times, given Coleen the room number. Had they moved her in anticipation of a kidnapping? Unlikely, she decided. Matthew's mother was already an unnecessary complication, a side plan not many people would bother to attempt. So where was she?

A sinking feeling in her stomach preceded the thought forming in her mind. She made her way back to the central nurse's station. It didn't take too long for a nurse to step away for a few minutes. Sitting down, Coleen quickly logged in with the credentials Ariel had made for her and ran through patient directories. She couldn't help but start with the least serious areas a patient might be moved to. Testing. Physical therapy. Surgery. ICU.

Then, there she was.

Coleen sighed. She picked up her empty clipboard, hugged it to her chest, and made her way to the Hospice rooms.

Coleen stood next to the older woman, silent, looking down at her, tears in the corners of her eyes. She'd seen this before, but she never got used to it.

Rhonda King was fifty-five years old. At least, in spirit. The body she was trapped in now looked closer to seventy-five. She was sedated to stave off the pain she must be feeling. An oxygen mask covered the lower half of her face. Coleen held her chart, looking over the information there. The cancer had come on quickly, ravenous. She had days left, perhaps. Maybe a couple of weeks. Order policy was to move such severe cases to a special wing for the dying, to avoid distressing the other elder care residents, and to give families privacy with their loved ones.

Coleen found herself automatically planning a care regimen in her mind. Trying to think of treatments or surgeries that might give the woman a chance. She stopped herself. She couldn't do that. This woman wasn't her patient. Wasn't ever going to be her patient. She couldn't take Rhonda King away from the Order and hope to give her any kind of peace at the end. If she regained consciousness at all, she would only be scared and confused. In a lot of pain. In unfamiliar places.

"Excuse me," said a voice behind her. Coleen managed to stifle a jump, and turned. An old man stood behind her. Where he had hair, it was white, but most of his crown was now bare. His white coat was well worn, formed to him like a glove after years of use, but perfectly clean. "You must be new here?" he said, making it a question.

"Yes, um, just a couple of days," Coleen said, stepping aside. The old doctor took his place at Rhonda's side, reaching down to feel her pulse rather than just looking at the machines beeping beside her.

"Known Mrs. King long?" he asked.

"Mother of a friend," she said. "Just thought I'd stop in and check on her."

The old man smiled. "I appreciate that. Lots of people around here are too busy for that these days." He adjusted the older woman's blankets, checked the fitment of her mask. "Good thing you came when you did. I don't think you'll get many more chances."

"No," she said. "I don't think so either."

"Fine woman, Mrs. King. Been looking after her for more than ten years now. She couldn't ever get up and do much, not after the attack that put her here. But if you went to her room to visit her, you always came away feeling like she was the one taking care of you. Shared a lot of my own troubles with her. Sure gonna miss her," he said.

"I, uh...I suppose I ought to be on my way now," Coleen said. Whatever time Rhonda King had left, this man would make sure it was as comfortable as it could be.

"Yes, I suppose so," the old doctor said, stepping back and looking at her. He seemed more troubled looking at Coleen than he had at the dying woman. "They'll be here for you soon."

Coleen started and turned to him. He looked a little ashamed. "You see, I had to report it to someone," he said. "You're not one of mine, and I couldn't take any chances. If anyone found out you'd been here, I might not be allowed to take care of my patients anymore." He dug in a pocket and brought out a keycard. "I don't think you meant to hurt anyone, though. Lycan of your strength, you wouldn't have needed to sneak in wearing doctor's clothing, would you."

"You knew," she said.

"We're doctors. We meet people at their best and their worst. We take care of those with secrets and those begging to be known. You learn to see people. I expect you knew I'm not human as quickly as I knew about you."

Jackson took a last look at Rhonda King and squeezed her hand. "Take good care of her," she said.

"I will," the old doctor said. "On your way out...please leave me something of the soldiers you're about to run into to work with."

Chapter 34

"Cleric King," said Saint Lindon, walking up to Matthew. "I've lost contact with my men in the west Hunter's tunnels. Requesting permission to go investigate."

Matthew was flipping through a series of security feeds on a small tablet. An exercise in futility, he knew. He'd warned the Order Intelligence team assigned to this operation to prepare for cyber-attacks from Ariel Ikeda. They'd all gone pale and stared at each other. He switched the view to the west tunnel cameras. The dust on the floors hadn't even been disturbed.

"That's the team that reported contact with the Order Vampire, right?" he said.

"Yes, sir."

"Then he's already done with them, and we can't help. Let him come to us." Matthew knew he was making a biased decision. If it had been Order troops, he'd have at least tried to collect the bodies. He just couldn't muster as much care about SOJ heretics.

Besides, this increased the chances that he could deal with Blood himself.

"As you say, sir," said Lindon. His face showed that he knew what was going through Matthew's mind, and he didn't bother to hide his displeasure.

Matthew had chosen a room not far from High Cleric Postan's chambers as his HQ. Based on what Matthew had reported about the night in Ariel Ikeda's apartment, Postan theorized that Dylan would ultimately head there, either to attack Postan himself, or to hunt for the scroll that bound the Inquisitor to the service of the Order. Matthew hoped to arrest Dylan evidence in hand, preferably without violence.

Suddenly Lindon's hand flew to his comms earpiece, and his face became a mask of concerned concentration. "King!" he said. "There's been an assault in the medical wing. Someone tried to access your mother's room."

"What?" Matthew snapped, snatching his earpiece off the table and tuning it to the frequency Lindon indicated. Team Epsilon, two Order and two SOJ operatives, had responded to an intruder alert entered by a physician, suspecting it might be connected to Dylan. They had encountered a tall, blonde woman dressed as a doctor, emerging from Rhonda King's room. She had fled the moment she'd seen them, disappearing down a hall that led to the ambulance bays. Epsilon pursued and was ambushed as they entered the garage. By a werewolf. The woman's scrubs and coat had been found discarded. She had been a Nether in disguise. Three members of Epsilon were in emergency surgery.

"Coleen Jackson," Matthew growled. He started toward the medical wing, but Lindon stopped him with a hand on his chest.

"With all respect, sir—"

"Carter went for my mother!" Matthew said. "I have to get to her!"

"I understand, Cleric King," Lindon said, lowering his voice. The half dozen Order and SOJ operatives in the room were looking at the pair. Lindon rested his hand on Matthew's shoulder and led him back to the HQ monitoring station. "And this is probably exactly what he wanted. Distraction. Drawing leadership away. Look, if a werewolf had wanted to hurt your mother, it would have, and it didn't."

"I didn't think he'd go this far," Matthew said, trembling with anger. "I need to go take care of her."

"I'll send extra security, with your permission. But we need you here. I can't operate in the Cathedral without your authority. I can't arrest Carter if and when he shows up. We need you here."

Matthew slowly brought himself under control. He nodded. "Yes…notify security. And have them check the ID cards of all the staff on the floor."

Lindon turned and got on comms with the medical wing, updating them on the situation. Matthew was breathing hard, trying to process what was happening. His mother. That was a line he'd never imagined Dylan would cross. Maybe he was changed more than physically. Maybe Matthew would have to be ready to cross lines he hadn't considered before, too.

Matthew turned back to the monitors and began cycling through them, but he kept the earpiece in this time.

Chapter 35

Ariel's laptop screen glowed in front of her, heatsinks almost as hot as the coffee she'd ordered. Everything of real value to her fit in the large backpack on the floor next to her chair. The EMP bomb she'd set in her apartment before leaving would have gone off about an hour ago, rendering useless all the electronics she'd been forced to leave behind. No matter. In her backpack were drives with terabytes of data and programs, custom electronics, and a few useful items of magic that she'd collected over the years.

She tabbed rapidly through programs, monitoring security feed overlays, alarm sensor settings, digital communications, whatever she could do to help Dylan and Jackson get where they needed to go. She'd managed to scrub Jackson from security feeds and recordings in real time. She'd cycled exterior cameras on police feeds so that Dylan could make it to the entrance to the Armorer's Way without being recorded and rerouted security patrols.

She couldn't do anything for James. She didn't know where he was. He hadn't contacted her since he'd disappeared. In the end she just looped the security feed to the tunnels nearest the Inquisitor's chambers. She didn't know what he and the Inquisitor were going to be doing anyway. She had begun to assume she wasn't going to see him anymore. He'd been locked up in servitude to the Order for a century. Why would he stick around once he was freed from their control? She blocked him from her thoughts. More important things to worry over.

Ariel had tried to help Dylan locate the scroll used to bind the Inquisitor, but there was no mention of it in any archival systems. The Inquisitor had said it was kept in Postan's personal chambers, and that was all they had to go on. She'd tried to find where the Inquisitor had hidden their Service Talismans, but they weren't showing up on any internal sensor grids.

She was so fixated on her screen that she'd lost all track of the people moving in and out of the coffee shop. She didn't notice when an unusually tall man walked in with his jacket hood pulled over his head. Or minutes later when two tall women came in, wearing hats and scarves that completely obscured their features. She didn't see the last man come in, bareheaded, but with something about him that made eyes slide off his features, like dreams off despair.

She didn't notice the identical charm each wore on their left wrist, a leafless tree worked in gold wire.

She didn't notice how they sat down at the same table, each glancing at her every few minutes in turn.

Chapter 36

James never fully lost consciousness, but he did slip in and out of memories, losing himself in time and place. He lived again the moment his Progenitor had brought him into the world of Vampires. He tasted blood on his lips that long ago had dried to dust in dark London alleys. He felt the sun on his face, before it became a death sentence to him. He felt love for one that he'd given up long ago. He felt loss for one he'd have to give up soon.

He felt as the Inquisitor injected liquid fire into his veins, igniting the dark blood that flowed through him. He screamed as his mind was hurled back into the present, into hateful reality and violent perception. His limbs slammed against restraints of iron and silver.

"Intravenous blood transfusion is quite different from oral ingestion, isn't it?" said a smooth voice in the dark, heavily colored with a German accent.

The bones in the Vampire's spine made snapping sounds as his back arched. "Why would you do that?" James screamed. He'd heard of this being done before. It was a relatively modern torture method used by Vampire Covens.

"Many reasons," the Inquisitor said, circling the steel table to which James was strapped. "To begin, we are pressed for time. You are still weak from your foolish run-in with Cleric Carter. This will restore your strength quickly."

The tattoos on James' skin began to smoke, attempting to burn away the foreign blood now coursing through his veins. Some of them, buckling under the pressure of the infusion, ignited into pale blue flames.

"Secondly, I need your skin, or rather those nasty tattoos in the skin, to react with sufficient volatility to the blood that your body begins to reject your own flesh. This will make removal much easier."

James heard little of this. His screaming drowned out all other sounds. It rose continuously in volume and supernatural power. Finally, the bulbs of the overhead operating lamp gave way, shattering and sparking in their sockets.

"But ultimately," said the Inquisitor, still circling like a jungle cat in the shadows of the forest, "I wanted to see just what it would do to you. I am not disappointed."

He stepped closer, his leering face illuminated only by the light of the flames that coursed over James' naked, pain racked body, and began to work. His tool of choice was a silver skinning knife, obviously old and well worn, but remarkably sharp. He sliced across arm and thigh and stomach with a rote precision, lacking any hesitation. As he peeled the flesh away, ember colored power ran along each incision, searing the skin even as it tried to knit and heal.

James' mind began to cross a line drawn in the sand of his psyche. On one side was his sense of self, his personhood, his life and will. On the other, a creature waited, laughing and deranged but unassailable. Unconquerable. A survivor. The line between was written in the language of madness. Pain was the force that chased James across the border of his being, into the arms of the creature.

His wails turned to laughter, violent and shrieking, as his skinless muscles strained against the metallic bonds holding him under the knife of the Inquisitor. Blood ran freely from the raw meat of his body, flowed down drains and tubes attached to the table, and was pumped back in by the cold machines whirring nearby.

The Inquisitor laughed with the Vampire. He'd crossed his own line centuries ago.

Chapter 37

Dylan stood over two unmoving operatives, one SOJ, the other Order. Some new kind of gun lay on the floor beside each of them. He wasn't sure if they were alive or not. He'd hit them pretty hard. Then he heard a pair of heartbeats and let out a breath of relief. He wasn't here to kill anyone if he could help it.

He'd been able to tell they were waiting for him around the corner of the tunnel leading toward High Cleric Postan's chambers. He'd heard them, smelled them, even felt their body heat on his exposed skin as he'd crept through the shadows toward them. When he'd moved on them, he'd surprised himself with his own speed, and had to pull back sharply as he struck. As he thought about it now, he realized if he'd hit them full on, the tunnel would be covered in gore and body parts.

He listened to their hearts beat as he waited for his own body to calm. It didn't want to. He felt a call within himself to hunt, to feed. The helpless pair on the floor. He wanted to hurt them. Consume them. He turned away in disgust at himself.

It was a subject he'd been avoiding thinking about. What was he going to do when this was over? When he'd freed his team from service to the Order, when he'd used these powers to help those he cared about, what then? He'd either have to accept what he was or find a cure. A cure he'd certainly never heard about to this point.

He made his way deeper into the tunnels underneath the Cathedral, moving shadow to shadow. He tried to think of a way to use the knowledge Jelena had given him to get in and out of Postan's chambers, to find the scroll and leave unscathed. *Don't force it,* said a honey warm voice in his mind. *Let the magic do as it will.*

Don't play around in my thoughts, they aren't fit for guests, he thought back. He wasn't sure if she actually had a backdoor into his mind or if he was talking to himself.

A familiar scent on the air staggered him momentarily. *King*. He was close by. Strangely close. Not in the chambers above, nor making his way to the Armory back the way Dylan had come. He was ahead. And not alone.

It was true, then. Dylan couldn't really be surprised. Matthew was a true Order devotee. His faith was actually enviable. Now that faith stood between Dylan and his goal. Along with half a dozen other Order and SOJ operatives.

He hoped to try to reason with Matthew one more time. He wanted give his brother every chance. He didn't know if Matthew would do the same and seriously doubted his new team would.

The flashbang grenade took him by surprise. It caught him square in the chest as he moved fluidly through the dark places. Someone up ahead knew what they were doing.

Dylan had been caught in a flash grenade once before, on a mission to eradicate a cell of a cult that worshipped zombies. That time, the blindness, the sound, the pain, they'd all struck faster than his mind could keep up. By the time he had realized what was happening, a team member was dragging him out of the room on his back, and he was mindlessly pulling the trigger on his revolver.

It didn't feel like that this time. His eyes wouldn't go blind to the awful light. His hearing had no upper limit. His mind processed stimuli as quickly as events happened. He had to take it all in, suffer every moment and sensation of the explosion. His emotions disoriented him. Faced with all that violent sensory input, he suddenly found himself blind with rage. He lunged forward, teeth and claws bared.

Whoever had thrown the grenade had expected that reaction. They came out swinging at the same time, aiming for where he would be, not where he had been. A silver tipped spike flashed in the light.

It was what Dylan would have done. Seventy-two percent of Vampires use their right hand to wrench a victim's head over and expose the right carotid artery. A Hunter holds their spike left-handed and aims straight ahead to hit the heart. The Hunter in Dylan remembered those lessons, taught to him in the Order gyms all those years ago. Dylan dodged left to avoid the spike. He brought his right elbow down on the man's collarbone. If the man was lucky, he'd be able to breathe until help arrived.

Something hit Dylan in the stomach. A firearm of some kind, but the foot pounds of impact were all wrong. A non-lethal then. His amped up body started to push through it, when his legs suddenly went weak. He looked down and saw a small silver spike sticking out of his abdomen, with a flashing crystal at the end of the spike. A modern Sicilian Spike?

Two agents charged him, one SOJ, one Order. The Order operative had a pair of iron and silver shackles at the ready. The SOJ had a large syringe of tranquilizer in his hand. Gritting his teeth, Dylan wrapped his hand around the silver spike. His palm hissed as the silver burned his skin. He growled and yanked it out. Instead of tossing it, he held on through the pain, and rushed the SOJ, slamming the spike into his bicep. The man cried out and dropped the syringe.

The Order woman threw the chain of the shackles around his neck from behind and pulled. Dylan could feel his strength returning, but it was slow, and she hauled him off balance. He tried to spin as he fell and bring her to the ground with him. Before any of that happened, some huge force slammed into his chest. He and the woman both went flying.

"Stay down, Carter," Matthew said. "This has to happen."

"Hi, King," Dylan said, rising to his knees. "New friends?"

"Cleric Carter, you're under arrest for heresy, consorting with Nether, and intention to harm Order Clergy," Matthew said, stepping closer. "Submit or letha—"

Dylan shoulder charged Matthew before he could finish, closing the distance before Matthew could counter. Normally Dylan couldn't do anything to Matthew with a move like that. Matthew was just too massive.

Matthew landed on his back two meters away.

"We need to talk about this, King," Dylan said. "You gotta know something's off here."

"I know you came for mom," Matthew said, walking slowly toward Dylan. "I know you left Ikeda with that bloodsucker."

Matthew slammed a fist down at Dylan's head. Dylan barely got his arms up in time, and the force half drove him to his knees.

"I know you lie on half your reports."

A front kick threw Dylan against the wall.

"I know you use magic you shouldn't touch."

Dylan caught Matthew's straight arm punch and held it. His eyes had rings of burning amber in them.

"I know that you're Nether, and I have to cleanse you," Matthew said, but all the anger had drained from his voice, replaced by pity and regret. "I'm sorry it came to this, boss."

"Yeah, me too," Dylan said.

He grabbed Matthew's outstretched wrist with his right hand and moved the other to the back of his shoulder, twisting and slamming Matthew face first into the wall. Matthew bounced off, spinning as he did, swinging out to take Dylan in the head. Dylan ducked and pounded his fists into Matthew's midsection. Matthew slipped his head to one side and used the momentum to bring his opposite leg forward. His shin crunched into Dylan's thigh, numbing it. Before he could withdraw, Dylan grabbed his leg and spun, pulling all of Matthew's two-hundred-plus kilos off the ground and throwing him down the hall.

Suddenly Saint Linden fell to his knees, gasping. Matthew and Dylan both turned to look at him. Dylan noticed the difference in the atmosphere first and put out an arm to steady himself against the wall. The air around them had become heavy, hard to pull into the lungs. Matthew looked at Dylan, confused. "What is this? What are you doing?" he said.

"Not me," Dylan said. He sniffed the air. There was a familiar scent. "King," he said, "I think you need to run."

Chapter 38

High Cleric Postan was a painfully old man. He rarely stood, preferring the comfort of the chair in front of his hearth. When needs forced him to walk, his presence was announced with the threefold sound of his cane and careful steps; tap, shuffle, shuffle. Tap, shuffle, shuffle.

The man who rounded the corner in the passageway stood straight and confident. No cane, no shuffling. The deep wrinkles of his face had smoothed. No surprise visible at finding half a dozen women and men assaulting each other outside the door to his personal chambers.

"Cleric King," he said. "I am disappointed."

"High Cleric," Matthew said, "I...we're in the process of arresting Cleric Carter. You shouldn't be here, it isn't safe. Cleric Simmons, escort High—"

"You're in the process of getting your ass kicked," Postan said, scowling. "I expected better!"

"King," Dylan said, "What the Inquisitor told us about Postan, about the higher Clergy. I think you know it's true. You need to get these people out of here right now. I'll handle this, just protect your team."

"I'm not going anywhere, Carter," Matthew said, reaching for the shackles on the floor, though the last few moments had leached the confidence from his voice.

"'Handle this'?" Postan said. "Insolence, even in the light of your suspicions confirmed? Cleric Carter, too long have you needed instruction in humility. Had you heeded earlier guidance, today's lesson need not be so harsh."

He raised a gnarled hand that seemed to smooth and grow vital as the seconds passed. "Remember that." He reached into a pocket in the folds of his robes, and brought out a large, ornate ring with a blood-colored jewel. He slid it onto a finger, and life visibly flooded into his body. With a flick of his hand, the walls began to change.

The shift in reality was sickeningly familiar. The gray stone walls, ancient and dark, became smooth, rust colored. The ceiling rose until it disappeared high above in a foggy haze. The entire Cathedral around Dylan and Matthew began to kaleidoscope outward, folding over and through itself. As the structure changed, so did Postan. His diminutive stature lengthened, rising to well over two meters tall. His humble gray robes became a cobweb veil around him, and bright rods of light circled his head.

"What are you doing?" someone cried, rushing in from the confusing spiral of hallways that fanned outward.

"Chronicler Miranda?" Dylan said. "Miranda, run! He's—"

The young woman with the librarian's glasses morphed smoothly, dusty whisps fanning out around her like sea fog. Her face glowed with the semblance of a cold night's dying fire. She spared Dylan a quick glance as she rushed across floors that became walls, walls that looped and swirled and returned to the ground. She was unperturbed by the changes in reality around her.

"Postan, you've exposed us! The Cathedral was never to be revealed in full form!"

"Where is the glory in that?" Postan said, still looking at Dylan.

"You. Must. Stop!" said the Demon Kinyr. She reached behind herself and pulled a fiery whip out of the fabric of unreality. She swung the blazing weapon at Postan, power and death radiating from the cord of the weapon.

Postan caught it easily in one hand. He turned his black eyes on Kinyr and the flames racing along the whip died. Postan's great, bloody wings burst into being, shaking the air as he stretched them wide. "Kinyr, your service to the Order Pure and tenure in the Red Cathedral are hereby ended. When the glory of the New Order is revealed, be sure you are not found in its grasp." With that, walls surrounded Kinyr, and disappeared into the floor.

Postan was turning his gaze back to Dylan when the bullet left Dylan's revolver. The sound repeated. Yet, Dylan had only fired one round. The thunderclap of that shot echoed, over and over, folding in on itself faster and faster. The bullet spun but slowed in its forward momentum as layer after layer of Nether unreality rushed past it. The round traveled between Dylan and Postan, but never seemed to get closer to the Demon as he flung room after room of the Cathedral at it, moving space past the round until it finally used up all its kinetic energy, and fell to the floor.

Dylan lowered the gun, then holstered it.

"Oddly silent, Cleric. No acidic remarks left to fling?" Postan said.

Matthew drew and racked his own sidearm, pointed it at Postan, lowered it, raised it again. Indecision, disbelief, and anger crossed his features. Anger at Dylan for being right, at Postan for his deception, at the Order for trading his faith for a lie. At himself for being wrong, at the helplessness he had brought on himself when he sought strength to protect. In the end, he dropped the pistol and charged at Postan with a roar.

"No," the Demon said, and wall after wall rushed up before Matthew, flinging him and the remaining members of his team back through layers of unreality, into the labyrinth that was the Red Cathedral. "Someplace more private, Cleric Carter? We need to talk."

Postan's private chambers fell from the whisps of gray high above. Dylan fought vertigo as the room enveloped him. Postan sat in one of a pair of wingback chairs in front of the fireplace and motioned for Dylan to do the same. It was a bizarrely human gesture coming from the Fallen Angel. Dylan looked around the chamber for a moment, before turning back to Postan.

"The scroll. Barnard August's binding spell. We'll get to that soon. Please, Cleric, sit with me. We need not possess such animosity for each other."

"No, I'm good, I'll stand. King?" Dylan said. "If he's not ok, there's gonna be a lot more than animosity flying around."

"Do you know, we actually fostered a certain distance between members of Hunter teams for centuries. It made inevitable deaths easier for all involved. Yet I always admired the ferocity with which you guarded your own team. A useful trait, if you invest it in the right allies. But yes, Cleric King and the others are, for the moment, safe. Lost and angry," he said, smirking, "but safe."

"Is this your 'temple,' then? Hiding inside the Red Cathedral this whole time?"

Postan looked around. "Hiding? No. The Red Cathedral has always been my temple, in its entirety. I've kept it partially manifested for over three hundred years now. Not many of my kind are capable of such a feat."

"I'm impressed as all fuck, really," Dylan said, circling the room. "Look, I obviously didn't come dressed for tea, so tell me what you want and why we aren't ripping pieces off of each other."

He felt far less confidence than he was showing. Klarisvan's temple had been a staggering, impressive force, a room where the Demon held absolute sway. Postan's temple was something else entirely. It seemed to be a place only connected to reality by Postan's whim. Postan's control over reality inside these walls was unlike anything Dylan had ever heard of. He only hoped the Demon would keep talking long enough to find the cabinet where the scroll was kept.

"I had plans for your Ouruqan friend, Cleric Carter. I think the way the game has played out, though, he's unlikely to be quite so inclined to follow direction anymore. Still, couldn't let you damage him. I had to step in."

"Shame. Sorry about that."

"He still has some value. However, this leaves an opening in the coming restructuring of the Order. I need someone to lead on the action level of the force. You...well, when I decided it was time to let that dolt Klarisvan dispose of you, you were just a Hunter slowly giving in to his Nether self. Something has clearly happened between then and now, and I'm looking forward to you telling me all about it. After you take control of the military branch of the New Order Pure."

Dylan stopped walking and turned to face Postan. "Are you seriously offering me a job based on my ability to survive an assassination? That you ordered? I am seriously in awe of your hubris. You should bottle it. Make a killing off selling it. You remember I killed that Demon, right? That I do that for a living? That I, and forgive me, but I am bragging, that I am one of the best in this whole organization at what I do?"

Postan's expression grew dangerous. "Do show some resp—"

"Counteroffer," Dylan said, resuming his orbit of the room. "Give me the Service Talismans my team and I signed and I won't kill you today. Or tomorrow, I'll give you all of forty-eight hours to get your ass back to the Old World. Oh," he said, looking genuinely annoyed, "I also need whatever you've got that binds the Inquisitor to this place, or he's gonna give me trouble, and I'm too busy to deal with that right now."

As he finished, a voice whispered in his earpiece. "You're close. There's a lot of interference, but something's spiking. Keep walking. Left, I think."

Ariel. Before he'd left her, she'd wired the inside of his coat with a web of sensors. According to her research, the scroll should emit an Ether signature unique to specific binding rituals. The rig she'd laced around Dylan would be able to pick it up if he got close enough.

"I have tried with you, Cleric Carter," Postan said. "I offered lenience for two decades as you played with magic beyond your worth. I kept you alive for longer than most because, as you say, you are good, extremely good. And now I have offered you power that my compatriots would never give to a human. The greatest sting is I begin to believe they are in the right." Postan rose from his chair and stepped toward Dylan.

"There!" Ariel said. "You're right on top of it!"

Dylan glanced to his left at an unassuming oak cabinet. It was neither ornate in appearance nor of heavy construction. It was perfect. He could grab everything inside, make a run for it, and sort out what he'd taken later.

He moved as fast as he could. His speed was considerable. Postan's was more so. He was so remarkably fast that Dylan had only a fraction of an instant to see the Demon appear and smile at him, before backhanding him hard enough to send him flying across the room.

Chapter 39

"King, what the hell was that?" Linden said. His sidearm was drawn, waving around wildly.

Matthew was running his hands over the stones of walls that he knew couldn't be there. He looked from one end of the hall to the other, but every time he looked back again the other way, the turn at the end of the hall had changed direction, or the hall disappeared into a silver fogged distance, or just decided to end, five meters away.

"King, answer me!"

"Linden, check the team comms, see if anyone's hurt," Matthew said.

"That was a Demon, King. A full-fledged Demon!" He lowered his gun. "How would a Demon break into the Cathedral to impersonate the High Cleric?"

Matthew hung his head. He was tired of trying to believe. "It wasn't impersonating him," he said. "That was the High Cleric. All along."

Linden could no longer decide what he wanted to do with his sidearm. He began to gesture with it in ways no Armorer would approve. "You mean, you work for Demons? And you know it? They always told us you Nether types were trying to redeem yourselves serving here, but seriously, to work directly under the orders of Demons?"

"I didn't know!" Matthew snapped. "None of us did. Wait, what do you mean, 'you Nether types'?"

"You know, what you all are," Linden said. "Nether touched. Untransformed. Like the SOJ hunts outside of the Order's ranks."

It had all been true, Matthew realized. It was a truth he didn't want to hold, still would not look at too closely, but it was there. And he just didn't have it in him to push it away anymore.

"Ok, look. We're gonna have to talk this out later, there's a lot you don't understand, and a ton I don't. But right now, please, will you check on the other agents."

Linden looked around, as if only then registering that the two men were alone in the hallway. "Oh. Crap. Yeah," he said. "Yeah, I'll find them. What are you gonna do?"

"I need to make a call," Matthew said. He started to step down the hall but thought better of it. More than a couple of meters from Linden was probably risking separation if the halls shifted again. He pulled a cell phone from his thigh pocket and stared at it for a few seconds, then thumbed the power button until it began to power up.

He turned to keep Linden in his peripheral sight, clicked on favorite contacts, and dialed. The line didn't even ring before the call was answered.

"I can see where you are even with it powered off, you know. Dummy," Ariel said.

"Then why didn't you make it ring or something?" Matthew said.

"You've been ghosting us, and I got mad at you. Now I see why, and I'm even more mad."

"I'm sorry, ok? Things just got…I don't know, nothing makes a lot of sense. We can talk about it later. Postan has Cleric Carter. I think we're in his temple"

"Weren't you gonna give Carter to him?"

"Yes, but not like this!" Matthew said. "You were all right, ok? Mostly. I don't know if Carter's in his right mind, but I need to go get him away from that Demon right now, so we can kick each other's asses later. Can you help?"

"Yeah," Ariel said, "just give it a second. He's in there looking for the Inquisitor's scroll. I think he's getting…hold on a sec."

There was a click as Ariel presumably switched to talk to Dylan. Matthew took the opportunity to snap his fingers at Linden and raise an inquiring eyebrow. Linden looked at him, face pale, and just shook his head. No contact with the other team members.

Suddenly Ariel's voice was back in his ear. "Dylan's in trouble! Hold on to something!"

Neon glyphs flashed across the walls around Matthew. Ariel was doing her temple hacking again, only she seemed much faster at it this time. Matthew had just enough time to pocket the phone and drop into a braced stance when the world lurched around him, a feeling of being compressed into a ball even as his eyes told him the universe was shooting away from him in all directions. There was a shock of atmospheric change and he was standing in front of Postan's fireplace. He registered three things in the space of a racing heartbeat. He was facing the wrong way. Linden was there with him, screaming. And something was coming at him from the left, painfully fast.

Interlude - Ariel

The clouds erupted. Rain poured out of the night sky. The cloaked figure standing in front of the Red Cathedral placed her baby on the steps, slammed her balled fist against the door, and ran for the trees in the park across the street.

The baby cried. The door opened. A prophecy was undone. For a while.

Chapter 40

Hacking a Demon's temple took significantly more concentration than anything else Ariel had ever done. She still hadn't figured out how she even did it. None of her key trackers or system logs worked right last time. But she could do it. She got Matthew in. And apparently the guy standing next to him. Oops. She made a mental note to at least figure out the radius part later and got ready to transport everyone out at Matthew's signal.

It was just too much to think about. She didn't notice as the customers in the coffee shop went slack faced and blank eyed in unison. She didn't hear them all get up at once and shuffle out the front door.

All except the four tall strangers at the table, who were staring at her. They waited until everyone else had left. Then they moved together, toward her.

They were unnaturally silent, as if the room was muted. They moved with frightening speed. She might not have been able to do anything about them even if she'd noticed the threat.

Seconds later the shop was empty. The only sounds left behind were Ariel's computers still running at the booth she had been sitting in.

Chapter 41

In the history of the Order, no Hunter had ever had to face more than one Demon in their lifetime. Therefore, no comparison of the strength of different Demons had ever been made.

Dylan knew the difference now. Klarisvan had been bone shatteringly powerful, possessed of both physical and magical strength unlike anything Dylan had ever faced before. Had Dylan stayed in the good graces of the Order, his story, the killing of such a powerful creature, would have become legend.

Postan made Klarisvan look like a flailing child. Where the lower Demon had been fast, Postan was instant. Klarisvan injured; Postan broke. He moved like an incarnate force of Nether itself.

All Dylan had managed to do so far was get his arms in front of a few of Postan's blows. Dylan was taking the worst beating of his life, but Postan didn't even seem to be trying hard. Sickeningly, he realized the Demon was just playing with its food. Every piece of furniture in the chamber was broken, the jagged edges stained with his blood. Every piece, except that cabinet. There was some satisfaction in that. That's where important things were kept. Maybe a lot of important things. If he could just get to it, he could try to break for the door.

There was no more door. He looked for it when he could, trying to maintain some grip on his sense of position in the room, but all the walls were solid, rust colored stone. It was, and it wasn't, Postan's chamber. The fireplace was there, chairs, the cabinets and shelves, but the stones of the walls were immense red blocks, like poured concrete, reaching up past the edges of vision above. Painful acceptance began to spread in Dylan's chest. As soon as he got bored, Postan was going to finish him.

Then it was over. Dylan's ears rang and his vision swam. He was lying on his back, staring up into the fathomless depths above. No one was hurting him.

"In the end, I suppose you are the proof of why the old Order must pass," Postan said. He was standing by the fire, looking at Dylan. He was bizarrely calm, as if he hadn't been trying to kill Dylan seconds earlier. "That drive to 'do the right thing', that need to destroy that which you do not accept as natural. It was useful, so useful, when the people feared that which they did not understand."

He looked down into the coals of the fire. "Not so anymore. Science, economy, politics. Especially politics. The world is now reduced to numbers. Humans see the Order as a relic of superstition, even as they secretly desire our protection. No matter. We can adapt to this dry, magicless world. Even politics." He turned back to Dylan with a smile. "I can, at least. You, clearly, cannot. Goodbye, Cleric Dylan Carter."

Dylan's body had been healing, but not nearly fast enough. He reached a hand up to his ear, hoping for enough time to tap his earpiece and give Ariel a warning to run, to hide. His finger came away from his ear bloody. The delicate electronic device had been crushed in the melee. It was hard, knowing he had to face his end having done no good at all, at the last.

"It would be so cool to shoot you right now," Dylan said, "but you broke my gun hand. That was a real dick move, do you understand that?"

With a look of utter disappointment, Postan stepped forward, claws growing from his fingertips. "I suppose I'm doing both our species a favor," he said. "Nether forbid anyone should inherit that insolent tongue of yours."

Neon green light illuminated the side of the Demon's face and he wheeled on its source. On the wall was a glowing glyph Dylan didn't understand but recognized. It was a variation on one of the glyphs Ariel had used to break into Klarisvan's temple. In rapid succession, glyphs covered the walls. Postan spun around, looking for a some new enemy and finding none. "What foul trick is this, Cleric?" he screamed. "What sorcery beyond your understanding do you employ against me now?"

"Not me. But for sure beyond my understanding." Dylan smiled. "You're so screwed."

Dylan's elation was short lived when Matthew materialized into the room facing the wrong way. Before he could call a warning, Postan moved with the unearthly speed he had displayed earlier, flying at Matthew with a swipe of his claws, like a lion bringing down an intruder to its territory.

Matthew somehow brought his forearms up in front of the blow. The sound of the impact was like a truck slamming into the stone walls of the room, but Matthew stood his ground. His instincts took over, and he spun, connecting to Postan's jaw with a backhand strike. "Carter?" he said, looking around the room, his eyes snapping to his friend.

"Watch out!" Dylan shouted, but couldn't get the warning off in time. Postan struck with a backhand of his own, much less sophisticated than Matthew's, but magnitudes more powerful. Matthew was thrown across the room, tumbling over and through piles of broken furniture, until he crashed into the wall next to Dylan. "Hey, buddy," Dylan said.

"What have you done, Carter?" Matthew said. Then he saw the blood all over Dylan, and concern showed on his features.

"Don't worry, got him right where—oh shit!" Dylan said, seeing Postan charge across the room.

Matthew King was a natural protector at his core. He'd always been the biggest person in the room. His mother had taught him that meant he had a gift he could use to help others. To do for them what they couldn't. Sometimes that meant a fight. Sometimes, it meant he was the shield. Matthew put himself between the Demon and Dylan, letting the Fallen Angel rain blows down on his back that would have crushed normal humans. Matthew also had a heritage, and in that moment he began to accept it. The Ouruqan, his ancestors, were the only beings on earth that could fight a Fallen one on one. Matthew could protect, even from Postan.

Postan seemed willing to test Matthew's strength to the fullest. He slammed his fists down time and again, brutal, punishing, and relentless. The constant barrage left no room for a counter. Eventually the Demon would change tactics, take some advantage. Both men knew they couldn't give Postan that chance.

Years of fighting together had given the two Hunters a shared understanding of each other's tactics. Dylan moved his hand to the hilt of the long-bladed knife on his belt. "Go!" he yelled to Matthew. Matthew rolled to his right, swinging back with his left elbow as he moved. He barely clipped Postan's jaw, but it was enough to break the Demon's rhythm. Dylan came up with the knife in his right hand, plunging it into Postan's ribs. Postan wrenched away, screaming. The knife went with him, smoke roiling out of the wound where the blade pierced his flesh.

The two men rushed into the gap in the Demon's defenses, raining blows onto the Nether creature. Matthew fought with precision and discipline; Dylan fought with a speed gifted by his transformation. Matthew caught the Demon's return strikes in his hands with a strength he hadn't known he possessed, and Dylan used the openings he made to strike with his own claws, eyes glowing red in the pale light.

They'd have stood a chance against other Fallen Angels.

Postan ran the New World for a reason. He roared with rage, and slipped a gap in both men's defenses, catching each by the throat. He squeezed. Matthew gasped, but his Ouruqan physiology withstood the pressure. Dylan's body didn't. The small bones and cartilage of his throat made cracking sounds, and blood burst from his mouth. Postan tossed him away like a dead rodent, then slammed Matthew to the ground and began to beat him into the stone floor.

Dylan landed on the floor, limp and flailing. He was still in there, in his mind, somewhere, but he'd taken about as much damage as his body could stand. He couldn't move anymore. He hardly felt the pain anymore. Except in his stomach. Oh, that hurt a lot. Where the hunger was beginning to wake.

A figure moved in his peripheral vision, blurry and indistinct. Saint Linden. He'd been hiding in a pile of rubble since he'd materialized in the room with Matthew. He was moving low and quick, trying to get to Dylan, to drag him away.

He was ill rewarded for his humanity. As he bent over Dylan, a feeling clawed the inside of Dylan's chest. His heart raced, while his mind retreated farther behind an animal that lived within him. Dylan was wounded. Hungry. Thirsty.

Linden knew. He saw it as he took hold of Dylan's coat to pull him away. He'd seen the look in the eyes of Vampires before, just before they'd taken his friends. His scream was just as short as theirs had been, cut off in a strangled sound, just like theirs.

Dylan drank the magic of mortal life without restraint or control. Deep inside, he raged at the total loss of his humanity. There was no stopping it. Linden's life flowed into him. Bones that couldn't knit quickly enough before now snapped into place. Organs regenerated. Strength filled him. And the magic. Oh, most of all, the magic. The room was alive with it. Always had been, he realized, but beyond his power to see. Especially that fireplace.

He made some effort to lay Saint Linden on the floor gently. There was still a drop of life left in the man, if only just. Dylan couldn't ask his forgiveness. So he would try to make the most of what had been unwillingly given.

He reached an open palm toward the coals smoldering in the hearth, a great inferno of magical power to his enhanced sight. He pulled the magic from it, the heat, the swirling fire, the power Jelena had shown him how to control. His hand raged with the strength of it as he drew the pistol Tomlinson had given him.

Postan felt the shift of power in the room. He tried to change targets, to leave Matthew on the floor and go for Dylan. Matthew didn't allow it. His hand shot up, grabbing a great fistful of the Demon's robes, holding him fast as he tried to leave.

Dylan let all the stolen magic in his hand flow into the round he fired. Postan saw it, saw the power of it, and raised his hand in panic. Waves of reality flowed between him and the bullet flying toward him, stretching the distance, slowing the shot. Dylan had banked on that reaction.

He reached out his own hand, took the power from the shot, and yanked himself forward with it. Postan tried to shift his focus, but Dylan was coming on too fast. Vampire slammed into Demon and a halo of flame exploded outward from where they met.

The two beings cast aside all pretense of defense as the room caught fire around them. Dylan's claws dug smoking furrows across Postan's face, while his own arms ran slick with blood leaking from long, painful lacerations. They seemed so evenly matched.

Not quite. Never that. In one hate-fueled push, Postan slammed his claws deep into Dylan's stomach, then closed his fist. His long fingers wrapped around Dylan's ribs, locking him in place. Pain coursed through the Vampire like nothing he'd yet felt. For all his hate and anger, for all his desire to rip his enemy to shreds, his strength was leaving him, faster than even his blood-fed Vampire physiology could replenish it.

The ring. Realization bloomed like a dark flower in his gut. Dylan looked down at the hand that disappeared into his abdomen. Postan's ring was within his chest, feeding off his life, pulling everything from him. He met the Demon's black eyes. "Goodbye, Hunter," Postan growled. "You lose."

Two giant hands closed around the ghost gray arm between Vampire and Demon, and squeezed. Bones snapped in the Demon's arm. With a furious roar, Matthew twisted his hands in opposite directions. Postan's arm tore apart, the flesh cracking like concrete. Postan screamed in pain as Matthew wrapped his arms around him. He lifted the Demon in a crushing bear hug and slammed him against a wall. Dylan fell to the ground, gasping for air. He tried to pull the severed hand out of his stomach. It wouldn't let go. The fingers were still locked tight around his ribs. Not a dead stiffness, but a living, active grip.

"Carter!" Matthew yelled. "Carter, get out of here! Go!" Postan had his feet on the ground again and was pushing back against the big man. Stone cracked and snapped under Matthew's feet as the two tested the limits of their strength. "Run!"

Dylan knew Matthew was right. He wasn't going to beat Postan. He also didn't have the scroll. He couldn't leave empty-handed. Yet the room was an inferno now, and he couldn't find the cabinet holding the scroll in all those flames. Maybe it had even burned up. What would happen to his team then, if he had nothing to trade the Inquisitor?

Empty-handed. Dylan laughed, looking at the severed arm that disappeared into his flesh. No, he had exactly what he needed. He had the Demon's ring. That, he was certain, was worth something. Postan should have let go.

Dylan had become a battery of sorts for the Demon's ring. It drew power from him as fast as he produced it, leaving him able to do little more than kneel on the floor. He reached for the gun lying next to him, surprised at how heavy it felt. He wasn't going to be able to do much with it. Not by himself.

"Hey," he heard himself say, almost drowned out by the roar of the flames. "I know I was a little cranky before. It was a really rough night, and I apologize. I was wondering if you would mind helping a fella out. *Moja ljubav.*"

Three aching heartbeats passed. He heard a woman laugh, a chanting in archaic Serbian. He couldn't understand the words, but he could feel the pull in the core of his being, like a hand reaching into his dreams to pull him from one to the next.

Dylan pointed the heavy revolver at the wall. He wasn't able to put any of his own magic into it. That was all going to the ring. That didn't matter. Jelena had more than enough to spare. He pulled the trigger

The wall of the chamber exploded outward, and Dylan went with it. Jalena's power yanked him into empty space. He began to fall. The top of the Cathedral. Somehow Postan's chambers had been at the very highest point, though he'd always had to go underground to access them. *Now that's just some weird shi—*

He hit the pavement with a crunching sound.

Chapter 42

Dylan was jolted awake. He was strapped to a gurney, in the back of some kind of vehicle. An ambulance? Another bump made him cry out in pain.

A woman looked back at him from the driver's seat. Coleen Jackson. "Hold on, Dylan, it's gonna be ok," she said. From the frantic way she was driving, Dylan wasn't sure of that.

"Coleen," he said. "Why are you naked?" Then his world went dark again.

Less than an hour later he awoke to Coleen trying to surgically remove the hand from his abdomen. Unconsciousness would not come again to save him from the pain. The more progress she made, the more his regenerative powers were able to strengthen him. He felt every second of the bone saw that took his ribs from him.

Two days later Dylan was standing in a deeply wooded area of upstate Illinois, breathing in the cold air. He still had phantom pain in his ribs, even though Coleen assured him that the bones had grown back and all wounds had healed. He was physically whole, if not psychologically.

He didn't turn at the sound of crunching leaves behind him. He had felt the Demon the moment she had walked into the woods. "So, what's the real name?" he said. "I don't wanna use Miranda anymore."

The woman stepped up beside him, staring at the same point in the forest as he was. "Kinyr is what my Brothers and Sisters call me," she said. "That will do."

Dylan nodded. "That'll do then. I take it my proposal was accepted?"

"What makes you think I'm not just here to kill you?" she said.

"You're doing a piss poor job of it if you are. Besides, I think you really wouldn't like that ring to end up on the black market."

"You wouldn't like it either, if you let such power fall into unworthy hands," Kinyr said, scowling. "You would face just as much evil and destruction as my kind would, with Postan's ring on the hand of some unfortunate vessel. So, yes, your proposal of a trade was accepted."

"That'll make things considerably less bloody going forward," Dylan said. He hoped the Demon couldn't tell how much worry and fear he'd been carrying, or how it had fallen away at the prospect of a peaceful transaction. Looking strong was one thing. Taking your hits to prove it was less appealing than stories made it sound.

"What about the Cathedral, about Postan letting it off the leash? I haven't really heard much about that. Nothing, to be precise. How did you spin control something that big?"

"It only affected those inside the Cathedral," Kinyr said. "Your timing saved more people than you realize. That late at night, almost no one was there. I wish I could go on believing you did that on purpose, it seemed so clever. Ah, well," she sighed. "A half dozen humans inside the Basilica went insane They are being cared for. In seclusion, of course. Another four...well, you surely heard the reports of that crazed Vampire on the streets. They were folded into that casualty count. You wouldn't believe the tithes that have been coming in, people asking for more Hunters, for more protection, for blessings."

"Great. Some of the best work I ever did for the Order was because I tried to get away from it. Awesome. I'm sure this isn't going to keep me up nights at all," Dylan said. "Alright, let's get this over with, I need a drink."

Kinyr took a leather satchel off her shoulders and dropped it on the ground. "We dug it out of the ashes of the Postan's chambers. The Inquisitor's binding scroll was surprisingly well warded, even I was shocked to find it whole. For my part, I do not advise giving it to him. He is a terrible evil to unleash on the world again. We did your kind a favor when we bound him."

A man in a light gray suit walked up to Dylan's other side, smiling and humming a tuneless song. "I'm not so bad, really, am I, Kinyr? I thought we both enjoyed our little chats by the fire. Well, until you pulled the branding irons out of it, I didn't enjoy that part as much."

Dylan lifted the satchel off the ground and held it out to the Inquisitor. "Make good on your part, Inqy. I'm a little touchy today, and standing between you two makes my skin crawl."

The Inquisitor held out a small wooden box. "Three Service Talismans, whole and untampered. Destroying them, or whatever you intend to do, is your responsibility. I can't do all the work for you."

Dylan took the box and made it disappear inside his coat. "Don't let me find you inside Chicago again. I'll leave you alone only so long as I think you aren't a danger to me or mine."

"There are eight billion people in the world, Dylan. Honestly, what makes you think I would start with you?" the Inquisitor said. He smiled and walked away, whistling.

"It's not too late, you know," Kinyr said. "The Red Cathedral will be under new management now. Postan has already been collected by the other Elder Demons. I don't believe their intent is his healing and comfort. You could come back with me. We—"

Dylan turned to face her, and she flinched as she saw his eyes, liquid smoke and predatory. "Goodbye, Kinyr," he said, walking away.

"Wait!" she called. "The ring! The ring, you bastard!"

Dylan turned and looked from her to a large oak nearby. He nodded at it, and Kinyr turned to follow his gaze. She was confused for a moment, then shot an incredulous look at him. "Under the tree?" she said. "You grew a tree over it? An oak?"

"Wasn't easy," he said. "Wasn't even sure I could do that, but low and be-fuckin-hold. You can have it back when the tree dies in a few hundred years."

To his surprise, Kinyr laughed. "You have served our purposes whether you will it or not, Hunter," she said. "A few hundred years. Yes, that sounds just about perfect."

Epilogue

"I don't know if we're gonna find James for a while. Or if we even want to," Coleen said. She was shuffling through Order reports obtained on the underground market, mostly bought from operatives looking to make money off the chaos of the Order's restructuring. "The only thing I can find that maybe sounds like him are reports of a skinless Vampire wreaking havoc on a few neighborhoods the night we escaped. The Order was in no shape at the time to hunt it down, and it escaped." She looked up at Dylan. "Could that be how the Inquisitor freed him from the Order's control?"

"Oh, that does sound like Inqy," Dylan said, sipping coffee. He was staring at a laptop. "James is off the ally list, for now. We're still gonna need help finding Ariel."

"Matthew, then. Find him yet?"

"Good chance," he said, spinning the laptop around.

Matthew King was sitting on a too small bed in a too small cell. That was fine with him. He'd been allowed to visit his mother once, a week ago, and then to attend the funeral two days ago. He didn't really feel the need to do anything else.

No more Order, for him, at least. Nothing to believe in. His friends were gone. His whole family. Rotting in a cell felt just fine.

"Matthew King," said a flat, dead voice at the cell door. The guard. He ignored it. They'd come in and get him if they really wanted him.

"King. You have a visitor."

That got his attention. Prisoners here didn't get visitors. He got up and looked at the guard through the small window in the door. His face was oddly slack, and his eyes glassy. "What do you mean?" Matthew said. "Who?"

"Candyman," Dylan said, stepping out from behind the guard. "Cool trick, huh? Very old-fashioned Vampire hypnotism thing."

Matthew sighed and walked back across his cell, sitting on his bed. "Go away, Carter."

"Can't do that, buddy. Gotta break you out."

"Don't want to break out. Nothing for me out there."

"And I can't take no for an answer, King. I need your help."

"With?" Matthew said impatiently.

"Ikeda's missing."

Matthew shot up from the bed and grabbed the bars on the door's window. "What do you mean?" he said. "The Order got her?"

"No," Dylan said. "We don't know who. We've got some leads, me and Jackson, but we need you. No one hunts like you. You gonna help me get our girl back?"

Matthew smiled. He gave a sharp push on the bars, and the door snapped off its hinges. He stepped out and dropped it to one side. "Let's go," he said.

Glossary

- Northumbria – A kingdom in Northern England from 651-954CE.

- Ealdmodor – Grandmother.

- Sunu – Son.

- Lugh, etc. – Old Irish god of, among other things, oaths.

- Karteus mekia dai – Combat magic, phrased in a variant of Old Angelic.

- Krathnaem – A spell of breaking, phrased in Fallen Angelic.

- Moja ljubav – "My Love". Serbian.

- Kijivu – Grays, a race of people from the stars.

Order Pure Ranks

- High Cleric – The top ranking official in charge of a Cathedral of the Order Pure.

- Senior Cleric – A high ranking Cleric authorized to give instruction or orders to lower ranking Clerics.

- Cleric – A person who has shown sufficient dedication in working for the Order and passed exams designed to test knowledge of Order teachings. Comprises the majority of persons employed at a Cathedral.

- Junior Cleric – Someone seeking certification as a Cleric employed in any of several departments of the Order Pure.

- Shepherd – A special department tasked with seeking out recruits for Hunter groups.

- Battle Priest – A retired Hunter, well versed in advanced magic and tactical combat skills. Often assigned to guard special resources at a Cathedral.

Sons of James Ranks

- Saint – A high ranking field combat specialist in command of a group of lower ranking SOJ operatives.

- True Believer – A skilled fighter in a Nether hunting squad, answerable to a Saint or higher ranking SOJ official.

www.ingramcontent.com/pod-product-compliance
Lightning Source LLC
Chambersburg PA
CBHW061525310726
48972CB00008B/2332